JOURNEY TO CASH

What Reviewers Say
About Ashley Bartlett's Work

Cash Braddock

"There were moments I laughed out loud, pop culture references that I adored and parts I cringed because I'm a good girl and Cash is kind of bad. I relished the moments that Laurel and Cash spent alone. These two are really a good match and their chemistry just jumps off the page. Playful, serious and sarcastic all rolled into one harmonious pairing. The story is great, the characters are fantastic and the twist, well, I never saw it coming."—*Romantic Reader*

"This book was amazing; Bartlett has a knack for being able to create characters that just jump off the page and immerse themselves into your heart."—*Fantastic Book Reviews*

"Ashley Bartlett was able to leave me hanging on every word and then at the end just like a junkie from the book… I was hooked and craving more!"—*Les Rêveur*

The Price of Cash

"The chemistry between Cash and Laurel is fantastic. This match has tension, heartache that pulls you deep into their dilemma. You want them to go for it and damn the consequences. It is so good! The whole book is fantastic, the love story, the crime, supporting cast, really top notch. Ashley Bartlett has written a fabulous follow-up. I cannot say enough good things about this one. I am absolutely hooked on this series!"—*Romantic Reader Blog*

"This series is like nothing else I have ever read in this genre and it just keeps getting better. It's a solid storyline that keeps me guessing as to what will happen next. Cash and Laurel's emotions are highly charged and you can feel the chemistry brewing between them. I was hooked and kept praying they would just launch themselves at each other. 5 stars"—*Les Rêveur*

Cash and the Sorority Girl

"I live for this series. Live. For. It! I love the paradox that is Cash. This amazing human being with her genuine spirit just pulls to me. On the flip side, she's a drug dealer so there is the conundrum you find yourself, as the reader, in. It's glorious."—*Romantic Reader Blog*

"Be prepared for an emotional rollercoaster. Because in reading this book, there are a few things I can guarantee. 1. You are going to laugh. A lot. 2. The sarcasm is phenomenal, and one of the main reasons I adore this series. And 3. Be prepared to feel emotionally destroyed afterwards because honestly, this book is all heart, but there are some hard to read moments. Is it worth it? F*ck yes!!!"—*Les Rêveur*

Dirty Sex

"A young, new author, Ashley Bartlett definitely should be on your radar. She's a really fresh, unique voice in a sea of good authors. …I found [*Dirty Sex*] to be flawless. The characters are deep and the action fast-paced. The romance feels real, not contrived. There are no fat, padded scenes, but no skimpy ones either. It's told in a strong first-person voice that speaks of the author's and her character's youth, but serves up surprisingly mature revelations."—*Out in Print*

Dirty Money

"Bartlett has exquisite taste when it comes to selecting the right detail. And no matter how much plot she has to get through, she never rushes the game. Her writing is so well-paced and so self-assured, she should be twice as old as she really is. That self-assuredness also mirrors through to her characters, who are fully realized and totally believable."—*Out in Print*

"Bartlett has succeeded in giving us a mad-cap story that will keep the reader turning page after page to see what happens next."
—*Lambda Literary*

Dirty Power

"Bartlett's talents are many. She knows her way around an action scene, she writes *memorably* hot sex, her plots are seamless, and her characters are true and deep. And if that wasn't enough, Coop's voice is so genuine, so world-weary, jaded, and outrageously sarcastic that if Bartlett had none of the aforementioned attributes, the read would still be entertaining enough to stretch over three books."
—*Out in Print*

"Here we have some rough and tumble action with some felons on the run! A big plus is the main characters were very engaging right from the start. …If you like your books super chocked full of all manner of things, this will be a winner. I definitely ended up enjoying this wild and woolly whoosh through the world of hardcore criminals and those who track them. Give it a try!"—*Rainbow Book Reviews*

Visit us at www.boldstrokesbooks.com

By the Author

Sex & Skateboards

Dirty Trilogy

Dirty Sex

Dirty Money

Dirty Power

Cash Braddock Series

Cash Braddock

The Price of Cash

Cash and the Sorority Girl

Journey to Cash

JOURNEY TO CASH

by
Ashley Bartlett

2021

JOURNEY TO CASH
© 2021 BY ASHLEY BARTLETT. ALL RIGHTS RESERVED.

ISBN 13: 978-1-63555-464-9

THIS TRADE PAPERBACK ORIGINAL IS PUBLISHED BY
BOLD STROKES BOOKS, INC.
P.O. BOX 249
VALLEY FALLS, NY 12185

FIRST EDITION: JANUARY 2021

CREDITS
EDITOR: CINDY CRESAP
PRODUCTION DESIGN: SUSAN RAMUNDO
COVER DESIGN BY MEGAN TILLMAN

Acknowledgments

Since the start of this series, the world has shifted in seemingly unfathomable ways, but for those of us already living on the fringes it has only been a confirmation. Rules and laws were always intended to keep the powerful in power and the rest of us down. Like Cash, I knew from a young age that society wasn't made for me. Once I accepted that, the entire edifice needed to come down. I built my own morals and laws based on what I knew to be true and good and righteous. And, like Cash, I sometimes had to shift those boundaries as I learned. It isn't always easy or comfortable, but I've found that ignoring my own morality for the comfort of others is far worse.

This book—this series—is the product of my friendships. Sydney, thank you for answering all my questions and also for your handsome face. Carsen, thanks for calls after midnight when you've already spent the whole day on the phone. Hearing your laugh gave me the fuel to write for a few more hours on desperate nights and also added years to my life, probably. Ruth, you keep me grounded. You see the parts of me I hide and you never cringe. I love you all.

I've been with Bold Strokes for most of my adult life. Rad and Sandy, I'm so thankful for you. Cindy, you're the bestest editor and an excellent friend. I love when you coddle me and I love when you don't.

Finally, my readers. Thanks for staying with me and Cash to the end. I've had a great time and I sincerely hope you have as well. I'd promise not to break your hearts again, but I think you kind of like it when I do.

Dedication

For my wife.
I'm not entirely certain why you stick with me,
but I'm awful glad you do.

CHAPTER ONE

It was an unremarkable Friday in June when I opened the door to an unremarkable woman. She was in her late forties, maybe. Her sweater set and khakis were nice in an understated way. She looked like a process server, which, considering the year I'd had, wouldn't have been surprising.

"Cash Braddock?"

"Yes."

"I'm Marjorie Braddock." She hesitated, waiting for a response before continuing. Suddenly, the fifteen missed calls I had from Clive made sense. "Your mother."

"Oh. Umm, hi." That was how I greeted my mother after twenty-three years. "Come in?" I stepped back. I didn't know how to act so I reverted to bland politeness.

"Thank you." She stepped inside.

I led her into the living room. I hesitated before sitting in my usual armchair. Would she think I didn't want to share the couch with her? Did I want to share the couch with her? I had no idea how to occupy space with a woman who had carried me in her womb, which wasn't entirely surprising. She had abandoned me, after all.

"Would you like something to drink?" I pushed myself up out of the chair. "I can make coffee." Did she drink coffee?

"I'm good, thank you." She twisted her hands and stared intently at me. "You're probably wondering what I'm doing here." Her eyes were bright and earnest.

"A little. Clive called me a bunch yesterday and today. I'm guessing he knows you're here?"

She nodded. "I'm staying with him."

"Cool."

"I think he wanted to warn you I was coming. He asked me not to come yet, but I didn't want to wait any longer. I needed to see you. I know I have no right, but I'd like to get to know you a bit. Sorry, I'm rambling." She started to pick at her thumbnail. "If you're open to it, I'd like to stick around for a while."

"Cool." Apparently, my vocabulary had been reduced to one word. I gave myself a mental head shake. "Where do you live now?"

"Del Mar. It's a little town above San Diego," she said. I nodded. That had been the extent of my polite questions. The silence stretched. "I moved there when I got married."

"You're married?"

She smiled. "For almost ten years." Faint lines appeared in the creamy softness of her skin. I wondered if I would show those same wrinkles in twenty years.

"Any kids?" It hadn't occurred to me that I might have siblings until I asked the question. Then again, it hadn't occurred to me that my mother was alive and clean.

"No. Just you."

My phone rang and I had never been so fucking happy for my phone to ring in my life. "Sorry." I dug the phone out of my pocket. It was Kyra. "I have to take this." Marjorie nodded. "Hello?"

"Hey, Van got stuck at school so he can't meet the art movers. Any chance you can meet them at the gallery?"

"Aren't they due at three?" I glanced at the time. That only gave me twenty minutes.

"Yeah." There was a pause. I assumed Kyra was also looking at the time. "Shit. Never mind. I'll just ask them to push back the delivery an hour or so."

"If you do that, we won't have time to get the final pieces hung." Those three pieces weren't the end of the world or anything, but we wanted the opening to be perfect. My mother caught my eye. Whoa. My mother. That was weird. I suddenly needed to get the fuck out of there. "It's fine. I can get there by three."

"It's okay. I didn't realize what time it was. We'll just have to work with a later drop-off," Kyra said.

"Great. I'll be there in fifteen." Hopefully, Marjorie couldn't hear Kyra's side of the conversation.

"Cash," Kyra said.

"Yep. See you then." I hung up.

"You have to leave?" Marjorie asked.

"Sorry." I stood to highlight the speed at which I needed to leave. "My friend and I are opening an art gallery. Tonight is the opening of our first show."

"Wow. An art gallery. That's impressive." She stood. "Well, I uh, suppose I should let you go. It's been—You look—Thank you for seeing me. Can I give you my phone number?"

"Sure." I dug my phone back out and opened my contacts. I handed it to her.

She carefully typed in her name and number before handing it back. "I hope you'll call so we can actually sit down together."

"Right. Yes. I'll do that." I didn't know if we were planning a business meeting or a family reunion. I walked her to the door and held it for her.

She paused and turned before walking out. "I'm sure this is a lot. I've had time to think about it, but you haven't." She shook her head. "Anyway. I won't bother you again. It'll be entirely up to you." Her hand came up. For a panicked moment I thought she wanted to hug me. Instead she touched my cheek briefly with the tips of her fingers like she was afraid any more would do damage. She smiled a brittle smile and let her hand drop. "Good-bye."

I nodded, torn between acknowledging the weight of the moment and wanting to sprint away. Marjorie walked to a sedan at the curb and climbed in. I closed the door and had to brace myself against it. My heart was racing and my hands trembled. I wished I had answered Clive's calls or listened to his voice mails. Maybe it was good I hadn't because I never would have answered the door.

My phone rang. I pulled it out and looked at the screen. Kyra again. "Yeah?" I slid down the wall and sat on the floor. Everything felt shaky, precarious.

"What was that?"

I took a deep breath and prepared to explain how my world had just shifted. But then I didn't. I couldn't deal with it. Saying it was far too much acknowledgment.

"Cash?"

"Nothing. It was nothing. There was someone at my door and I needed an excuse." I knew she wouldn't be satisfied with that, but hopefully she could let it simmer untouched like I was planning to do. "I'll be there in fifteen."

"You sure?"

"Yes."

"Okay. Thanks."

Ten minutes later, I parked in one of our two spots behind the gallery. I made sure to keep the other space clear enough for the truck. The building backed up to an alley. The west side of the building was accessible for vehicles. The east side had a narrow strip of garden. It was mostly overgrown planters spilling flowers. There was also room for a small table and two rickety chairs.

I left the gate open for the delivery guys and let myself into the small office that overlooked the garden. Kyra had clearly been the last to leave the night before because the surface of the desk was tidy. She'd left detailed instructions for Van, which was great because I needed just as much guidance as her boyfriend did, but I rarely admitted as much.

At five after, the rumble of a large truck carried down the alley. The art movers came in through the gate. I gave them Kyra's instructions and watched them carefully place each piece in the appropriate locations. I'd wanted to hire an assistant to handle that sort of day to day task, but Kyra insisted we should handle it ourselves and use the money for better wine. I didn't know shit about wine and was generally too lazy to be so present, but when the movers handed me the invoice and shook my hand, it felt real and valid. Like I'd earned my name on the door.

Van arrived not long after and I helped him hang the last pieces. The main gallery space had been finalized two days before the opening. Kyra had overseen that. My ego was quite comfortable with her having done so. The final pieces were split between the smaller room that branched off the main floor space and the narrow loft upstairs. Per Kyra's instructions, the loft pieces needed plenty of breathing room. After much discussion Van and I decided that meant they needed lots of space because they were big. Too bad she hadn't left detailed instructions about that part. Hanging them made me very aware that Van had muscles and I did not. But I could use a level with the best of them. We were doing a final check of the lighting when Kyra arrived.

Van wolf whistled. "I mean that in the most respectful way. Like, you look real successful and empowered. Not like you look bangable."

"So I don't look bangable?" Kyra looked down at the tight cocktail dress she was wearing. Her undercut was freshly buzzed, and the curls piled on her head had a glossy sheen.

"I didn't say that. You look more than bangable. Like bangable and also audacious," Van said.

I climbed down the ladder. "Smooth, dude."

"Thanks. I know."

"Neither of you are dressed for tonight," Kyra said.

Van and I looked at each other. She was correct. "And?" Van asked.

"You guys aren't planning on wearing shorts and T-shirts tonight." Her tone suggested it would be extremely unacceptable to make that choice.

"You are really good at this state the obvious game we're playing," I said.

Kyra rolled her eyes and huffed. "When were you planning on changing?"

"I have my bag in the office." Van nodded at the back of the building.

"I wasn't entirely prepared when I came over. I need to run home," I said.

"Yeah, what was that about earlier?" Kyra asked.

I kicked around the words in my head but couldn't bring myself to say my mother had shown up on my doorstep. I really tried. Honest. "It's a long story. I'll tell you about it tomorrow though."

Kyra stared at me like she was pulling apart my syntax to find a lie. After a moment, she nodded. "Okay. Get out of here. Hurry back."

"Will do." I sketched a quick wave and left through the office.

It took me thirty minutes to change clothes and style my hair and give myself a pep talk that this whole idea wasn't bananas. Clothes and hair took about ten. Removing cat hair from my outfit was three. The rest was pep talk. Spending the majority of my savings on a business with a questionable survival rate was responsible and not a bad idea. It was all going to be fine.

When I got back to the gallery in my pale pink blazer and indigo jeans, I couldn't decide if I was a massive douche or the pinnacle of cool. But then I walked in and Van let out a long low whistle.

"So I'm bangable?" I asked.

"Totally, bro."

I looked over Van's teal chinos and linen shirt. The shirt was unbuttoned about halfway down his chest. "You're looking pretty great yourself."

"When you're done fawning over each other, there are cases of wine and beer in my car that need to be moved inside," Kyra said.

"But we've barely fawned." I did my best to look sad and confused.

"Cash, people will start arriving literally any minute. If you don't get those cases out of my car before that happens, I will throat punch you." Kyra propped her fists on her hips and gave me a look that suggested she would not hesitate to throat punch me just to prove her point.

The door opened and a couple in their early sixties came in. They were almost immediately followed by a group of Van's grad students. I grinned at Kyra and backed away. In the time it took me to move six cases of booze inside, the gallery filled to about a third of its capacity.

Kyra introduced me to a million people. I retained exactly zero of their names or faces. People continued to arrive. The sun dropped enough to fill the room with warm light. Van had been right about using it to our advantage. I glimpsed Nate and Robin and Andy but couldn't manage to actually speak with any of them. I watched Andy acting very sophisticated with a champagne glass filled with sparkling water and hitting on a woman in her early twenties. Robin intervened. Andy pouted.

CHAPTER TWO

On one of my circles around the gallery, I passed the office. Above the murmur of the crowd around me, I heard Lane's voice. My initial confusion at hearing her voice coming from the office was immediately overshadowed when I heard the urgency and hint of fear undercutting her tone. I went into protector mode.

"Lane, everything okay in here?" I rounded the corner and froze.

Lane stepped in front of Laurel like she was shielding her. "She's just leaving."

"No, I'm not." Laurel tried to get around Lane.

Lane's jaw tightened. "Yes, she is." She turned and forcibly pushed Laurel toward the back door.

"Stop it, dammit." Laurel planted her feet. "Cash, I'm sorry to just show up like this. I just need to talk to you for two minutes." She tried to lean around Lane to see me.

Lane leaned with her. "Tonight matters. You don't get to show up unannounced and demand her time. You gave up that right." She looked back at me. "I'm sorry. I didn't know she was going to show up here."

It took me that long to realize Lane was shielding me from Laurel. Not the other way around. It also took me that long to speak.

"It's okay. Thanks, Laney." I reached out to her.

Lane took my hand and squeezed. "It's not okay. You don't have to be nice to her."

"It's fine. Give us a couple minutes. If I'm not out in five, you can come in and kick her ass." I grinned.

Lane rolled her eyes. "Fine." She turned back to her sister. "You get two minutes." She skirted around me to get out the door and I finally was able to see Laurel.

I immediately wanted to leave the room. Laurel had two black eyes, a purple bruise along her jaw, and a dark line across her throat. Her arms were scraped and bruised.

"So I see things are going well for you."

She took a shuffling step forward. She was favoring her left leg. "I didn't know it was your opening night. I'm sorry."

"Laurel, what happened?"

"Henry Brewer is back." She held my gaze. "Reyes or Agent Michelson will contact you tonight or tomorrow. I just needed to tell you myself."

"Henry did this?"

She took a slow breath and nodded. "He was trying to kill me. We don't know much of anything so we—they—I mean. They have to assume you or Nate or Clive could be his next target."

"How bad are you hurt?"

She half shrugged. Her T-shirt was thin and I could see the outline of a white bandage on her shoulder. "Mostly just bruises."

"It looks like more than that."

"You don't need to worry about me. I'm fine. I just didn't want you to hear it from a stranger," she said as if she wasn't a stranger. "That's all." She held up her hands in placation. The same dark line stretched across her left palm. Henry had tried to strangle her with something. "Lucas will make sure you're safe." She turned and headed for the door.

"You know that's not fair. You don't get to stop by after seven months, drop a bomb like that, and leave."

She stopped but didn't turn. "What else am I supposed to say?"

I tried to come up with a rational answer. "Well, I don't know. But that's fucking shitty." I didn't know why I was surprised at that. "I guess that's your MO."

"I guess so. I'm sorry." She walked out. I saw her shadow blend into the trees out back before she disappeared around the side of the building.

"You okay?" Lane asked from behind me.

I turned toward her. "Not really."

She came all the way into the office and hugged me. "I'm sorry. I tried to get rid of her."

"It's okay. Not your job."

"Yeah, but I'm the one who told her we were at the gallery tonight." She squeezed me once more, then let go. "I mean, I didn't think she was going to show up here but still."

"In that case, yeah, totally your fault." I grinned.

"You're a dick."

"Did she tell you what's going on?" I asked.

"No. She only got here a minute before you came in. We were arguing over her barging into your opening with her face fucked up." Lane hugged herself. "Is she okay?"

I shrugged. "She said she was, but you saw her. Did you hear what we were talking about?"

"Of course. I was eavesdropping. Someone tried to kill her? Who is Henry Brewer?"

"My old business partner. He was a sheriff up in El Dorado County. He used to steal drugs from the evidence locker for me to sell."

"Oh, shit. Isn't he the one who tried to kill Laurel last summer?"

"Yep, that's the one."

"So your ex-girlfriend just showed up after disappearing for months to tell you your old business partner is back and hasn't gotten any less homicidal? Did I get that right?"

I stared out the window at the darkened yard with its collection of romantic, terrifying shadows. There was a breeze picking up. Or maybe Laurel was still out there. Or maybe Henry was. "Also my mother showed up this afternoon and asked if she could get to know me." I tore my gaze away from the yard. Lane was staring at me, stunned. "Hoo boy. I've been trying to say that out loud for the last"—I checked my watch—"six hours or so."

"Cash."

"It's okay. I'm okay. It's just been a long day."

"What are the chances I could take you home?"

I forced a smile. "Slim. I have to be here until we wrap up."

"Yeah." She pursed her lips and nodded. "Is there anything I can do to help?"

I shook my head. I just needed to get through the next few hours and then I could go home. Laurel hadn't said it was unsafe to go home. "Shit. Yes, actually."

"What?" Lane perked up at the possibility of helping.

"I need to give Nate and Robin a heads-up, but if I go out there, I'll never make it through all those people."

"I got you." She pulled out one of the refurbished chairs in front of the desk and directed me into it. "Chill here for a minute. I'll be right back."

I did as I was told. I slid down in my chair to lean my head back. It was stupid comfortable. When we were furnishing the gallery, I'd introduced Kyra to my former client Patricia. The gallery's bank account took quite the hit, but Kyra and Patricia had chosen exquisite vintage furniture. Patricia said I deserved it for forcing her to buy from Jerome. She wasn't wrong.

"Congratulations, man." A warm hand gripped my shoulder for a moment. I opened my eyes. Nate was pulling out the chair next to me. He held out a beer, which I gratefully took. "Lane said you needed this."

"Thank you, Dr. Xiao."

He laughed. "I told you to stop doing that."

"You told me to stop telling people. You never said I couldn't call you doctor privately."

"You are exhausting."

"Aww, thanks."

"So what's up? Lane said you needed to tell me something."

I took a drink of beer, but it didn't give me courage. "Laurel just showed up to tell me Henry made an appearance. He wants revenge or something."

Nate looked at me. I looked back at him. The looking went on for quite some time.

"What?" he finally asked.

"Laurel had the shit kicked out of her by Henry. She said she was fine, but he was aiming to kill her so that's not great. She said Reyes or Michelson would contact us soon because we might be targets too."

"Nope. Fuck all of that. I'm not doing this shit again."

"We could hop a plane to somewhere with warm beaches and fruity drinks."

Nate nodded and pointed at me. "I like it."

"Great," I said.

"Of course I'm moving in like a month and you hate fruity drinks."

"And there are a bunch of people we love who we would be leaving vulnerable to an unhinged ex-cop."

"But we could. That's the important thing," he said.

"Exactly. We're making the choice to stay. We have autonomy."

Nate nodded seriously. "Autonomy."

"Who has autonomy?" Robin asked.

Nate and I turned to the open doorway. "We do, dammit. We control our own destinies," I said.

"Damn right you do, honey."

Nate stood. "Robin's turn?"

"Yeah, but stick around. We should probably game plan this."

"Right." He pulled out the chair for Robin.

"Is game plan a verb now?" Robin asked.

"It is," I said.

Robin sat. "What do we need to game plan?"

"Remember Henry?"

She nodded. "Asshole cop who tried to kill Laurel and got you two arrested."

"He's back and up to his old tricks. Well, not all of them. Just the attempted murder part," I said.

"Huh?"

"Henry tried to kill Laurel again and now he's probably gunning for us. Usual summer shenanigans." Nate flashed an impish grin.

"I'm not following. You guys are being too cavalier and I don't know how seriously to take you."

"Oh, yeah, no. It's real serious. Laurel looked like she'd been hit by a truck." I started to point at my own body where Laurel was injured but gave up when it became a whole body thing.

"You saw Laurel?" Robin asked.

"Yep. She was here like ten minutes ago. Lane booted her ass."

"Aww. Your knight in shining armor," Nate said.

"Yeah, she's my hero." I smiled dreamily at him. He smiled back.

Robin touched my knee. "Cash. Focus."

"Sorry."

"Henry attacked Laurel?" she asked. I nodded. "And he might want to hurt you or us?"

"Yeah. Laurel didn't have much info. Just that it would logically follow that if he wants to kill her, he might also want to kill me or Nate. She said her old Sac PD partner or her FBI contact would likely be contacting me."

"How worried do we need to be?"

"I honestly don't know. For now, just be aware. Make sure Andy is aware. As soon as I know anything, I'll tell you."

"What about Nate?" Robin looked over at him. He was perched on the edge of the desk. He seemed surprised at her question.

"What about him?" I asked.

"Well, Andy and I have each other. And you and Lane are next door. But Nate lives alone."

Nate shrugged. "I'm fine. He doesn't even know where I live."

I scoffed. "Yes, because finding out where someone lives is so difficult."

"I can take him." He looked entirely unconcerned.

"You can take a gun-loving, trigger-happy former cop who thinks you betrayed him?" I asked.

Nate grinned nervously. "Maybe I should just stay at your place. You know, so the lady folks feel safe."

"Good idea," I said.

"Yeah, and you can reach things off high shelves and open pickle jars," Robin said.

"And take out the trash," I said.

"And tell us to calm down if we get hysterical," Robin said.

Nate wrinkled his nose and shook his head. "I don't know. That seems like a lot of effort."

I shrugged. "Okay. You can drink beer and watch dumb movies with us."

"Much better."

"I better get out there," I said.

"Yeah, go sell some art." Nate held up his beer. I saluted him with mine.

❖

Robin texted ten minutes after they left to let me know there was a police cruiser outside our place. It was still there when I got home. Nate was parked in the street almost blocking my driveway, but not quite. I carefully angled into my spot. I walked over to the cop in the cruiser.

"How's it going?" I asked.

"Everything is quiet," he said.

"I assume you're here because of the whole death threat thing?" He looked at me strangely. Maybe Robin was right and I was being too cavalier about my imminent death. "Yes, ma'am. Sergeant Ionescu had me stationed here."

"Do you have any information on the threat level?"

"I'm sorry. I don't." He turned his computer screen so I could see a photo of Henry in his dress uniform. "I was only given a name and a photo."

"All right. Have a good night." I walked up to the house. I didn't know what the protocol was when a cop was staking out your house to protect you. I was more familiar with the staking out to intimidate and subtly threaten you approach. Should I give him a bottle of water? A cookie?

I let myself into the house. The TV was on and Lane was in her spot on the couch. I could see Nate's feet hanging off the end. My spatial awareness suggested his head was in her lap.

"Hey," Lane said. She paused the movie.

I came around the couch and saw that Nate was lying on a pile of pillows propped against Lane's side. He had a bowl of popcorn on his stomach.

"How's it going?" I asked.

"She's way less freaked out by the cop babysitter outside than I am," Nate said.

"And he's way less freaked out about the homicidal former cop who could be sitting in the backyard watching us right now than I am," Lane said.

"So you're both indulging in irrational fears based on the weight of history but very little current evidence."

"Yep."

"Definitely."

"And that's why you're watching a slasher flick?" I looked pointedly at the TV.

"Yeah, the only way to deal with fear is to lean into it," Lane said.

"And you aren't going to have any trouble sleeping?" I asked. They looked at me like I was out of my mind.

"We're not sleeping. This here is the beginning of a terror filled all-nighter, man." Nate put up his hand.

Lane high-fived him. "Terror. Filled."

"Are you guys just using this as an excuse to do the *Scream* marathon you've been talking about?"

"How dare you, sir?" Nate did his best to look offended.

"Yeah, basically," Lane said.

I laughed at them. "I'm going to bed." I stood. "Don't stay up too late."

"Okay, Dad," Lane said.

I flipped her off. They started the movie back up after I closed my bedroom door. Nickels was sprawled in the center of my bed. She stirred at the sound of the door closing, then put her head back down. I stripped to my underwear and climbed in bed. Nickels scooted closer until she was tucked in my armpit. She started purring.

Lane had opened my window. A warm breeze floated through the room. I could hear faint sounds from the street. The white noise of traffic and music and voices blended with the movie playing in the other room until it was all just a pleasant hum.

I closed my eyes and tried to sleep, but I couldn't. What normally would have been peaceful wasn't. My mother had tilted my world a scant inch and I was telling myself the resulting shift in gravity wasn't catastrophic. But it was Laurel who had unapologetically fucked me right up. Because she cared. Like she always had.

They were two women who should have loved me without reservation, but neither loved me enough to stay. And when I had made my peace, when I had started to do well, when I didn't need them anymore, they sauntered back into my life.

Chapter Three

"No offense, but I was kind of hoping I'd never see you two again." I sat across from Reyes and Duarte. They'd snagged a window table at Old Soul.

"Rude." Duarte grinned.

"Who told you I was polite?" I asked.

"You seem pretty chipper for someone who was just told their life was in danger," Reyes said.

I shrugged. "Living in the patriarchy means some dude is always trying to kill me."

Reyes shook his head, but I saw the grin he tried to hide. "This threat is a little more specific than that."

Nate sat next to me and handed me a cup of iced coffee. "What did I miss?"

"Death threats, the patriarchy."

"This is serious, you guys," Reyes said.

"Okay, how worried do we need to be?" I took a sip of coffee and tried to look invested.

"What did Kallen tell you?" Reyes asked.

"Not much. Henry tried to kill her. He probably wants to kill me and Nate and, I don't know, whoever else he blames for destroying his life and making him a fugitive," I said.

Duarte nodded. "That's a decent description, actually."

"What do you guys know?" Nate asked.

"Kallen was out hiking when Brewer ambushed her." Reyes aimlessly spun his glass of tea. "She fought back. It's possible she broke his fingers or hand. She almost certainly broke his nose. She definitely stabbed him in the side." He finally looked up. "We've been checking hospitals and clinics, but nothing so far. We also don't know anything about his targets or his motivations yet."

"Well, he considers it personal," I said.

Reyes huffed. "Yes, definitely."

"How'd you know that?" Duarte asked.

"Last time he tried to execute her," Nate said. "On her knees. With a gun. Mobster style. It was a business transaction. Cash said this time he tried to strangle her. That's intimate, personal."

"Which is why we think he might come after you two or Clive. Really anyone who he blames for the trajectory of his life," Reyes said.

"But that's all speculation?" I asked.

Reyes shrugged. "Yeah."

"What are you guys doing about it?" I asked. Reyes and Duarte seemed confused by the question. "You called me to update us. So update us. What's the plan? How are you going to catch him? Are you going to park a cruiser outside my house until you find him? Are you covering anyone else's residence?"

Reyes nodded a couple times. "For the time being, Sac PD has a cruiser outside your place." He looked at Nate. "And Davis PD is covering your apartment. EDSO are doing the same for Kallen and Mr. Braddock."

"EDSO?" Nate asked.

"El Dorado Sheriff's Office."

I tried to figure out why Laurel would have an El Dorado sheriff escort, but couldn't. "I don't understand."

"What part?" Reyes asked.

"The El Dorado sheriffs."

"Hey, they have just as much investment in catching him as we do." Reyes shrugged. "More, maybe. To have one of their own become a cop killer, or an attempted cop killer is bad news."

"No. Laurel. Is she in El Dorado County?" I asked. Next to me, Nate shifted uncomfortably.

"Yeah, Placerville." Reyes looked confused at my confusion. "You know that's where she's been, right?"

I frowned and shook my head. I felt like crying suddenly and I couldn't quite process why. I needed this meeting to end. "No, but it doesn't matter."

Nate briefly touched my knee under the table. I nodded that he could take over. "So is someone meeting with Clive to tell him why there's a cop parked at his farm?" he asked.

"Yeah. Do you remember Agent Michelson from the FBI field office?" Reyes asked. Nate and I nodded. "He's at Braddock Farm with one of the EDSO investigators right now."

"And how long is this going to go on for?" Nate asked.

Duarte raised his hand a couple of inches off the table like he was asking permission to speak. "We don't know. The FBI, Sac PD, and EDSO all have open files on Brewer, but we haven't had any significant leads in the last year. This is the most contact anyone has had."

"But you're going to do something, right? We can't live in a police state forever," Nate said.

"It's not exactly a police state to have police protecting you," Reyes said.

"I'm a six-foot Chinese dude with a criminal record. Feels like a police state to me." Nate looked pointedly at Reyes. Reyes shrugged and leaned away from the table.

"Brewer dropped his cell phone when he attacked Kallen. The FBI team is working on unlocking it. We're hoping we get some information from that," Duarte said.

"Well, you can call Davis PD off my place. I'm going to stay with Cash until this is resolved," Nate said.

"Great. I'm sure they have other uses for those resources," Reyes said. There was a hint of irritation in his tone. Nate's comment about police states had clearly pissed him off.

"I assume you'll keep us apprised of the situation?" I stood.

"Of course." Reyes stood when I did. Duarte scrambled to follow suit. "Thank you for meeting with us."

Nate and Reyes nodded at each other. It was all very tension filled. I didn't know if it was me reeling from the revelation that Laurel apparently left me to live a scant forty miles away or the polite masculine energy radiating between Nate and Reyes, but regardless I didn't like it.

I grabbed my coffee and left. Nate followed me. We started walking back to my place. The air held the promise of heat for the afternoon.

"He was being a dick, right?" Nate asked.

"Yeah. Definitely."

"I don't care if he's a cop. He's Latinx. He knows exactly what it feels like to be a brown dude threatened by a police presence." His voice rose in a hint of anger. In all the time I'd known him, it was the only real display of anger I'd seen.

"What can I do?"

"Nothing." We waited at the corner for the light to change. Nate tapped the light pole as if it would make things go faster.

"You're allowed to be pissed about this," I said.

"Thanks for the permission to get angry?" The light changed and he took off.

I hustled to catch up. "I'm just saying you're not in the wrong."

"It doesn't matter. How are you doing?" he asked.

"Fine."

"Wow, so we're both just going to be masculine about our emotions?"

"Huh?"

"Kallen left you to find herself. I thought it was mostly a proximity thing. Like she couldn't stay in Sac and you're in Sac. But she went to the next county, which kind of suggests that it had nothing to do with proximity."

"Cool. So you're not going to let me lie to myself about this at all?" I asked.

"Oh. I didn't know that's what we were doing."

"I mean, we could like talk about our feelings and shit, but also what if we buried them deep down instead?"

"Sounds fucking dope."

We turned up the walkway to my front door. We could hear the *Mario Kart* music before we even opened the door. Lane and Andy had cleared the living room floor and covered it in pillows and blankets. A reverse fort, if you will. Lane was lying on her stomach with her feet crossed in the air behind her. Andy had pulled a cushion off the couch to set up a lounge chair of sorts against the couch front.

"Oh, man. Staying the weekend at your house is the best." Nate bumped his shoulder against mine. "Guys, I want in on the next game." He vaulted over the couch and landed on one of the remaining seat cushions. Lane and Andy made grunting noises in affirmation.

"You want a beer?" I asked Nate.

"Not right now," he said without turning away from the screen.

"I think Mom's out back having one though," Andy said.

"Cool. Thanks, tiger." I grabbed a beer and went out back.

Robin turned at the sound of the door. "How did it go?"

"Okay. They don't have any info and we're going to have a cop babysitter until they sort it out."

She sighed. "Oh, fun."

"It could be worse." I sat next to her. She gave me a questioning look. "I could have a seemingly perfect woman pretend to be my girlfriend but really she's an undercover cop investigating me. Or I could have my secret girlfriend actually be a cop who is here to use the cover of protecting me so she can spend the night, but then she experiences such cognitive dissonance from being in a relationship with me that she leaves, literally abandoning the city she's lived in her whole life."

"What an oddly specific hypothetical of worseness."

"I'm imaginative."

"I like that about you," she said.

"Aww, thanks."

"So I take it the gallery opening went well? Aside from the hypothetical ex-girlfriend showing up."

"Yeah. Kyra already sold like six pieces. It's pretty great."

"I'm so proud of you, Cash." Robin took my hand and held it. "You've done something really cool."

"Thanks." I smiled. Coming from Robin, it mattered. "I need to tell you about something. I need friend advice."

"What's up?"

"A couple hours before the gallery opening, my mother showed up here."

Robin cocked her head and stared at me. The realization slowly overtook her expression until she uttered an erudite, "Huh?"

"Yep. That mother."

"No." She said it very authoritatively. Like she'd considered all the possibilities and simply decided against my mother reappearing.

"Yeah."

"What did she want? Was it weird? How did she look? I thought she was dead?"

"She wants to get to know me. And it was super fucking weird. I kinda thought she was dead too."

"Wasn't she a drug addict?" Robin asked.

"Oh, yeah. Big time. She looks fine now. Clean. Happy."

"That's wild. What are you going to do?"

"I don't know. That's why I'm telling you about it. What the hell do I do?" I asked.

"How did you leave it?"

"Kyra called with a gallery thing and I pretended I had to leave right away."

"Nice. Very mature," she said.

"She told me she would like to hear from me. She's staying with Clive. I guess I should call her? Should I call her?"

"If you want to." Robin shrugged. "It's totally up to you. If you're curious, then go for it. If you're not, it's okay to say no thanks."

"There's not really anything I want from her."

"That's good. It means you'll be more impartial if you do call her."

"I feel like I should care more than I do."

"Maybe your lack of feelings has all just been leading to this moment." Robin sipped her beer. "Or, you know, you're a deeply broken person because your mother abandoned you at a young age and that's why you lack normative emotional responses as an adult."

"It's a real toss-up."

"Guess we'll never know." She held out her beer and I tapped mine against it. "Have you talked to Clive about it? Are you talking to him at all?"

The door behind us opened. We turned in time to watch Andy, Lane, and Nate rush outside.

"Mom, guess what?"

"What, bud?"

"We are going to put wood slats in the back of Gracie-Ray," Andy said. Nate and Lane nodded enthusiastically.

Robin looked at me in question. I shrugged. "I thought that was the plan all along," Robin said.

"So did I," I said.

A week after getting the truck for her birthday, Andy declared that she was going to replace the wood in the bed. It had been seven months. "No, I mean, yeah. But we were waiting because I had to save up for supplies and then we were waiting because of the weather, but look." Andy pointed at the sky.

"It's summer," Lane said.

It certainly was.

"Great. What do I need to do?" Robin asked.

"Nothing, honestly," Nate said.

"Yeah, I've got the plans Lane made me." Andy held up the hand-drawn specs Lane had given her for Christmas. "We just need to make a hardware store run."

"You guys don't mind?" Robin glanced at Nate and Lane.

"It'll be fun," Lane said.

"Yeah. Plus the lady folks need an escort." Nate nodded confidently.

"Hey, Nate, what's the difference between oak and pine?" Lane asked.

"Excellent question. Andy, why don't you take this one?" Nate clapped his hand on Andy's shoulder.

"Oh, no." Andy made a pained face. "I couldn't possibly use my lady brain to understand something so complex."

"Right you are. Well, we better go." He gestured grandly to the door.

Lane crossed her arms. "Hey, Nate, what's the difference between an orbital sander and a belt sander?"

"If you have to ask me, then maybe you're not qualified to do this," he said.

Lane grinned. "Hey, Nate, should we stain or varnish the wood?"

"Yes?" He held the door open in the hope Lane would stop asking him questions.

I turned to Robin. "There's no part of this that can go wrong."

CHAPTER FOUR

Nate texted for me to open the side gate when they were a couple of blocks away. Robin helped me wrestle it open. We hadn't opened it since we built flower beds five years earlier.

"Well, this is going to be a problem." Robin stared out at the street with her hands on her hips.

"What?" I dropped the gate and hustled to stand in the opening with her. My car was parked in the driveway leading to the gate. "Hmm. Yeah. That's going to make it hard to drive back here."

"Andy can move it," Robin said.

"That's the whole point of having children, right? So they can move vehicles when you've had too much to drink."

"Of course. That's why I had Andy."

"I'll grab my keys for her." I went up the steps to my back door.

"My beer's almost gone," Robin called after me.

"I got you, girl." I pulled my keys off the hook by the door, snagged two beers from the fridge, and went out front to wait for Andy.

A minute later, they pulled up at the curb. Andy turned down her stereo and leaned out the open window of Gracie-Ray.

"Hey, Cash, you planning on moving your car?" she asked.

"I thought I told you to turn down your stereo when you're a block or two away," I said.

"I forgot."

"She's right, you know," Nate said.

I pointed at Nate and nodded. "Someone is going to steal your stereo."

"Message received." She rolled her eyes. "Can you move your car now?"

I held up my keys. "No, but you can."

"Why?"

"Because I cannot currently operate a motor vehicle," I said. Lane laughed.

"We were gone forty-five minutes!"

"And we drank another beer while you were gone. That means we have had two beers in about ninety minutes. What is the legal cutoff?"

Andy took a deep breath and blew it out. "One alcoholic beverage per hour unless you are under the age of twenty-one in which case any alcohol puts you over the legal limit."

"Very good." I'd always been responsible about booze and driving, but Robin and I had agreed to be extra clear about following the rules since Andy had gotten her license. Largely, we were finding it a convenient excuse for our own laziness.

Nate laughed and climbed out of the truck. "I'll move your car."

Lane crawled out after him. "I'll direct you into the backyard, Andy."

"Thanks, guys." Andy put Gracie-Ray in reverse and backed up so Nate had room to pull out.

I left them to play musical cars and went through the gate to the yard.

"They get it sorted out?" Robin asked.

"Yep." I handed her a beer. "We should probably think about food at some point."

"Because it's midafternoon and we're already unable to drive cars?" Robin asked.

"That and they're all going to be occupied and won't realize they are hungry until they are starving."

"Aww, you're a good dad."

"Fuck off."

Andy's engine revved and Lane started directing her into the yard. They managed to bypass the planter beds, which was pretty excellent. Nate followed the truck and closed the gate. Andy climbed out. The three of them stared at the pile of supplies in the truck bed.

"You ready?" Lane asked.

"Heck yeah I am. What do we do first?" Andy asked.

Lane pulled the plans out of Andy's back pocket and studied them very seriously. "Unload the truck."

"Wow. Really using those engineering classes," Nate said.

"Yeah, it's good I drew up these plans." Lane held them up.

"Give me that." Andy took the plans and set them on the deck.

"Keep an eye on this. It's very important," she said to me and Robin.

"On it," I said.

We watched them unload the truck. Lane kept everything in very specific piles. Wood and strips of metal were propped on the flowerbeds. Tubs of chemicals and brushes were placed on the ground underneath. Hardware was gathered on the edge of the deck next to the specs.

Nate and Andy hauled out the piece of plywood lining the bed and tossed it aside. They started deconstructing the bed, which apparently required removing about fifty bolts from under the truck. Our view quickly became a pair of Vans, a pair of retro Nikes, and Nate's leather high-tops sticking out from under the truck.

"So I know the mom reappearance is a big deal and all, but can we discuss the Laurel reappearance?" Robin asked.

"We could, but what if we didn't?"

"Or, conversely, what if we did?"

"Fine. What do you want to know?"

Robin sat up straighter. "Everything. What did she say? What did you say? How did she look? Was it weird? Are you still in love with her?"

"Oof. Okay. She said Henry attacked her and she didn't want me to hear it from someone else."

"Why would that matter?"

"I don't know. It seemed like a stretch."

"And what did you say?"

"That it was shitty to disappear then show up and drop a bomb then disappear again."

"And?"

"And she agreed it was shitty and left."

"So why did she really show up?"

I shrugged. "I don't know, man. I've been asking myself the same question since last night."

"Maybe she was scared. You said she looked really bad."

I took a sip of beer and sat with that hypothesis for a moment. "Like she was looking for comfort?"

"Yeah. You two kind of built that habit. Even if you're doing well, having someone try to kill you with their bare hands would mess you up. Maybe she just wanted to feel safe."

"That is not helpful."

"Why not? I just solved it. I'm a genius."

"Yeah, but in a way that makes me want to heal her and also really fucking pisses me off because she gave up that right. And why do I give a shit? She's a dick. So I'm pissed at myself in addition to being pissed at her."

"So I guess that answers my other question."

"Which one?"

"Are you still in love with her."

"No," I said.

"And it's an obvious yes."

"How the hell did you reach that conclusion?"

"Because it takes a lot to genuinely piss you off."

"It does not. Hair trigger here." I pointed at myself.

"Uh-huh."

"That doesn't mean I'm still in love with her." I sounded petulant as fuck, which was very annoying.

"You can be mad at her and still in love with her. Love is a complicated emotion."

"Super. Thanks for that."

"I don't know what to tell you. I'm just offering brilliant insight. I can't help it if you don't like it," she said.

"It must be difficult to be so brilliant."

"It's no walk in the park. I can tell you that."

I rolled my eyes. "That was an eye roll. In case you missed it."

"Oh, I caught it," Robin said.

"Hey, Cash," Andy yelled.

"Oh, thank God." I yelled back, "What's up, tiger?"

"Can you grab the WD-40?"

"You got it." I went inside. I was reasonably certain I had WD-40 under the sink. I pushed the curtain to the side. It was dark. I really needed to install a light of some sort. I turned on the flashlight on my phone. The blue can stood out among the various other chemicals stacked behind the barrier I'd made to keep Nickels out.

Back outside, Andy's Vans had shifted about forty-five degrees to the right. As I approached, there was a clunk as someone dropped a bolt into the container they were using.

"See? I told you to use torque," Lane said.

"Yes, yes. You're very smart and good at the science," Nate said.

"Don't you have a PhD in science?" Andy asked.

"Yep. PhD in science. The school said, 'Don't you want to narrow your focus?' And I said, 'No thanks. I'm studying all of the science.'"

"Hey, Andy." I held the can low so she could see it. "I got you a present."

She scooted out to grab the can. "Thanks, dude."

"Happy to help." I went back up to the deck and dropped into the Adirondack next to Robin.

"I've given it a lot of thought and I think I've arrived at the proper solution."

"Robin, are you letting me believe that you have some solution to the conundrum of my mother reappearing after twenty-three years or my ex-girlfriend showing up or my old business partner trying to kill me, but then all you're going to say is like nachos?"

"No." She huffed. "I was going to say tacos."

I laughed. "Did I steal your thunder?"

"Yes. Ya jerk."

"Tacos sound great. Are we making them or ordering them?"

"Making. I'm proud that Anderson is so invested in her truck, but I can be proud without watching the entire process."

"Excellent."

"What are the chances you have all the ingredients for tacos in your fridge?" Robin asked.

"Well, last time I looked I had a wedge of Parmesan, a case of beer, approximately four dark chocolate bars, and an apple, singular."

"So, high chances?"

"Definitely."

"That's more stocked than your fridge usually is."

"The cheese, chocolate, and apple are all Lane's."

"Ah, yes. That makes more sense."

"Do you think Nate will go to the store for us?" I asked.

Robin shrugged. "It's worth asking."

"Hey, Nate," I yelled.

"Just a sec," he yelled back. After a minute, he rolled out. He had a very charming streak of grime from his jaw to right below his eye. He came up the deck and leaned against the railing. "What's up?"

"We're going to make tacos," Robin said.

"Love that."

"But we are missing a few ingredients," I said.

He raised his eyebrow. "And you two can't drive."

"We cannot," Robin said.

"So you want me to drive you?"

"Or just go for us?" Robin stuck out her bottom lip in a pitiful manner.

"You know charming me isn't going to work. Why are you trying?"

"I don't know." Robin grinned. "I thought it was worth a shot."

"Fine. What do you need?"

"Tortillas. The little street taco ones. Chicken, cilantro, onion, lime," she said.

"Cotija." I turned to Robin. "Should we do peppers and onions too?"

"Oh, yeah. Green and red bell pepper. Black beans to add to the peppers. Tortilla chips."

"More beer." I liked to remember the important things in life.

"Salsa," Robin said. "Do we want to make guacamole too?"

"Heck yes we need guacamole."

"Avocado. More onion and lime."

Nate shook his head. "I thought you said a few ingredients?"

"Yeah. That's like less than fifteen. So you can still go through the express lane," I said.

"Are there any ingredients you currently have?" Nate asked.

"Hot sauce," Robin said confidently.

"And?"

"And I think we've got four varieties?" She sounded less confident on that one.

"Wow. Okay. Would you care to write this down for me?"

Robin rolled her eyes. "Fine. I'll go with you." I looked at her in question. "What? I can be nice."

"What do you want from the store that you think I won't approve of?" I asked.

"Nothing."

"Smooth, lady. Real smooth." I winked.

"I'll make sure she doesn't buy more ice cream than will fit in the freezer," Nate said.

Robin looked scandalized. "Cash Braddock, I tell you my secrets and you share them with him?"

Nate offered his hand to help Robin up. "If that's your shameful secret, you're doing just fine."

Andy took a bite of street taco and leaned back against the railing. Her legs were stretched across the full width of the step she was sitting on. "You guys are the best."

I saluted her with my own taco. "We know."

"So how are things going with Gracie-Ray?" Robin asked, ever the indulgent mother.

Andy pointed at Lane to answer, her cheeks puffed with the remaining half of her taco.

"Great. We've got the old base removed. Next we're going to put in the wood to make sure everything is square before staining and varnishing," Lane said

"Ha! I knew we had to stain and varnish," Nate shouted.

"But you still don't know the difference between oak and pine."

"It's a trick question. They're both wood. There's no difference." Nate triumphantly held up his beer.

"Seriously?" Robin asked.

"What? Like you all know the difference?"

"Pine's faster burning, like kindling. Oak is slow burning," Robin said.

"The hardness," I said.

"Pine's soft. Oak's hard," Andy said.

"Screw you guys." Nate ate an entire taco in one bite in what I imagined was protest of our assholery.

Lane laughed.

I almost felt bad for mocking him. "In his defense, he grew up in Arizona and New Mexico. I'm guessing they didn't have a fire going all winter."

"It's still common sense," Lane said.

"I'm going to have to agree with Lane. We never had a fire when I was a kid and I still know the difference," Andy said.

Nate shook his head. "But you're a lesbian. Lesbians have knowledge."

"That was a broad generalization, but it benefits my people so I'm going to agree," I said.

"Thank you." Nate pointed at the guacamole. "Now pass me the guac."

CHAPTER FIVE

The squad room at Sacramento PD looked exactly like it had the last time I'd been there. It smelled the same. It sounded the same. Without realizing I was doing it, I looked for Laurel at her desk, but it wasn't her desk anymore. Duarte grinned at me instead. He hopped up and crossed the room to me. He'd graduated to button-ups that fit him properly. His tie was perfectly knotted with a tie pin holding it in place. When he got closer, I realized the pin was a tiny little octopus, which seemed like a very Duarte choice.

"Hey, Cash. You want a cup of coffee or water or anything?"

"I'm good, but thanks."

"Cool. You guys are in conference room B." He pointed to one of the doors that lined the wall.

"There's a conference room B?"

Duarte laughed. "We have labels on the conference rooms and interview rooms now. It's all very fancy."

"Sounds like."

I found the correct conference room and glanced back at Duarte. He nodded and waved me inside. I walked in and found Laurel sitting at the table alone. Nothing says Monday morning like a bright and early meeting with your ex at a police station.

She seemed as surprised to see me as I was her, which was silly considering we had been called in for a meeting together. I just thought I'd have more time to prepare. As if ten more minutes could have made me ready.

She was wearing chinos and a T-shirt with canvas shoes. There was nothing exceptional about the outfit, but that made it all the more exquisite. Her pants were cuffed above her ankle. Her T-shirt clung to the lines of muscle in her back and shoulders. The bandage I'd noticed before was visible at the edge of her collar.

"Hi," she said.

"Hey." I sat three seats down from her, but I could still smell cedar and salt. This was going to be torture.

"I'm sorry I ambushed you before. That wasn't cool."

I shrugged and stared at the table. "It's fine."

"It's not. I should have waited and let Reyes tell you."

"Why did you, then?"

"I wanted—" She shook her head. "I don't know. I guess I wanted to make sure you were okay."

Well, that pissed me right off. I turned to look at her. The bruising around her eyes and along her jaw had gotten darker. "You talked to Lane before showing up. Why not ask her if I was okay?"

"I needed to see you. I knew I wouldn't be able to trust hearing it."

"No, you wanted to make yourself feel better. You were feeling shitty and vulnerable and you came to me for comfort."

"That's not—"

But I didn't get to find out what she was going to deny because Reyes walked in.

"Sorry to keep you guys waiting." He set a file on the table and sat across from us. "The FBI lab was able to get into Brewer's phone. We're still processing all the info, but it's clear that he is exclusively interested in you."

"As in me or as in the two of us?" Laurel asked.

"The two of you. There was nothing to indicate that Xiao or any of your family members are in danger."

"That's good," I said.

"It is, but the notes and photos we recovered suggest a deep fixation." He placed a hand on the closed file in front of him. "He has been stalking the two of you for months. Brewer wants to kill you. He's been unsuccessful, but I'm certain he will try again."

"So what?" I asked. "He's not the only person who wants to kill us. We both have our fair share of enemies."

Reyes shook his head. "The depth of his obsession is pathological. An FBI profiler is working up an analysis right now, but it doesn't take a psychologist to know that he is completely unhinged." He made meaningful eye contact with Laurel, then me. "I'm scared for you."

"Did the phone give any insight into where he's been living?" Laurel asked.

"Nothing yet."

"So we just wait until you arrest him or he kills one of us? Solid plan. Love it," I said.

"I've asked Michelson to put the two of you in a safe house where you'll have twenty-four seven protection," Reyes said.

I laughed. Laurel laughed. Oh, good. Common ground.

"I'm not hiding. I can help you find him. I'm your best chance," Laurel said.

"Absolutely not. We don't use people as bait," Reyes said.

"It doesn't matter. I'm not getting locked in some random safe house in some random location for who knows how long," I said.

Laurel rolled her eyes. "They would put us in a hotel or a condo. It's not like they would ship us off to a black site."

"Oh, I'm sorry. Are you advocating for this now?" I asked.

"No, I'm just saying there's no CIA bunker to sequester us in."

"So your issue is the assumption of a bunker, but sequestering is fine?" I was being a petty asshole. I knew it and I didn't care.

"Hey." Reyes snapped his fingers at us several times so we would look at him. It was like we were five-year-olds. "We don't have time for this. I know this isn't ideal, but it's the best way to guarantee your safety. An officer will escort each of you home to pack a bag." He stood. "We will meet back here in two hours."

"No, I'm not going," Laurel said. She stared Reyes down.

"We're not using you to draw him out. It's just not going to fucking happen," Reyes said.

Laurel stood and squared her shoulders. "Okay. Don't include me in the investigation. But I'm not going to a safe house. You can recommend it, but you can't force me."

"I'm not going either," I said.

Laurel groaned. "God, you're stubborn."

"Seriously? So it's okay for you to skip on a safe house, but I have to go? That's absurd and you know it." I crossed my arms. They were both towering over me, but I didn't care.

"Let us protect you." Reyes shifted to speak directly to Laurel. "I can't investigate this if I'm worrying about you."

Laurel smirked and shook her head. "You'll do just fine. You're perfectly capable of investigating while worrying. This is hardly the first time I've had my ass kicked."

"This wasn't some basic ass kicking." Reyes waved his hand up and down. "He strangled you. He stabbed you. Twice."

He stabbed her? She neglected to mention that detail.

"I'm fine. And even if I wasn't, I still wouldn't go to a safe house. You're blowing this way out of proportion."

"I am not. This dude is batshit and he's basically writing fan fiction about murdering you," Reyes yelled.

Laurel laughed cruelly. "Do you hear yourself?"

"Yes, I do. And I know how this sounds. But his notes are terrifying." He held up the case file and shook it. It was very dramatic. "This guy is a trained law enforcement officer with a stockpile of weapons and equipment and a psychotic fixation on my best friend who hasn't called me in three goddamn months."

Laurel and I stared at Reyes, waiting to see if his diatribe would continue. Or that's what I was doing. She looked like she was processing.

"I'm sorry," Laurel said.

"No, you don't get to do that. Don't patronize me."

"I'm not. I really am sorry." Laurel looked at me, then back at Reyes. She sat back down. "I handled leaving all wrong and I hurt just about everyone I could hurt. And by the time I figured it out, I was too ashamed to come back."

"Dammit, Kallen." Reyes came around the table and hugged her.

I stood. "Well, this has been enlightening, but I'm going to take off. Let me know when you catch Henry."

"Hold up." Reyes let go of Laurel. "It's not safe for you."

I shrugged. "Whatever, man. It's your fault he is in the wind. I did my part."

"How is it his fault?" Laurel asked.

"All the Sac PD officers are at fault. If you guys didn't have such a bullshit toxic culture, maybe someone would have listened to me the night you arrested me and Henry got away. Anyone who participates in and benefits from that culture and doesn't fight against it is at fault for it."

"Christ, I forgot how obnoxious you are," Reyes said.

I forced a grin. "Yeah, it's annoying to have someone point out systemic power structures."

Reyes took a deep breath. "Can you just cool it for a minute? Your self-righteous anger isn't going to protect you. When Brewer comes after you, explaining that it's my fault isn't going to stop him."

"You're not wrong," I said.

"So let me keep you two safe." He turned around to look at Laurel. "Please. We will wrap this up as quickly as possible."

"I'm sorry. I still can't do it," Laurel said.

"Neither can I. I just opened an art gallery. I have to be there. Plus, there's a lot going on in my life. I can't just dip out." I tried to keep my tone even and non-confrontational. I was mildly successful.

"Let's compromise, then," Laurel said. She slugged Reyes in the shoulder. "Everything will be okay. You can keep the patrols outside our residences. Hell, you can assign us bodyguards if you have the resources."

"You know damn well that we don't," he said.

"Whatever. Monitor us however you see fit. If Henry escalates in any way, we can revisit the discussion. Cool?"

"Cool," I said.

"Okay. But any escalation and I'm locking you in a room," Reyes said.

"Does that mean I can leave?" I pointed my thumb at the door.

"Not quite. Let's review some security protocols." Reyes went back to his side of the table and sat.

I didn't move from my spot by the door. "We already shut down the safe house idea. What other security protocols could there be?"

"I'd like you to have the officer posted outside check your place before you enter every time you get home. I'd also like the officer to do a sweep of the perimeter of your house every hour."

"Okay, sure."

"You should also nail the back gate shut," Laurel said.

I gave her a look. I did not need her helping. "It only opens from the inside."

"She's right. Any deterrent is a good thing," Reyes said. "And keep your phone on and charged at all times. Tell Robin or your business partner your schedule and check in with them regularly."

"Can I just tell my roommate?" I asked.

He gave me an odd look. "As long as they can easily contact me."

"It's Lane. She's still living with my sister," Laurel said.

His eyes went wide. "Right. Okay."

"Anything else?" I asked with as much exasperation as I could muster.

"Just be aware of your surroundings. Don't go out alone. Be smart."

"Fine. Whatever." I rolled my eyes extra good to make sure they saw. "What about Laurel? What dumb shit does she have to agree to?"

Reyes looked at Laurel and half-smiled. "I'd like her to move in with me until this is resolved."

She stared at him. After a minute she nodded. "Yeah, I can do that."

"Really?"

"Yes. I'm living in a B&B, but I can stand a couple days of your crappy coffee."

"Neat. Now can I go?" I asked.

"Yes." Reyes stood. He was still being weird and reluctant about the whole thing, which I didn't understand. He'd done his part. If I got killed, it wasn't on him.

I left the conference room.

"Wait, Cash." Laurel hustled to follow. As we waited for the elevator, she watched me. The doors opened and we got on. There was no one else. When the doors closed, she turned. "I was hoping we could talk."

"I'm good, thanks," I said.

"I did a shitty thing and I'd really like to explain."

"You already explained. You needed to find who you are when you're not a cop. You didn't want me around for that journey. You left. That's it."

"And I was wrong," she said.

The doors opened. "Yep." I walked out and turned toward the parking lot. Laurel followed.

Once we were out of the police station, away from cop ears, she started talking again. "I know you're upset. And you have every right to be."

"I'm not upset."

She slowed, then caught up again. "You're not?"

"Nope."

"Great. Then let's be together again." She called my bluff.

"Nope."

"Why not?"

"Because you left."

"Cash, stop, please."

"I can't. I'm busy." We got to my car and I hit the fob to unlock it.

"I came back for you."

"No. You came back because Henry Brewer tried to fucking kill you."

"No." She stepped in front of me so I couldn't get in the car. "I mean, yes. But I took a job up here for you."

"Without ever talking to me or consulting me about it. Kind of like your decision to leave in the first place. I'm glad to see you learned." I reached around her and opened the door.

"Cash."

I went around her and climbed in the car. She took a step back as I pulled out of the space. She looked sad and lost, but that wasn't my problem anymore.

Chapter Six

I set an iced coffee the size of my head on the table in front of Kyra and collapsed into the chair across from her. The wrought iron chair listed to the side before settling in the soft ground.

"Hey, friend. How did it go? Swimmingly?" She plucked the straw wrapper from the top of her drink and crumpled the paper.

"Yep. Swimmingly. It went fucking swimmingly."

"This might be me reading too much into it, but I'm kind of thinking it didn't go swimmingly?"

"Gosh. You're so astute. I can't get anything past you." The chair started to sink again. We really needed to do some proper yard work. Then again, all our time and money had gone into the gallery itself. I half stood and adjusted the chair.

She grinned and stared at me. Took a long drink of coffee. "Well?"

"Well what?"

"Are you going to tell me about it?"

"It was just weird. Laurel insisted on following me out of the station. She went on and on about how she did a terrible thing leaving me and it was a mistake and she came back for me. It was bullshit."

"How is that bullshit?"

"She was forced to come back when Henry tried to off her. It had nothing to do with me," I said.

"Maybe there's more to it?" Kyra's tone was far too gentle and kind. I wasn't ready for gentle and kind.

"There's not."

"Did she explain at all?"

"No. I left."

"You left?" she asked.

"Yeah. She followed me to my car and kept going on about her feelings and shit. And my feelings and shit. I don't need her to tell me I'm angry. I'll decide when I'm angry."

"Wow. Sounds like you've got it all figured out."

"Yeah."

"I meant that sarcastically," she said.

"Oh."

"You obviously don't have it figured out. You're all in a tizzy."

"I'm not in a—"

"A tizzy, dammit. I know this because I asked an innocuous question about how your meeting with the police detective went and you answered with a rundown of Laurel behavior."

"Oh."

"So what would you rather talk about? The uncomfortable meeting with the police about your former business partner going rogue? Or the woman you're still hung up on?" She bit her straw and smiled sweetly at me.

Well, when she put it that way. "The police."

"You're sure?"

"Totally."

"Okay, tell me how your meeting with Reyes went."

"There's not much to tell. Nothing surprising, at least. Henry Brewer apparently is real fixated on me and Laurel."

"Not feeling great about that," Kyra said.

"Nor am I. But he doesn't have anyone else in his sights, so that's good."

"Feeling better about me. Worse about you."

I shrugged. "I know I should be freaked out, but I'm weirdly not. If he wants to kill me, he's got plenty of opportunity. Not much I can do about it."

She scrunched up her face. It looked kind of involuntary. "That's the worst take I've heard in a long time."

"It's the truth. I'm not going to be a dumbass. I'm aware of my surroundings. I'm going to listen to all the stupid advice Reyes gave me."

"Reyes should keep you locked up until they find this guy."

I grinned, then forced myself to stop. Kyra probably wouldn't find it nearly as funny as I did. "He tried."

"He tried to lock you up?" She was confused.

"No. But he tried to put me and Laurel in a safe house. We declined."

"Cash. Why? What the fuck?"

"We opened a business three days ago." I gestured at the building. "And I have a life. And I don't particularly want to be locked up with my ex-girlfriend until they find a guy who has been hiding for a year and likely can continue hiding for years to come."

"You tried to gloss over that whole don't want to be locked up with my ex-girlfriend thing, but I heard it and I'm not ignoring it."

"Whatever."

"If I think you're sacrificing your safety because you don't want to have a couple of uncomfortable days with Laurel, I'm going to lock your ass up myself."

"It's not like that. I mean, it's definitely one of the reasons, but not the only one. Or even the biggest."

"Uh-huh." She seemed skeptical.

"It's not. And we both promised Reyes that we would go willingly if there was any escalation," I said.

"Escalation? Last time, he tried to kill Laurel. And from what you told me and what Robin told me after you didn't tell me shit, I'm pretty sure he was trying real hard. At this point, wouldn't escalation just be succeeding?"

"Calm down."

"Did you seriously just tell me to calm down?"

I squinted at her and grimaced. "Maybe."

"Okay, when you're done being a douche, I'm open to hearing the plethora of ways you are keeping yourself safe." She crossed her arms and leaned back.

"Fine. Look at your phone. I shared my location with you. I also shared it with Nate, Lane, Robin, and Van." Kyra pulled out her phone and tapped the screen. When I presumably showed up next to her, she nodded. "Lane is aware of my whereabouts at all times. I texted her when I left the police station to go to Old Soul for coffee, then when I came here. I'll text her when I leave and tell her where I'm headed next."

"What about Reyes? Does he know your location?"

"Yes. I shared my location with both him and Duarte, the other detective I don't outright loathe. And, yes, I texted to let them know I was doing so."

"And they still have a cop watching your house?" she asked.

"At all times, ma'am." I put my hand up in a Boy Scout salute.

"It's supposed to be three fingers, you poser."

I altered my salute. "Sorry. I was never too good at following codes of conduct."

"You don't say."

"Maybe if I'd joined the Boy Scouts, it would have helped." I grinned. "But, you know, heterosexism, the patriarchy."

"You're not taking this seriously at all."

I took a deep breath. "I am. Promise." I grabbed her hand. "Don't worry about me. I'm doing everything I can to stay safe while not letting this entitled asshole disrupt my life."

She sighed and squeezed my hand. "Okay. I just like you is all."

"Hey, I like me too. I'm real fun."

"Is there anything I can do?"

"Not really. Just let me pretend everything is normal for a bit." I leaned back in my listing chair. "We have a meeting scheduled. What's going on? How are we doing?"

"We sold four more pieces over the weekend. That brings us to about a third of our current holdings."

"That's like good, right?"

"That's really good. That's a couple mortgage payments."

"We're killing it." I gave her an enthusiastic high five. The chair shifted again.

"Okay. That's it." She stood. "We're going inside."

"What? Why?"

"Because you look like you're about to get sucked into a hell dimension or something."

I crossed my ankle over my knee. I was sitting at about a seventy-degree angle. My abs were getting a nice little workout. "Nuh-uh."

"Cash." She put out her hand.

I rolled my eyes and took her hand. "Fine. But only because you want to."

"Dipshit." She led me inside our office. "I need you to look at a couple portfolios anyway. I scheduled studio visits for us next week. I'd like you to be somewhat familiar with the work before we go."

"Okay, fine. I'll look at art." I dragged my feet a little.

"You have it so tough."

"I know."

In the office, Kyra cleared the edge of the desk of all two items and set a stack of portfolios in front of me. "They're in order of studio visit so don't mix them up."

"It's gross how organized you are."

"We play to our strengths, friend. You're good at looking at pretty pictures and charming white women. I'm good at managing us."

I opened the first portfolio. Kyra sat behind the desk and opened her laptop. I flipped two pages. They were photos of sculptures. I turned three more pages.

"Whatcha doing?" I asked.

"Working," Kyra said without looking up.

"Wanna play?"

"No, we're working right now, sweetheart."

I closed the portfolio. "I'm bored."

"You literally said you wanted a job where you got to look at art all day and decide in your heart whether it was good or not."

"I take it back. I want to read poetry in the sunshine."

"Well, we invested six months and a fuckload of money and effort into this so we're going to do the gallery thing right now." Her tone was unnecessarily patronizing.

I huffed. I sighed. She still didn't look up from her laptop. "Fine."

"If you look through all three portfolios, we can go check out the summer menu at Citrus & Salt."

"Fuck yes we can." I opened the portfolio again and actually looked at the art this time. The sculptures looked supple like flesh. There was something obscene, almost pornographic about them. About halfway through the portfolio, I realized the pieces were all metal. They were welded and smoothed and painted to look like skin, organs, but they were solid. "Okay, this shit is wild."

"What is?" Kyra finally looked up. "Oh, Nevada Tarr's work? Aren't they fantastic?"

"Yeah. Are these all sex organs?"

"Some of them. They're all physical markers of gender." She came around the desk and leaned over me. She flipped a couple of pages until she found a series of oatmeal colored strange shapes. "These are all glands."

"Oh, cool. I like it."

"They're all to scale, which is just neat. Especially when you compare the clitoris to, well, basically everything else."

"Oh, yeah." I waggled my eyebrows at her.

"You're such a child." She ruffled my hair.

"Whoa. Hey." I leaned away from her and finger combed my hair into place.

She grabbed the back of my neck and squeezed. "Chill, dipshit."

"What if a hot girl walks in here right now and my hair is all unkempt? Can you imagine?"

"We're closed so I doubt a girl, hot or otherwise, is going to walk in. Also, uh, hello." She waved a hand up and down her body. "Hot girl right here."

"Whatever. A hot girl I have an interest in sleeping with who has an interest in sleeping with me."

"Now you're just narrowing the field way too far. I doubt Laurel Kallen is going to walk in here again anytime soon," she said.

"Huh?"

"I'm pretty sure she's the only hot girl you have an interest in sleeping with."

"Nuh-uh."

"Yeah, okay." She rolled her eyes and went back behind her desk.

"I'm not interested in sleeping with Laurel."

"Right. Of course not."

"Kyra, I'm not." I sounded super believable.

"I totally believe you."

"Whatever." I set the Nevada Tarr portfolio down and picked up Dana Reed's. It was an abstract oil painting exhibit. I looked at the first three pages before realizing I wasn't actually looking at the paintings, just flipping through them. I went back to the beginning and forced myself to study it. There were swirls of orange and slashes of blue.

I wasn't interested in sleeping with Laurel. I wasn't interested in anything with Laurel. She'd left when she had no real reason to. And then she came back and wanted to pick up where we left off. Like I could just forget that she broke my heart and abandoned me. Especially when we were finally free of Sac PD, free to be together without reservation.

I was halfway through the portfolio staring at thick purple spatters. Dammit. I turned back to the beginning. This was going to be a long process.

"How's that portfolio treating you?" Kyra asked ten minutes later.

"I keep getting distracted and not seeing the art."

"Why's that?"

"Because you're a dick who insists on pointing out that I might not be entirely over Laurel."

Kyra laughed. "Oh. Sorry."

"No, you're not."

"I'm not. But you've done some real good work there. Can I buy you a beer and some fried pickles?"

I took a deep breath. "Yeah, okay."

CHAPTER SEVEN

It was a drive I'd taken countless times in the last decade. Everything was the same. Even the differences—the restaurants with new names, the ever changing art galleries, the requisite new stop sign—were the same. I just didn't know what I was driving to.

It had been almost a year since the last time Clive and I spoke about anything with real substance. He told me Henry was a good guy. Henry, who was currently being tracked by about five law enforcement departments. Henry, who had tried to kill Laurel twice now. Henry, who was currently stalking me.

"How you holding up?" Nate asked.

"I don't know. It's weird," I said.

"Yeah. That's not surprising."

"I don't really know where to focus. Like I've got an abundance of weird and I can't decide what to dread or think about or prep for." We went by the last vestige of civilization in Placerville. The hills began to slope naturally instead of the abrupt cuts into hillsides from gold mining and nineteenth century development.

"Any idea what you're going to say to Clive?"

I tapped the steering wheel and tried to find an answer. "I guess it depends what he says. Like if—just spitballing here—he says 'oh, Cash, I was so wrong and you were right and I went to therapy and got a degree in gender studies to better understand why what I said was wrong,' then maybe I'll just forgive him and move on."

Nate laughed. "Just spitballing?"

I grinned. "Yeah, but if he says nothing or asks if I've calmed down and decided to forgive that nice Henry boy, then maybe I'll just leave and move to Costa Rica. I mean, things aren't ideal here and apparently Costa Rica is nice."

"Awesome. Not at all extreme."

"That's what I'm thinking. Perfectly reasonable expectations and responses."

"Literally no room for disappointment." He nodded supportively. "And what about Marjorie?"

"I still don't know what I want from her."

"Do you have to want something?" he asked.

"She's my mother. I feel like I'm supposed to want something from her."

"And you've always been a stickler for things you're supposed to want or do."

"I don't like it when you tell me the truth about myself. It is very inconvenient," I said.

"I do it just to fuck with you. I like to stock up on truths just for fun."

"Dick. I think I preferred Robin's response."

"Which was?" he asked.

"That I'm deeply broken because my mother abandoned me."

"Oh, yeah. Much better than pointing out a logical fallacy, which suggests you don't owe her anything."

I saw the familiar sign for Braddock Farm up ahead. I knew I could turn around, go back where I came from. Or keep driving. We were only an hour from Tahoe. Nate would indulge me in a weekend at the lake. But the turn was inevitable. I'd eventually have to take it. Better now with one of my best friends and a looming death threat to act as a buffer. I turned on my blinker.

Nate reached over and tapped his fist against my shoulder. "I got you, man."

"Thanks." I took a deep breath and turned at the farm stand. I didn't recognize the kid in the booth. But then, I wouldn't. The kids I had a vague chance of recognizing had probably graduated and moved on. I pulled up in front of the house. Shelby's car was parked next to Marjorie's sedan.

"Okay, your codeword is persimmon," Nate said.

"My codeword?" I asked.

"Yeah, like if you want to get out of here, work persimmon into the conversation."

"How the fuck am I supposed to use persimmon in conversation?"

"I don't know, but if we choose a normal word, you might say it accidentally," he said.

"But if we choose a word I never say, I won't be able to use it in conversation."

Nate sighed. "Cash, we are on a farm. Just ask if they are growing persimmons. But more importantly, I was joking."

I punched his arm. "You're a dickwad."

"Yes, yes, I am."

I climbed out. Nate waited while I grabbed a six-pack from the back. It was from a brewery near the gallery. I'd always brought beer from Sac for Clive. I didn't really know why I continued the tradition except it was habit. Plus, Clive taught me to never show up at someone's house empty-handed. Most of his life lessons had been good. Aside from the latent sexist bullshit, of course.

We walked around the house to the patio overlooking the valley below. Clive, Shelby, and Marjorie were chatting and looking out at the sea of evergreen trees.

"Cash, Nate." Clive stood out of the same instinct that had driven me to bring beer. He hesitated, then we both stepped forward. He wrapped his arms around me. He smelled the same, felt the same. It dulled my irritation, but the last year had already worn it down to a familiar shine. At the core I was still angry that Clive dismissed my perception, my version of Henry over his own scant history with the Boy Scout version. I was still angry at myself for letting Henry's facade continue long enough to establish the legitimacy of the ruse. Clive let go of me and hugged Nate. It looked like there was something seeking in Clive's grip to compensate for the stiffness in Nate's.

In the space of time it took me to watch them hug, Shelby threw her arms around my neck with such force I had to swing her to stay on my feet. She kissed my cheek loudly.

"Hey, Shelby."

"Oh, Cash. I've missed you." She pulled me in tighter and whispered, "It's getting weird here. I don't like it."

"Have you been kidnapped?" I whispered back. "Because you know you can leave at any time, right?"

She squealed. "Shut up." She let go of me to slap my shoulder. I grinned. She threw herself back in my arms.

"Enough of that. My turn," Nate said.

"Nate." Shelby squealed again. She abandoned me to tackle him. He picked her up and spun in a complete circle.

"Hey, that's not Nate. It's Dr. Xiao," I said.

Shelby put her feet down to stop their motion. "No." She grabbed his face. "Really? Officially?"

"Really officially." Nate smiled.

"Congratulations, Dr. Xiao." She kissed his cheek. "Look at you. So fancy. Did you get taller? I think you got taller."

"I sure feel taller."

"Dr. Xiao?" Clive asked.

"Yep." Nate nodded.

"Congratulations. Very impressive." Clive grinned.

"Thanks."

"You're a doctor?" Marjorie asked.

"Sorry. Marjorie, this is my buddy Nate Xiao. Nate, Marjorie Braddock, my mother," I said.

Nate leaned over the table to shake her hand. "It's nice to meet you."

"You too. So did you just finish med school? I'm not sure how all that works," Marjorie said.

Nate sat in one of the empty chairs. "Actually, I just finished my doctorate."

"Oh, so you're going to be a college professor?" she asked.

He shrugged. "At some point, hopefully. Right now, I'm interviewing with research institutions. I kind of missed all the deadlines for teaching positions."

"Why's that?"

Nate gave me a look and I nodded. He waited until I sat to turn back to Marjorie. "Cash and I had to wrap up our business. It was time intensive when I would have been traveling for interviews."

"Wrap up how?" Marjorie asked.

"We sold it," I said.

"You did?" Clive sounded surprised.

"Yep. But I couldn't very well send her off solo to meet with our buyer," Nate said.

"He's not the friendliest of fellows," I said.

Clive put up his hands. "Back up. Give me the whole story."

"Remember Jerome St. Maris?" I asked.

Clive looked displeased at my question. "The guy who punched you that time?"

"That one, yeah. He's a little excitable."

Nate laughed. "That's ol' Jerome. Excitable."

"We sold him access to our supply line in exchange for a large portion of his profit. Our only caveat was that he had to sell our product exclusively. That stabilized his customer base."

"He was selling inconsistent crap, which made him hemorrhage customers," Nate said.

"Within a few months, he was able to hold the customers he stole from us in the first place. So we sold him our client list and direct access to our pharmacist and supplier, our brand, essentially," I said.

"How does one sell an illegal prescription drug brand?" Shelby asked.

"What do you mean?" I asked.

"Like it's intangible. You don't exactly have a logo. What is your branding?"

Nate looked at me. I shrugged. He shrugged back. "It's basically our reputation," he said.

"Yeah. Like we vouched for him. And directed customers to him," I said.

"And in exchange, he paid us a ton of money. I paid off a bunch of my student loans. Cash bought a building. And all we had to do was barter away our morality." Nate blindly put up his hand and I high-fived him.

Clive awkwardly cleared his throat and glanced at Marjorie. "So that's how you opened an art gallery?" he asked.

"Yep. Do you remember my friend Kyra from college?" I asked. Clive frowned and shook his head. "Kyra Daneshmendan. She's a painter. Persian. Hecka queer."

Clive nodded slowly. "She has that haircut." He waved his hand past the side of his head. "Shaved on one side."

"Yeah. That's her. She has some experience curating, but she's been ensconced in painting the last few years. And I clearly needed something to do. A gallery seemed like a natural fit for us."

"I'm sorry, what business did the two of you run?" Marjorie asked.

Everyone looked at each other awkwardly, but I knew I was the one who had to answer. "Drugs. We were drug dealers," I said.

"Oh," Marjorie said.

Clive looked like he was vacillating between angry and ashamed. Shelby was intently studying the view. Nate was fine. He shared my value system.

"So why did you decide to sell the business?" Marjorie asked.

"A number of reasons. Mostly because we no longer could justify it to ourselves," I said.

"And Cash's ex was a cop," Nate said.

I kicked him. "I didn't stop for a girl. It was a moral issue."

"A hot cop," Nate whispered.

"Wow. I'm so glad I brought you along for this," I said to him.

"So you dated a cop and that inspired you to become a law-abiding citizen?" Marjorie asked.

I turned to Clive. "I brought beer. Maybe we should break into it."

He shot out of his chair. "I'll get the bottle opener."

"I'm sorry. I didn't mean to sound blasé. I was really asking," Marjorie said.

"It's fine. It's just a bit more complicated," I said. Nate let out a short, loud laugh. "Do you want to tell the story, dickwad?"

"No, ma'am." He put his hands up.

I rolled my eyes at him. I was sure it made an impression. "I started dating a woman last summer. Then I found out she was an undercover detective building a case against us."

Clive came back outside. He set a Pellegrino in front of Marjorie and opened beers for the rest of us.

"I'm not certain that qualifies as an ex. That's horrible," Marjorie said.

"Terrible." Nate nodded. "Unforgivable, really."

"I hate you," I said. He just laughed. "She arrested us and we brokered a deal to act as confidential informants in exchange for, you know, not going to jail."

"Come on. Get to the sexy part," Nate said.

"Oh, yeah. I love sexy parts," Shelby said.

"There's a sexy part?" Marjorie asked.

"Well, we were working real close on cases and—"

"I'm sorry." Clive set his beer down hard. "Did you get back together with Laurel?"

"Yep." I nodded once to emphasize the definitiveness.

"What the hell is wrong with you?" he asked.

"Lots, probably."

"She put you in jail."

"I broke the law."

"She lied to you."

"And she apologized," I said.

"How can you just forgive someone for lying about the fundamentals of who they are?" The last time we had talked about this, Clive had been lost. He'd been confused, searching for clarification but unwilling to listen to my explanation. He was clearly still uninterested in listening to me, but now he was angry.

"She didn't lie about that."

"She didn't even tell you her real name," he shouted.

"Names aren't who we are." I knew I should stop trying to piss him off, but he was making it so easy. It felt compulsory.

Nate cut in before we could dig deeper. "Listen, Kallen lied about a lot of shit, but she never lied about loving Cash. She gave up her career because she couldn't reconcile the two. As far as grand gestures go, that's a big one." He squeezed my thigh under the table.

Clive angrily drank his beer and said nothing.

"She quit being a cop?" Shelby asked.

"Yeah. The same day she got us released from our CI obligations," Nate said.

"Wasn't that like her entire identity?" she asked.

"She thought it was. But she realized it wasn't," I said.

"So you're together now?" Marjorie asked.

I shook my head. "She left me."

"After all that?" Shelby sounded bummed.

"After all that."

"Oh, Cash." Shelby came around the table to hug me.

"Thanks."

"So who is the man who threatened you and Clive? Is he related to this drug business?" Marjorie asked.

"You mean Henry Brewer?" I asked. She nodded. "He worked with us. He blames me and Laurel for ruining his life, which is why he came back to terrorize us."

"What do you mean? I thought the threat was gone? That's what the sheriff said," Marjorie said.

"The threat to Clive is gone. Henry is still very much stalking Laurel and Cash." Nate very carefully avoided looking at me or Clive as he spoke. "He's misogynistic and fixated. Granted, he's always been a horrible person and this is simply a symptom of his entitlement, but him behaving exactly as you would expect doesn't make it any easier to deal with."

I loved Nathan Xiao.

"That's certainly extreme. We've all known men like that, but most of them stop before attempted murder," Marjorie said.

"That's why I love Clive. He's secure enough in himself that he doesn't need to control vulnerable people to feel masculine." Shelby leaned over to squeeze Clive's shoulder.

"Yes, he's always been like that." Marjorie smiled.

Clive's shoulders relaxed infinitesimally. I was well aware that focusing on areas of success rather than critiquing was the way to change minds, but I just didn't have it in me to praise Clive for behaving like an adult. It was my failing and I was comfortable with it. He was a grown man with a twenty-two-year-old woman for a best friend. She could take on the burden of teaching him. I was done.

We stayed for another hour before I asked Clive if they grew persimmons. In that hour we talked about nothing. I thought I might find some familiarity in Marjorie, but there was nothing. She reminded me of my aunt, her older sister. Her hands were reminiscent of my grandmother's. The cadence of her speech was Clive's. But she was a stranger.

CHAPTER EIGHT

A t the knock on the door I cycled through all of the unfortunate possibilities. My family, the cops. But then I realized Lane probably forgot her key again. With our recent attention to security, she couldn't break in like she had in the past.

Of course, it was none of those people. Laurel was on the porch turned away from the door. The arrogant cut of her shoulder blades was familiar and obnoxiously sexy. She was talking to my uniformed watcher for the day as he checked her ID. The cop handed the ID back.

"Thank you, Ms. Kallen. I hope I didn't alarm you."

"Not at all, Officer. I appreciate the vigilance." Laurel turned and half-smiled at me. "I'm sure you're loving this security."

"Big fan. What do you want?" My tone was decidedly lacking in warmth.

"Everything okay, Ms. Braddock?" the uniform asked.

"Yes, thanks. Ms. Kallen will be on her way shortly," I said. He nodded and went back to his car.

"I was hoping we could talk." Laurel put up her hands in placation. "Not about us or anything involving relationships or emotional states or morals. I swear."

"Then what?"

"Can we talk inside? Please."

I hated myself. "Fine." I stepped aside.

"Thank you." She came in and I closed the door.

"You want a cup of coffee?" I asked.

"That would be great."

I nodded toward the living room and went into the kitchen to grab another coffee. When I came back out, Laurel was in her usual spot on the couch looking uncomfortable with how well she fit. I handed her the mug.

"So talk." I sat across from her.

"I want to catch Brewer."

"Great idea. I'll alert the media and the FBI."

She leaned forward. "Your sarcasm is getting lazy."

"I'm existentially tired. What do you want from me?"

"I think we can access Brewer in different ways than the cops and the feds can," she said. I waved my hand for her to continue. "When we initially tried to find him last summer, most people were reluctant to believe that he could possibly have done the things we claimed, but when presented with evidence, they were more willing to talk." Nickels emerged from Lane's bedroom and made a beeline for Laurel. "Hello, my darling." Nickels jumped on her lap, already purring in anticipation. "I've missed you." Laurel scratched Nickels's head and stared deeply into her eyes.

"Laurel? The Brewer investigation?"

"Sorry. His colleagues were pretty pissed off that he made a mockery of their department once they found out he'd been helping himself to evidence." Nickels flopped and stretched across Laurel's lap. She rubbed the cat's tummy. "They wanted to kick his ass."

"I remember. Sheriff Tolson was personally offended."

"Yeah, he took it hard. His family is close with Brewer's family."

"I take it the family didn't jump at the chance to help you arrest their golden boy?" I asked. And then I wondered why I was asking questions. She was already reeling me in and I hadn't even noticed the hook.

"They basically stayed quiet. They weren't going to obstruct us, but they weren't going to help us in any way. His grandmother, however, actively fought us. She refused to show up for scheduled interviews. She wouldn't answer the door when we went to her house. She released hellhounds that nearly took Reyes out."

"Hellhounds you say?"

"Hellhounds, Rottweilers, whatever," she said.

Nickels got tired of the effort it took to keep her eyes open. Her purring ramped up. Traitor.

"So we'll just go to her house and ask her to pretty please tell us where her murderous grandson is and, based on her previous behavior, we can assume that we she will immediately draw us a map and give us a phone number?"

Laurel rolled her eyes. "Or you can go tell her you want that bitch Kallen to pay for what she did to you and precious Henry. See if she bites."

If nothing else, it might piss him off enough to make a move. Henry was a mama's boy. And if his collection of knitwear was any indication, he was probably a grandma's boy too. "Seems thin, but I'll give it a shot."

"Reyes said Brewer has been stalking us for months." Laurel suddenly looked vaguely guilty. "But he left his laptop unlocked last night and I kind of helped myself to the files. Brewer's been stalking us for at least nine months. His notes go back to September, but he might have been keeping tabs on us before that."

I did the math. Hoo boy. "He knows we were together."

"Oh, yeah." She pressed her lips together.

"Shit. Sac PD knows too, don't they?"

She nodded slowly, deliberately. "Yep."

"But they haven't said anything to you?"

"No. Not yet, at least."

"I'm sorry."

"I'm not. It might screw up a few cases." She shrugged. "But up until the end, I did good work. Those convictions will hold." She caught my eye and held it. "But I can't, I don't regret our relationship."

"So." I waited.

"So let's use it," she said.

"How?"

"Tell Grandma Brewer you were in a sexual relationship with me. Tell her it is enough to create doubt around her grandson's case. If you can just talk to him, the two of you can clear his name and get revenge on me."

"You are a devious motherfucker, you know that?" I asked.

"I'm aware."

"I don't hate this plan. Except for the Rottweiler threat."

The faint scowl she'd been wearing since I saw her in the art gallery office lifted. "You'll do it?"

"Yes. But only to nail Henry. This doesn't mean anything."

She nodded. "Okay. You don't want to acknowledge that I'm still in love with you, that's fine."

"See that wasn't cool." I pointed.

She shrugged. "I won't mention it again."

"And you have to be honest about everything Henry related."

"Done. I copied the files off Reyes's computer. I'll let you read them."

"I'm not talking about the very illegal file stealing, which I absolutely do want to read. I'm talking about whatever freaked Reyes out so much he's got you living with him. I'm talking about the fact that Henry apparently stabbed you and you didn't mention it."

She looked at her thigh. It wasn't bleeding so it clearly wasn't important. "It's not like it's a secret."

"Sure. Being stabbed isn't worth mentioning. Just a regular Tuesday."

"It was a Thursday."

I raised my eyebrows. "Yeah, that's the important detail."

"Okay, what do you want to know?"

"Tell me about him trying to kill you. The actual injuries. I'm not working with you if I'm not aware of your physical limitations."

"Okay. I was hiking. He came up behind me and tried to strangle me with a piece of wire. I managed to get my hand up in time to get between the wire and my throat." She held up her hand so I could see the bruising. "I threw my head back and probably broke his nose. He eased up long enough for me to break his grip on the wire. He slugged me in the face a couple of times." She pointed at the bruising on her face.

"And the stabbing?"

"That's when he pulled out a knife. A little guy. Only five inches or so."

"That's not little."

"Whatever. I didn't see him pull it out. So he throws a left hook to distract me and gets my thigh with the knife. I realize he's seriously trying to kill me—"

"You didn't realize that before with the strangling?"

"Well, yeah. But that requires some element of surprise and he'd lost that. With a knife you just have to get lucky."

"Lucky. Right."

"Anyway, he twists the knife and yanks it out. I go down. He kicks me a couple of times then gets on top of me. He stabs me again, but I roll to the side enough for him to get my shoulder instead of my chest, nail him in the balls, pull the knife out, and stick him in the side with it." She extended two fingers and motioned like she was stabbing me in the ribs. She stopped an inch from touching me and I was briefly disappointed. "He falls over. Then I shove him off the path and down the side of the mountain."

"You shoved him off a mountain?" Dammit. That was hot.

"There was another path below. It was only like twenty feet down."

"Cool." I kind of hated myself for being impressed.

"So then I picked my ass up. Tied my shirt around my leg. Saw his phone on the ground. Grabbed it and ran. You know the rest."

"You ran down a mountain after being stabbed in the thigh?"

"I didn't have much of a choice. Plus, I didn't run down a whole mountain. I wasn't far from the parking lot and there was cell reception. The rangers met me halfway. I probably only ran two miles. Adrenaline is a great drug."

"Totally. A couple days ago, I was helping Andy and Lane sand wood for the truck bed and I got a gnarly splinter. I pulled it out all on my own. Just grabbed the tweezers and yanked out that motherfucker." I extended my right index finger so she could see the very serious red dot in the center of my finger pad. "I didn't even feel the throbbing until afterward."

"Whoa. And you didn't have to go to the hospital or anything?" She grabbed my hand and inspected the dot. Then realized she was holding my hand and abruptly dropped it.

"Yeah." I rubbed my hands together like that would remove her touch. "So I get adrenaline."

"Sounds like basically the same thing."

"Okay, when do we want to go manipulate old lady Brewer?"

"As soon as possible. She's in Camino. She's isolated, but not too far out. There's a fire access road behind her property. I can monitor your conversation from there. The recording won't be admissible in court, but I no longer care about that."

"You're going to wire me?"

"Of course. I'm not going to risk your safety."

Right. Because she was in love with me. "What if Henry is following us?"

"That's the part I'm not sure about. I can't figure out how he's keeping tabs on both of us. And I can't shake him if we don't know how he's tracking us. In fact, I should leave soon. He's probably watching your place right now. The longer I stay, the less he will believe that you want to crucify me."

"So we need to figure out how he's stalking us, but we need to do it without being seen together?"

"Pretty much."

"Can you send me the files you took from Reyes? We can FaceTime once I look them over. Unless you think he's tracking us digitally."

She shook her head. "Digital Forensics already checked all my electronics. Brika is confident Brewer's not cyber stalking me. Reyes said they were going to check you out too."

I nodded. "He texted earlier and asked me to call him."

"Okay, so have Sac PD clear your computer and phone. Text me if you're clear and I'll email the files."

"And right now I need to make a show of throwing you out?"

"The louder the better."

"Screaming match. Got it."

"According to his psych profile, his misogyny is deeply rooted. He thinks women are inferior and likely connects masculine gender presentation with superiority."

"That's why he and I always got along. I was the right kind of chick."

"Right. And the wrong kind—anyone challenging his masculinity—is an object to be used either sexually or emotionally or physically."

"Aside from telling you my problems and asking you to take on my emotional labor in the middle of the street, I'm not really sure how to demonstrate that."

"You could just get physically violent with me. It'll show him that you've evolved."

"Well, that's not great."

"It'll be fine. Just shove me. I'll stumble. You'll shout. No big. And it will assert your masculinity and physical superiority. He will eat it right up."

"I get what you're saying. I'm just not sure it will work. First, you're equally masc. Second, I'm not remotely physically superior. And finally, I feel super uncomfortable assaulting you. I like to play to my strengths and I'm not good at assault."

"Those are fair points."

"I will, however, forcefully grab your arm and walk you to your car."

"I like it. Secret chivalry masquerading as violence."

"That's me."

She carefully scooted Nickels off her lap. Nickels appeared quite inconvenienced by this shift. Laurel stood and shoved her hands in her pockets. "Right arm, if you don't mind. I pulled out a couple stitches on Monday and Reyes is still fussy about it."

"Yeah, he's super unreasonable, that guy," I said. We walked to the door. I took a deep breath. "Ready?"

"Call Reyes as soon as I'm gone, okay?"

"You got it." Standing in her space was doing obnoxious things to my central nervous system. It seemed to think we should be doing something other than throwing her out. I cupped her right arm and flung open the door.

"Jesus fucking Christ. I'm leaving okay." Laurel made a show of trying to yank her arm out of my grip.

"Not fast enough." I pulled her outside and she stumbled.

"You are such a dick, you know that?"

"I'm aware." I dragged her down the steps.

The uniform climbed out of his cruiser. "Everything okay, ladies?"

"It's fine," I said.

"Fucking fantastic." Laurel jerked her arm out of my grasp.

I pointed to her truck. "Leave."

"I'm going."

I shoved her lightly. "Not fast enough."

"If you'd stop manhandling me, I could go faster."

"If you left my house when I told you to, I wouldn't have to manhandle you," I shouted.

"Whatever." She backed away, still making eye contact.

I turned and stomped back inside. I slammed the door as Laurel started her truck up. The sound threw me back a year and I thoroughly did not appreciate it.

CHAPTER NINE

I'd bullied Lane into attending some sorority event for her own good. She needed to get out. Encouraging her to go had nothing to do with the FaceTime call I had scheduled with her sister. Absolutely nothing. Just like the extra ten minutes I spent making my hair into a casually unkempt quiff instead of a constructed pomp so I would look good, but not like I tried to look good.

I was stretched out on my bed with a harem of pillows behind me and my inconstant cat at my feet. While I waited for Laurel to call me, I read through the files she had emailed an hour before. They were mostly unfiltered notes from Henry's iCloud account. Detailed notes.

CB, 2/07, 10 a.m. Drinks coffee on back deck with Robin Ward.

CB, 2/07, 11:30 a.m. Nate Xiao picks CB up.

CB, 2/07, 11:45 a.m.–12:30 p.m. CB and Nate meet Jerome St. Maris at Old Soul.

CB, 2/07, 1:00 p.m. Nate drops CB at home.

CB, 2/07, 5:45 p.m. Drives to CSU Sacramento. Picks up Lane Kallen.

CB, 2/07 6:15 p.m. CB and Lane return home and stay for remainder of evening.

Turns out reading boring, detailed notes about your own movements on days you barely even remember is disturbing as fuck.

FaceTime popped up to let me know Laurel was calling. I answered.

"Hey, your computer passed inspection too?" At Laurel's voice, Nickels raised her head.

"Yep. But after reading some of these notes, I kinda wish it didn't," I said.

"It's creepy as hell, right?"

"Creepy is an understatement."

Nickels stood and stretched. She walked up and stuck her head around the computer to find the source of Laurel's voice.

Laurel grinned when Nickels's face filled her screen. "Hey, Nickels. How's my favorite girl?"

Nickels meowed and hit the screen with her paw.

"Whoa there." I pushed her paws off the computer.

"Aww, she missed me."

I deserved some sort of award for not saying I did too. Or calling her a dick for leaving me. "Apparently." When I wouldn't let the cat continue to bat at the screen, she sprawled dramatically at my side.

"So how much have you read?" Laurel adjusted her laptop and I got a glimpse of Reyes's IKEA bachelor living room. I also got a look at her full outfit. She was wearing salmon colored cutoff chinos with another paper thin V-neck. And in my expert lesbian opinion she wasn't wearing a bra, which seemed very unfair to me, specifically.

"Not much. Just what I did in February."

"Did you read the list I created with dates?"

I opened the folder she'd sent. One document was labeled Chronology. That seemed promising. "Chronology?"

"Yeah."

I opened it. It was a list of dates starting September eighth and ending last Friday. It was filled out through the end of September. "What am I looking at?"

"He's got separate notes for each of us. In September we were in the same city so there's a lot of overlap. When you get to November, we were in different cities, but he's still got detailed notes on both of our movements."

"How did he know where you were?"

"Not sure. That's what we have to find out. He documented me driving to Marin, which presents more questions than answers."

"So we're just going through to figure out how he's watching us?"

"Basically, yeah. Did he have an accomplice? He's not tracking us digitally, but what if he's tracking our vehicles? Does he have access to our bank accounts? Maybe he's using cameras? If so, where are they?"

"Got it. So the day I read in February, he knew when I was in the backyard and when I left the house, but there was no information about what I was doing inside," I said.

"Which means he's got a sightline into your backyard, but not your house."

"He also knew Nate picked me up and that we met Jerome for coffee. And that I went to pick up Lane at Sac State in the evening."

"If he was physically present, he could have watched the backyard, followed you and Nate, seen you with Jerome, followed you and Lane," she said.

"Or if he had an accomplice, they could have done all that."

"Now we need to look at what I did that day. What was the date?"

"The seventh."

Laurel nodded and started clicking. I opened the appropriate file and started reading.

LK, 2/07, 7:30 a.m. LK goes to Stinson Beach.

LK, 2/07, 8:00 a.m. LK runs Mount Tamalpais.

LK, 2/07, 10:25 a.m. Returns to Liam Salvi's house.

LK, 2/07, 11:00 a.m. Arrives at Corte Madera CHP Office.

LK, 2/07, 12:30 p.m. LK and Sergeant Moira meet for lunch at Cafe Cormorant.

LK, 2/07, 2:00 p.m.–5:30 p.m. Returns to Corte Madera CHP Office.

LK, 2/07, 6:15 p.m. Arrives at Mill Valley Clinic.

LK, 2/07, 7:15 p.m. Returns to Salvi's house. Stays for reminder of evening.

I finished reading and watched her read. The blue of her eyes was muted in the low light. The bruises under her eyes disappeared in shadow, making her look haunted. As she read she chewed the inside of her lip. It was a movement I'd never noticed before.

"I don't remember this at all. It could have been any one of a number of days," she said.

"Which I think begs the most important question." I paused for dramatic effect. "Why the hell would you spend two hours running up and down a mountain?"

She fought a grin. "Shut up. My therapist wants me to do physical activity."

"Yeah, but there's a massive difference between walking regularly and running up a mountain. And often enough that you're like yeah, that could be any day."

She rolled her eyes. "I like it, okay? It's pretty and challenging and it makes me feel good."

"Okay. Weirdo."

"I'm pretty sure all of this information could have been gathered from a tracker or something on my vehicle. The only exception is the trail run. I parked at Stinson so a tracker would just make it seem like I was on the beach for two hours."

"But he knew you went up the mountain instead of down the beach. So either he was there or he had a camera on you."

"Which matches the surveillance of you that day. He could have tracked you really easily with cameras. Backyard, front yard, and vehicle would cover it," she said.

"I was in Nate's car that day."

"If he put a camera on both our cars, he could put one on Nate's too."

"What about batteries and recordings?" I asked.

"Theoretically, he could piggyback off the car battery. Recordings could automatically upload whenever in range of open Wi-Fi. And at your house he could totally use a neighbor's power and Wi-Fi to operate those cameras. Wouldn't be difficult. Illegal, but easy." When she was pontificating about something she knew a lot about, her confidence was super hot. I found it quite distracting.

"Wow. Really not feeling great about the ease of surveillance. Or your awareness of it," I said.

"It was my job to know these things."

"Thanks. That makes me feel lots better."

"Whatever." She started clicking. She frowned in what I imagined was concentration. "We've got two image files for you that day. Do you see them?"

"No. I didn't know there were image files."

"There's a file labeled Documentation. It's organized by date."

I clicked back and opened the Documentation file. I scrolled until I found *02.07 CB 1* and *02.07 CB 2*. "At least he's super organized." The CB files were followed by *02.07 LK 1* through *02.07 LK 5*.

"Somehow that doesn't comfort me," she said.

"I'm trying to stay positive here." I opened the CB files and saw myself on the back deck having coffee with Robin. The second photo was me standing next to Nate and shaking hands with Jerome.

"All right. The angle of the backyard photo suggests it was shot from high up. A tree or a roof." She leaned in close and squinted at the photo, which almost gave me a look down her shirt. I forced myself to look away.

"Agreed."

"Angle of photo two is low," she said.

"Like a camera attached to the bottom of a car?"

"Exactly like that."

"What about the photos of you for that day?" I opened the files. Two of her in running gear. One fresh and one sweaty. Exact same angle. She looked unnecessarily hot in both photos. Her shorts were short. Her sleeves were nonexistent. Her muscles were popping. She'd been doing more than recreational trail runs.

"Jesus fucking Christ," I said.

"I know, right?"

"Yeah, totally." I had no fucking clue what she was talking about. I was pretty sure it had nothing to do with her being irritatingly sexy.

"It's just so creepy."

"So creepy." I clicked open the remaining three photos to see what was creepy. There was one of her outside a beige building. *CHP Marin Area* was painted on the side of the building behind her. The next was her at a cafe with a beefy older guy in a khaki uniform. Photo five was her walking into an office building. There was a sign next to her, but I couldn't read it without enlarging the photo. "Okay, so that solves the tracker versus camera debate."

"Yep. These all look like they were taken from the same height and distance." She frowned and clicked.

"So he was using surveillance cameras to track both of us. It's not that difficult to deduce."

"For that day, yeah. Let's pick a another day and see what we can glean."

"Okay. What day?"

"I don't know. March." She clicked. "Twenty-second."

"March twenty-second."

LK, 03/22, 8:15 a.m. Liam Salvi drops LK at Muir Woods visitor center.

LK, 03/22, 8:30 a.m. Begins run at Redwood Creek. Takes Canopy View to Old Railroad Grade to top of mountain. Returns on same route.

LK, 03/22, 11:15 a.m. Meditates off Redwood Creek Trail.

LK, 03/22, 11:35 a.m. Salvi picks up LK.

LK, 03/22, 12:00 p.m. LK and Salvi return to house.

LK, 03/22, 4:30 p.m. Private appointment at Mill Valley Clinic with Carolyn Plaskett.

LK, 03/22 5:30 Returns to Salvi's house. Stays for reminder of evening.

"It seems like he's got a lot more information on my movements this day," she said.

"Yeah. The whole knowing what trail you're on eliminates any sort of vehicle camera. He was either following you himself or had someone else following you. I mean, assuming there's no cameras on that trail," I said.

"There's not. The parking lot doesn't even have surveillance."

"Could he have installed cameras on the mountain? That would explain the super accurate trail names."

She slowly shook her head. "He could, but there are a ton of trails and I ran them at random. It would be difficult to cover them all. Even just the junctures between trails would be prohibitive. And he would need to regularly change out batteries and transfer recordings, which would be damn near impossible. There are rangers all over that area because there are so many hikers."

"Okay, so we're going with the theory that you were physically followed that day."

"And not the other day since he didn't note what trails I was on."

"Right. Because you were clearly on different trails?" I had no clue. I clicked back to the other day to see what it said.

"Yeah. I mean, same mountain, but they start in totally different places."

"Well, duh." A fact I was absolutely aware of before that moment.

"Hey, Cash, what mountain was I running on?"

"Runner's Mountain."

She grinned. "Yep. Nailed it."

I looked for photos and found pre- and post-run again. This time the sweaty photo was Laurel meditating on a wooden bench. She looked like a tool. I still wanted to make out with her, but that was irrelevant. The third photo was her in front of the same office building. The angle was a bit different and the sign was easier to read. That was it.

"This makes me want to punch someone," she said.

"Why's that? I mean, aside from the violation of being stalked."

"Mostly that. I remember that run. It was a gorgeous day. The top of the mountain was almost too hot, but the view was clear. You can never see far, but the fog lifted and it was just perfect." She shook her head. "And I'd been meditating seriously for a couple weeks, but that was the first time I had the courage to just sit on a trail in public and go for it. And this motherfucker was watching me. It feels tainted."

I didn't have a brilliant response to that. "Shit. I'm sorry."

"Why? It's not your fault."

"It kind of is. If not for me, you'd never have met Henry Brewer and been the focus of his obsessive bullshit."

"You're not responsible for his behavior. You know that, right?"

"That's not really true though."

"It is true. He would have snapped eventually. The dude is unhinged. We just happened to speak to his damaged psyche or whatever."

"Well, I'm still sorry."

"Thanks." Laurel adjusted her laptop screen nervously. "So what did you do that day?"

"Let's find out." I opened the Cash file for the same date.

CB, 03/19, 9:30 a.m.–11:00 a.m. Coffee on back deck.

CB, 03/19, 2:00 p.m. Leaves for meeting with Kyra Daneshmandan and Irene Terzi at S Street building.

CB, 03/19, 6:00 p.m. CB and Daneshmandan meet Van Bertram for drinks at Citrus & Salt.

CB, 03/19, 11:15 p.m. Arrives home in a Lyft. Stays for remainder of evening.

After reading, I remembered that day. I was pretty sure it was when Kyra and I bought the gallery building.

"That's pretty bare bones," Laurel said.

"And missing some pretty basic details. Just a sec." I grabbed my phone and went back in my calendar. "Yep. That's the day Kyra and I signed all the documents to buy the gallery."

"Which means he definitely didn't have any eyes or ears on what you were doing."

"But he also missed what we did afterward. Kyra and Van and I met for drinks, but after that we walked to Aglio for dinner. Then Kyra dropped me and Van off at the Depot because she had an early morning. I took a Lyft home and picked up my car the next day."

"That supports the video on the car theory."

"Exactly."

"And challenges the accomplice theory," she said.

"Also, it suggests he didn't put video on Kyra's car because there's no record of her driving us to the bar."

"Great." Laurel clicked and started typing. "So now we just need to do this for the other two hundred and forty something days."

"What?"

"I already did September, which means we've got just over eight months of notes to read," she said. I assumed she was exaggerating and we weren't going to actually read all eight months of notes. I was incorrect.

"Fuck Henry Brewer and his fucking bullshit."

"Yep."

"I'm going to make some coffee. I'll be back in a minute." I set the laptop on the bed. Laurel gave me an ironic thumbs-up.

CHAPTER TEN

Two hours later, I'd gone through a pot of coffee, ordered pizza delivery for both of us, and we'd knocked out three and a half months.

"I guess it's good we're not very exciting," Laurel said.

"Speak for yourself, man."

"We just went through an eleven-day stretch where all you did was drink coffee in your backyard, and have groceries delivered."

"I was doing a lot of exciting stuff though. It was just indoor stuff." Like reading dark poetry and being depressed. Those were important winter activities. Especially when the woman you were in love with had abruptly left you.

"Exciting indoor stuff. Right."

"No one goes out in January. It's cold. If I left the shelter of the heat lamps on my porch, I'd probably die."

"I went out in January."

"You went to therapy once a week, group therapy once a week, got your hair cut, and had ten business meetings in the entire month." I ticked off her activities on my fingers.

"I had a lot of shit to work through, thank you very much."

"I'm just saying people who live in beige subdivisions shouldn't throw boring stones."

"I don't live in a subdivision."

"It's a metaphor, Laurel."

She rolled her eyes and dove back into January. It was infinitely weird to see an itemized list of my ex-girlfriend's movements in the months following our breakup. Weirder still was reading through the lists with said ex-girlfriend. We were being careful not to ask what the hell the other was doing, which I had especially appreciated when we read December and I did nothing except mope and drink beer and cry. Thankfully, most of the crying had occurred indoors where Henry and his cameras couldn't document it. The moping, however, was well documented.

The guy Laurel had moved in with when she left Sac appeared to be an old buddy, but I'd never heard her talk about a Liam Salvi. According to Henry's notes Salvi was law enforcement, but there wasn't any other information. His insistence on not stalking anyone other than Laurel was very inconvenient.

Laurel broke the silent code first. "So why were you and Nate meeting with Jerome St. Maris so often? I thought you hated the guy?"

"My answer depends on how dedicated to the law you still are."

"I cannot be regulated by the laws of man," she said grandly.

"New you is fun."

"Oh, yeah. I'm a hoot."

I almost didn't tell her the truth, but then I couldn't think of a reason to lie. "We sold him our business."

"What do you mean?"

"We sold him everything. Our connections, our supply, our customer base."

Her eyes went wide. "Shit."

"How do you think I bought the gallery building?" I asked.

"I don't know. With a bank loan like a normal person?"

"Well, yeah. The business wasn't worth millions and Kyra insisted we buy in midtown. But we needed a down payment."

"You're like officially, officially not a drug dealer," she said.

"And you're like officially, officially not a cop."

"Well, I do consult with cops."

"So you're just officially not a cop?" I emphasized the single "officially."

"Correct. Only one officially."

"Is it weird?" I wouldn't have asked in the daylight. But it was pushing eleven and the house was still empty and Nickels wasn't awake to judge me.

"Yeah."

That was it. That was all I got. We kept working. The pizza went cold. So did the second pot of coffee. Around midnight, I heard Lane get home. She moved around for about twenty minutes. Nickels scratched at my door to be let out. I opened it and she ran for Lane's room. A few minutes later, Lane hit the lights and closed her door. My eyes got gritty. I fell asleep in mid March.

"Cash. Hey, Cash wake up."

I opened my eyes. The laptop screen seemed harsh in the muted warm light of my bedroom. "Shit. Sorry."

"It's cool. Look at the documents. April third."

I blinked a couple of times until my vision fully cleared. I pushed myself upright. Laurel had finished filling in March on our shared document, but April third was blank so I pulled up Henry's notes.

CB, 4/03, 9:15 a.m. Van Bertram arrives at CB's. They pick up supplies at Home Depot.

CB, 4/03, 10:15 a.m.–1:00 p.m. Bertram and CB sand building floors.

CB, 4/03, 1:00 p.m. Kyra Daneshmandan brings them lunch.

"What am I looking for?" I asked.

"Unless Brewer was standing inside and you didn't notice him, he's got cameras inside your gallery."

"Fuck. Seriously. Fuck that guy." I thought I'd burned off my rage at Henry, but it shot through me again. I could deal with a camera on my car. I could even maybe ignore the one looking into my backyard. But inside my gallery? Fuck that guy.

"Any idea how he managed that?"

"I don't know." I grabbed my phone again. "Kyra tracked all the work we did." I scrolled through the spreadsheet. "Any idea what date he definitely did not have cameras?"

Her eyes shifted to a different area of the screen as she scrolled. "March twenty-seventh he's got you and Andy going in the building for about three hours with no other information."

"I think that's the day Andy helped me take measurements so we'd know how much paint and shit to buy. Just a sec." I switched from Numbers to my bank app. "Yep. We walked to lunch. We parked in the back of the gallery, but left through the front."

"Okay so twenty-seventh to the third."

I switched back to Numbers. "The next day, nothing. Twenty-ninth was all planning and making calls and shit."

"Yeah, he's got you and Kyra in the back garden doing clerical work."

"Does he have anyone else meeting us?"

Laurel chewed her cheek as she read the notes. "Nope."

"We met with Patricia Chadwell that day. Inside the gallery. She runs a shop that refurbishes vintage furniture. She wanted to scope the space to put together a selection for us."

"I remember her. You laundered money through her, but we couldn't prove it."

I laughed. "I don't appreciate your allegations and I don't think Ms. Chadwell would either." Which was exactly why we had laundered money through her.

"Whatever."

I kept reading the spreadsheet. "March thirtieth through April first we had electrical repairs. The second, internet was installed. The alarm system went live when the internet did."

"So he either went in at night or whenever the building was empty," she said.

"Or he somehow went in with the electrician or the dude installing internet."

"Or he could have bribed either of them to do it for him."

So either Henry invaded my space or one of the people we hired had no moral compunction. Either way it sucked. "How do we find out?" I asked.

"We don't. I'll give the info to Reyes and have them follow up. They can check for cameras. With any luck, they'll be able to use the equipment to reverse track down Brewer. They have more resources than we do anyway."

"Can he do the same for the cameras in my neighbor's tree and on my car?"

"He could, but then Brewer would know we know about them. The gallery is something Reyes ostensibly might check on his own," she said.

"Right. Because we only know the location of the cameras based on the photos you stole."

She looked offended. "I didn't steal them. He dropped his phone. That's on him."

"I meant from Reyes."

"Oh."

"He's going to be fussy when he finds out you stole his files."

"Maybe." She shrugged. "I think he left them out hoping I'd snoop."

"Solid friendship you've got there."

She seemed unconcerned. "You want to call it for tonight?"

"No, I'm good."

"You sure?" she asked.

"Yeah, the faster we do this, the faster we find Henry's punk ass. I want to go back to drinking my morning coffee alone." I was tired of having my every move monitored. Well, not every move. Laurel seemed to have gotten the short end of the stalking stick. I only had him taking remote photos of me. "Shit."

"What?"

"What are the chances he has audio in the gallery?" I asked.

"Probably slim. Video is much easier to set up. Or just audio, but a combination would be difficult." She screwed up her face. "Actually, that's not true. He could bug the space pretty easily if he wasn't concerned about the audio and video matching up. Why do you ask?"

"It's possible that Kyra and I had a discussion in the gallery office about my feelings for you earlier this week."

Laurel swallowed visibly. "Oh."

I cringed. "Yeah."

"Did you say something that would negate what you're planning on saying to his grandmother."

"Maybe? I honestly don't know. Kyra was giving me shit and I blew her off."

"Well, I'll just make sure Reyes checks for bugs when he checks for cameras."

"And then we'll know if Henry possibly heard me talking?"

"Yeah," she said.

"Cool."

"Cool."

It was approaching the witching hour when I found an entry for Laurel that gave me pause.

LK, 05/12, 9:00 a.m. Arrives at CB's house. Watches.

LK, 05/12, 9:45 a.m. Returns to Shaw House in Placerville.

A few days later, she did it again.

LK, 05/15, 11:15 a.m. Arrives at CB's house. Watches.

LK, 05/15, 12:30 p.m. Returns to Shaw House in Placerville.

I was too old for all-nighters and we were on our way to one. And I'd run out of filters. "Hey, Laurel."

"Yeah?"

"What the fuck were you doing May twelfth and fifteenth?"

"Oh. Umm. You're reading faster than I expected."

"That's not really an answer."

"I told you I came back for you." She said it like it was the most normal thing in the world.

"There's a pretty big difference between coming back for someone and sitting outside their house and watching them."

"I wasn't watching. I was trying to get the courage up to go knock on the door."

"Why?"

"I can't say." She pressed her lips together and shrugged exaggeratedly. "I told you I wouldn't bring up my feelings. If I explain why I was at your house, I have to tell you my feelings." She was fucking obnoxious.

"Stop being weird and shit."

"Okay. I was there to tell you I'd moved to Placerville for a job because I wanted to be closer to you." She didn't even look at the camera. She just kept reading the documents on her screen and sporadically typing. "I wanted to tell you I was an idiot and I missed you and I was still in love with you. And tell you where I was staying in case you felt the same way."

"What the fuck?"

She finally stopped typing and looked at the camera. "I already told you all this. It isn't new."

"But I didn't believe you."

She shrugged. "Okay. That's kind of on you though. I was pretty straightforward."

"Seriously? That's on me?"

"Yeah."

I stared at the image taking up a quarter of my screen. The light was warm and crisp enough to show every angle and line on her face, but it still seemed washed out. I replayed every interaction we'd had in the last week, wondering if her vitality was simply gone or if it just didn't travel via FaceTime. "You're serious." Apparently, eighteenth time was the charm for me.

"Yes."

"I can't deal with that right now."

"Okay." She went back to working.

"That's it?"

"What do you want? I told you exactly how I feel. I'm respecting your dumb boundaries. I'm not asking for anything."

"You don't get to play that card. Announcing you're still in love with someone isn't a neutral statement. There are implied questions that accompany that declaration."

"Okay." She tugged at the collar of her V-neck, then pulled it taut to scratch her shoulder. She was definitely not wearing a bra. So that was one mystery solved for the evening. What a relief.

CHAPTER ELEVEN

I woke up to someone making a lot of noise in my kitchen. Which would have been fine, but I'd been up until dawn and I was officially old enough that all-nighters made me feel hungover. I rubbed my eyes and looked at the clock. It was after eleven. I found Andy in the kitchen putting together my electric mixer.

"Whatcha doing, tiger?"

"Oh, hey. Good morning. How the hell does this go in here?" She handed me the mixer with one beater attached and the second, unattached beater.

I took the mixer, ejected the beater, swapped them, and handed it back. "There."

"Thanks. I'm making waffles. But it's Mom's recipe. Do you remember Mom's recipe? It's been forever since she made waffles." She pulled a clean dishtowel from the drawer and draped it over the bowl she was about to whip.

"Why are you making them in my kitchen?"

"Because I'm making them for you. Duh."

Well, that cleared that up. "Cool. I'm going to find pants."

Andy looked pointedly at my boxer briefs with elephants wearing sunglasses. "I think we would all appreciate that."

"Hey, punk. You're in my kitchen."

"You don't live alone," she sang pointedly.

"Lane doesn't judge me for walking around in my underwear."

"Lane is nicer than me." She started the mixer.

"Whatever." I went back to my room and pretended to get ready for the day. Cutoffs and a T-shirt I hadn't been wearing for ten hours.

I debated a hat or fixing my hair, but then it seemed like a lot of effort so I didn't bother with anything.

"Coffee's ready." Andy nodded at the pot when I walked back in the kitchen.

"Thanks." I poured a mug and sprawled at the table. "So to what do I owe this dubious honor."

"Waffles from scratch are not a dubious honor, dickwad. And I'm hoping you'll help me put the final layer of varnish on the slats so Lane and I can install them next week." She started folding whipped egg whites into a bowl of batter.

"I would have done that without waffles, but I'll take the bribe."

"You did tell me I should be able to cook five solid meals before adulthood. I'm killer at grilling, but I don't have any breakfasts under my belt." She stopped folding to look over her shoulder at me. "Unless pouring cereal counts. Does that count?"

"It does not."

She went back to stirring. "Then I need a breakfast item."

"Can I do anything? Without infringing on your culinary autonomy, that is."

"You can get the waffle iron. I don't know where it is."

"What if I don't have one? You didn't really think this through."

"You do. I've seen it. But more importantly, I could go get Mom's."

"I stand corrected." I pushed up from the table and went into the pantry. I opened the step stool and climbed to see the top shelf. The waffle iron was in a box behind my extra French press and an electric kettle I didn't know I owned.

"Your phone is ringing," Andy called.

"Will you answer it? Unless it's an unknown."

"Who's 'Don't be an idiot'?"

Fuck. "Don't answer."

"Hello? Cash's phone, Andy speaking." Of all the times for her to remember phone etiquette. "Excuse me?"

I climbed off the stepladder and went back into the kitchen. "Andy."

"Why the fuck are you calling?" she asked.

"Andy, don't be rude," I said.

She shot me a look that was equal parts disgust and pity. "Cash wouldn't work with you. You're an asshole. Right, Cash? You wouldn't be that dumb."

I decided to full name her. "Anderson Ward, you know better than to speak to anyone that way."

"Whatever." She set the phone on the counter and walked out of the kitchen. I heard the back door open and close.

"Fuck." I picked up the phone. "Sorry about that."

"It's okay," Laurel said. "I take it she didn't know I was back in town?"

"It wasn't intentional. I assumed Robin talked to her. Robin probably assumed I did."

"Shit. I'm sorry. I should have handled it differently."

"You didn't do anything wrong," I said.

"I still feel bad."

"Don't. What's up?"

"Oh, I was calling to let you know the plan for ditching Henry."

"You talked to Lance?"

"Yep. He's in. He'll pick me up. We'll go out to lunch at one of the breweries on sixteenth. There's a car rental place with alley access. We'll grab lunch, I'll slip out the back and into the rental car."

"Perfect. When are you doing this?"

"Saturday. Tomorrow. I'll take 80 to Tahoe and stay the night."

"And I'll go see the delightful Grandma Brewer the next day?"

"Yep. Reyes will drop off a bag at Nate's. Can Nate run it up to you? It's got the wire I want you to wear and all the info for the grandmother's house."

"I'm sure he can. Does this mean Reyes is signing off on this little plan?"

"No. He thinks he's dropping off books and clothes you left at my place."

I chuckled. "He's going to be pissed."

"I'm okay with that."

"Did you talk to him about scanning for bugs in the gallery?"

"Yeah. He's going to call you today. I told him you wanted it checked right away," she said.

"Cool. Thanks."

"Of course."

"So it's okay if Henry follows me, right? Because if he loses you, he's probably going to be all over me," I said.

"Yeah. There's a risk because he might intervene if he sees you going to his grandmother's house."

"You said that before."

"I put a stun gun in the bag too. You know how to use a stun gun, right?" she asked like it was a totally normal skill.

"Why the hell would I know how to use a stun gun?"

"You were a drug dealer. It never occurred to you to use a weapon?"

"My words are a weapon."

"Wow. Okay. Well, in case your words don't work, there's a stun gun. Push the button and touch him with the sparky end."

"What if he shoots me?" I asked.

"He could do that now. Like literally right now. I didn't think you were worried about it."

"I'm less concerned about Henry shooting me and more about Grandma Brewer shooting me, honestly."

"I mean, it's a possibility. She's kind of the worst."

"Oh, great. Thank you. I feel much better." Shooting was no better than being pulled apart by killer dogs.

She laughed, then got silent. "Does Andy hate me that much?"

"No. She's mad at me, not you."

"It sounded a lot like she was mad at me."

"Yeah, it kind of did. But she doesn't have any context. I'll tell her what's going on. She'll cool off. It'll be fine," I said.

"You sure?"

"You seem far more concerned with Andy's opinion than mine or Lane's or anyone else's."

"I am. I like Andy better than the rest of you," she said.

Hard to argue that logic. "Yeah, that tracks."

"Let me know how it goes."

"With Andy? Or bugs at the gallery?" I asked.

"Both, obviously."

"Right. Bye, Laurel."

"Bye."

I did a quick look around the kitchen to make sure nothing was plugged in and ready to catch fire before following Andy outside. She was sitting on the back steps staring out at the lumber stacked in the yard.

"Hey, tiger."

"Why the fuck are you letting her back in?" Andy asked without turning around.

I wanted to deny the allegation, but I wasn't sure if I would be lying or not. "It's a long story. I'd like to tell you if you let me."

"Are you back together with her? Because she's an asshole. She's out of free passes."

I sat on the step next to her. "Right there with you, pal."

"So why's she back?"

"I used to buy drugs from a guy named Henry Brewer," I said.

"How is that relevant to Laurel?"

"Let me tell my story."

"Fine," she said.

"Henry was a sheriff in El Dorado County. He stole drugs from evidence and I sold them."

Andy turned from her study of the yard to blink at me. "You worked with a bad cop?"

I nodded. "A real bad cop. When we realized Laurel was an undercover detective, Henry decided the best solution was to kill her. Nate and I disagreed. Henry sent Nate off with a task. Then he tied me up and went to go execute Laurel."

"Are you fucking serious right now?"

"Yeah. He was a terrible person and we knew it, but we kept working with him. It was stupid and shortsighted," I said.

"So what happened? I mean, he obviously didn't kill Laurel."

"No. Nate and I intervened in time. We didn't realize her partner and half the police department were shadowing her." I half-grinned. "If you ask Laurel, she was never in any real danger. Of course, Henry shot her so I respectfully disagree with her assessment."

"He shot her?"

"Yeah. In the arm." I pointed at my left bicep to show Andy where Laurel had been hit.

"Whoa. That's kind of wild."

"It is. Anyway, Henry got away. They never found him. That was almost a year ago. Last week, Laurel was hiking and Henry jumped out and tried to kill her again."

"Tried to kill her how?"

"Umm. Well, he strangled her, she broke his nose. He stabbed her, she stabbed him. It was a whole thing. She's fine, but he got away. It has since become apparent that he has been stalking both me and Laurel for months."

"What the fuck, dude?"

I turned to look at Andy and realized she was crying. "Oh, man. I'm sorry. I should have been more delicate about that."

"Why are you worried about me? Shouldn't you be surrounded by armed guards or something?" She swiped at her cheeks.

"Can I give you a hug?"

She sniffled and nodded. I put my arm around her and squeezed. After a minute, she relaxed.

"Are you scared?" she asked.

"Not really. I feel violated. He's got cameras everywhere to watch me. Including inside the gallery, we think." And the porch we were currently sitting on, but it didn't seem prudent to tell her that. "He's got cameras on Laurel's car and where she was staying, but he also straight up stalked her. We're pretty sure he didn't spend much time tracking me. And, you know, he tried to kill her."

"So that's why she called? To talk about the psycho stalking you guys?" Andy kept her head tucked under my chin.

"Yeah. We're trying to figure out where he is. Detective Reyes, Laurel's old partner, wants to sequester us," I said.

"Sequester? Like hide you?"

"Yeah, exactly. But neither of us want to give Henry the satisfaction of scaring us into hiding, I guess."

"That's dumb. Just hide until they get him."

"They've been trying to get him for a year and haven't succeeded. I don't have an abundance of faith in law enforcement. And I'm not particularly keen on going into a safe house until they manage to find him."

Andy leaned away from me and straightened. "Oh, you dumbass."

"What? Why am I a dumbass?"

"You don't want to be stuck in a safe house with Laurel." She rubbed the remnants of tears from her cheeks.

"That's not it at all," I said. It sounded pathetic.

"You still want her?"

"Absolutely not. She was in town all of two minutes before she told me she made a mistake and wanted me back. I told her to take a hike."

"Isn't that exactly what you wanted?"

"Well, yeah. But I don't trust her to not get scared again."

Andy shook her head. "You're the one who taught me fear was a terrible guiding force."

"Okay, no. You don't get to use my own words against me."

"Sorry, pal. Just did." She stood and pulled her phone out of her pocket. She typed, then turned the screen to show me a message to Laurel. "Is this okay?"

I'm sorry I was rude. I hope you're okay.

"Yeah, that's perfect," I said.

Andy hit send. She walked back inside and called over her shoulder. "Waffles will be ready in fifteen."

CHAPTER TWELVE

Detective Reyes, Detective Duarte." I locked the gallery door after letting them in.

"Ms. Braddock, thanks for letting us look around," Reyes said.

"Of course. I understand you think Henry might have some sort of surveillance equipment here?" This farce was strange, but if Henry had mics, I wanted him to think this was legit. It was good I didn't know where his cameras were. I would have compulsively stared at them.

"We would at least like to rule it out," Reyes said.

Duarte set a small tool bag on the ground and started unpacking it. "Is there anything we can't touch in here?"

"All of the artwork, obviously. I'll grab some gloves for you in case you need to touch the walls."

"Great, thank you," he said.

I ducked into the office and snagged two pairs of cotton gloves. When I came back out, Reyes was itemizing the vents, smoke detectors, basically anything disrupting the wall space. "Here." I held out the gloves.

"Thanks." Reyes took them.

"Do you guys need anything from me? I have some work to do in the office."

Reyes looked up from his list. "Nope. When we're done out here, we would like to take a look in there, if you don't mind."

"Not at all. We open at noon today. It would be great if you finished out here before then."

Reyes looked at his watch. He'd said they would arrive at ten and the man was disgustingly punctual. It was 10:07. "We'll be done well before noon."

"Kyra will probably be in around eleven. Just a heads-up," I said. They nodded and started playing with sci-fi looking tools. I went into the office and started filling in spreadsheets Kyra had left for me. I'd been adamant that I wouldn't do any sort of paperwork when we started this business, but apparently my coded drug inventory tracking system had prepared me well for such a task. I was quite disappointed in myself.

Twenty minutes later, I was in the zone. And according to the neat lines of numbers on the screen, we were doing well. My phone started buzzing in the continuous way that meant it was ringing. It was too early for Van or Kyra and they both had keys. I dug it out of my pocket. Marjorie.

"Hello?"

"Hi. Hello. Cash?"

"Yeah." I stood, unsure of what to do with myself. "How's it going?"

"Okay. I'm all right."

"Cool." Back to my single word. I sat again.

"I was wondering if we could get lunch this week? I enjoyed meeting your friend, but I was really hoping for some one-on-one time."

I probably should have seen that coming. I thought about the conversations I'd had with Nate and Robin about spending time with Marjorie and I couldn't think of a reason to say no. "Sure. We could do that."

"Great. That's great. What does your schedule look like this week?"

I rarely had a schedule, let alone any idea what it looked like. "Umm, open I guess." That wasn't true. I had to shake down an old lady. "Except tomorrow. I've got a thing tomorrow."

"Okay. The day after tomorrow then? Some place downtown?"

"Sounds good. Any lunch preferences?" I shifted the small stack of papers on the desk like I was going to write it down. As if I couldn't remember lunch with my mother.

"Oh, I don't know. Let's keep it simple. Do you like tacos? There used to be a little taco stand up Sixteenth. I doubt it's still there, but something like that."

"That little outdoor taqueria with the huge Jarritos sign? Jalisco, I think." As if that didn't describe about twenty-three different taquerias. But there was only the one on Sixteenth.

"Yes, that's the one." She sounded far more excited than a little taqueria warranted, but the tacos were pretty great.

"Yeah, they're still open. And they still make awesome tacos."

"That's fantastic. Let's say one?"

"Cool. I'll meet you at one."

We hung up and I sat staring at the wall. Kyra had painted it a rich yellow that contrasted with the dark cherry doorframe. The gallery walls were white, but in here we'd decided to indulge ourselves.

I didn't know what Marjorie wanted from me. Maybe that was why I couldn't figure out what I wanted from her. It was like walking into that lunch with Clive on repeat. I couldn't create a reaction until I knew what I was reacting to. I tried to go back to my spreadsheets, but I kept getting distracted and losing my place. A dangerous proposition with spreadsheets.

Reyes stuck his head into the office. "You mind if we do our sweep in here?"

"No. That's cool." I stood and grabbed the laptop. "I can work outside." Since I was being so productive.

"Is that your personal computer or does it stay here?"

"Here. It's the business computer."

"Better leave it. Electronic equipment is great for hiding bugs."

"Right." Fucking Henry. "I guess I'll go get a coffee then. You want anything?"

"I wouldn't say no to iced tea. Herbal. Something with rooibos in it," Reyes said.

I didn't roll my eyes at him, which I thought was very big of me. "Rooibos iced tea. Got it."

Duarte walked in as I was repeating the order. "You doing a coffee run?" He seemed hopeful.

"Yeah. What do you want?"

"Hot coffee. Big, dark, and creamy. Nothing sweet."

"Okay, I thought Reyes sounded gay when he ordered, but that was next level gay."

"Since you prefer gay people, I'll take that as a compliment."

"Touché, pal. Touché."

By the time I returned, the gallery was empty, but I heard voices out back. I followed them and found Kyra and the detectives in the yard.

"Is that coffee for me?" Kyra eyed the big iced coffee in the cup tray I was carrying.

"Of course it is. Did you think I'd bring coffee for the boys and forget you?"

"I don't know. You're not cruel, but sometimes you're forgetful."

"Fair point." I set the tray on the table and handed out cups. "Does this mean you're finished inside?" I asked Reyes.

"Yep. Three cameras in the main gallery space. One in the office."

Kyra shuddered. I was tempted to join her.

"No mics or any listening devices though," Duarte said.

"That's good I guess." It was better than good, honestly. It meant I didn't need to re-examine my conversation with Kyra about my Laurel feelings. And more importantly, I didn't need to re-examine the feelings themselves. Feelings were best left unexamined.

"Hey, I know this blows, but don't get dejected," Duarte said. The pep talk didn't do much for me, but the fact that he was trying helped.

"Thanks, man."

"What are you up to this week?" Reyes asked. Why was everyone suddenly so interested in my schedule? "Inventing new ways to mess with the uniform outside your door?"

"You got me. I love to torture rookie cops who are the only thing standing between me and an incensed ex-cop."

"She makes a decent point," Duarte said.

Reyes shrugged. "Sorry. It's been a while since we actually talked. Aside from the gallery, what's going on in your life?"

I knew there had to be something happening in my life, but all I could think of was my plan to run off with Laurel and poke Henry's grandmother to see if a bear would wake up. "Not much, I guess."

"Oh, before we forget, Ionescu suggested we check your car and house for bugs too," Duarte said. "Do you mind?"

"No, that's fine."

Duarte checked his watch. It had a massive face and a floral motif. "We have a meeting in an hour, but we could do tomorrow."

"Oh, uh, actually I can't tomorrow." I stood. I used to be able to lie. I'd been a criminal, after all. "And you just reminded me I've got to go. Lane and I have a night planned and I need to go shopping for it." Technically, that was true.

"Okay. Just text me a good time, then," Duarte said.

"Right. Will do. Later, friends."

That went well. I played it hecka cool.

"Madam, I give you popcorn, three varieties of gummy candy—one sour—and four varieties of chocolate including two caramel chocolate, per your request." I held out my hand palm up to frame the selection of candy. "I give you an unhealthy amount of Chinese takeout." I shifted my hand to the other side of the coffee table. "I give you the gas station ice cream sandwiches that you are inexplicably obsessed with. We also have sparkling water and Mountain Dew." I gestured toward the kitchen. "And the pièce de résistance, salt and vinegar chips with a five-pound bag of M&M's." I pointed to the bags next to Lane on the couch.

Lane surveyed the spread with a keen eye. After a tension filled beat, she nodded. "This is acceptable."

I bowed. "For your viewing pleasure, Beverly has prepared a number of movie marathon selections. The *Legally Blonde* movies, *Pitch Perfect* movies, or reboots that anger men, e.g. *Ghostbusters*, *Ocean's 8*."

"Oh, man. Is Beverly stalking me? Because that's an excellent selection."

"Beverly pays attention."

"Since we are celebrating me surviving finals week, I'm going to have to go with *Legally Blonde*. I also like the positive sorority girl rep," Lane said.

"An excellent choice, miss. Though I must point out the irony that you were given the option to go out partying with your sorority sisters for this particular celebration, yet you chose to celebrate with me by watching sorority girls."

"The irony is noted."

"Then let's go to Harvard Law."

I started the first *Legally Blonde* movie. As the living room turned a bright shade of pink, Lane started opening cartons of takeout. She handed me the kung pao and took the sweet and sour. Before digging into her carton she snagged a piece of my chicken with her chopsticks.

"I have to make sure it's not poison." She popped it in her mouth.

"So benevolent of you." This was the disadvantage of not liking what she ordered, but her liking what I ordered. It was what I imagined having siblings was like. "Have you thought about your birthday?"

"What about it?"

"It's coming up and I'm pretty sure your sorority sisters are dying to take you out for it."

She shrugged and studiously watched Elle brush her hair. "I know."

"And you skipped out on the group post-finals celebration to watch *Legally Blonde* with me."

"I'm trying to, but someone keeps interrupting." She pointed at the TV then me with her chopsticks.

I laughed. "I'm just saying. I mean, I'm down to hang, but this is kind of a big deal. Maybe you should live it up."

"It's not really a big deal."

"Twenty-one is absolutely a big deal."

She finally turned to look at me. "I'm just freaked out."

"About what?" I was pretty sure I knew, but I figured I should ask.

"Drinking in public."

I nodded. "Yeah. I get that. But you don't have to drink in public."

"It's my twenty-first birthday."

"So what? There's no rule about drinking on your twenty-first birthday."

"You just said it was a big deal," she said.

"I did. But it's the going out with your friends and celebrating the fall of the final bastion of childhood. It doesn't have to be about getting drunk if you don't want it to."

She nodded a bit. "I'll think about it." She shoved a bite of chicken in her mouth so she couldn't talk.

"That's all I ask."

We made it through the first round of Chinese and Warner breaking up with Elle. When we hit the LSAT study montage, Lane dug into the gummy worms. She bit and stretched her first worm viciously before tearing its head off.

"If I go out, will you be on call? You know, just in case?" she asked without looking away from the TV.

"Yes. Of course."

"And I can turn on my location and you can make sure I'm okay?"

"Yes, totally."

"Does that make me a complete wimp?"

"Not even a little bit. I think you should go at your own pace for all this, but I also think you've been spending a lot of time with a retired drug dealer who is rapidly approaching thirty and probably not nearly as fun and willing to engage in dance parties as your sorority sisters. So maybe try that out for a bit."

"Shhh, Elle's about to find out her LSAT score." Lane threw a gummy worm at me.

"Okay. Whatever." I ate the gummy worm.

"Thanks, Cash."

"Any time, pal."

CHAPTER THIRTEEN

The driveway to Grandma Brewer's house was around a blind turn. There was no mailbox, no sign, no fence. There was just a break in the trees and a narrow unpaved road. I turned and the sudden sound of the gravel shooting under my tires was overwhelming and loud. Or maybe that was blood rushing in my ears.

I resisted the impulse to call Laurel and confirm that my wire was transmitting. It was. I'd pulled off at Clive's fruit stand to check a few miles back. If it stopped working, she would call me. But I still wanted to call and check. I needed to do something to mitigate my nerves. I drove over a sketchy bridge with an anemic creek running under it. The driveway widened and became a turnaround. The house was modest and dark. I knew Henry's grandfather had built the place, but it lacked the charm I was expecting. He must have built it in the early seventies. The roughhewn porch was covered in pine needles. The only bright spot was a vibrant green State of Jefferson flag, which didn't exactly allay my fears. Fifty miles east or fifty years in the past would have made it a Confederate flag, but Northern California was a strange place.

The door opened as I was stepping up on the porch. Based on Laurel's description, I was expecting a shotgun-toting blue haired lady. Grandma Brewer was not that. Her shoulder length brunette hair curled under at the ends. A swath of freckles stretched across her cheekbones. She was wearing a linen shirt with small flowers embroidered along the neckline that matched the cornflower blue of her bright eyes. Hell, she was wearing Birkenstocks.

"This property is private." She smiled in a way that negated the heft of her statement.

"I'm aware of that. I'm looking for Mrs. Brewer, Henry Brewer's grandmother," I said.

She cocked her head questioningly. "That's me. I'm Melody Brewer. How do you know my Henry?" She put out her hand.

Henry Brewer's scary-ass grandmother was named Melody? "We went to high school together. And I was his business partner." I shook her hand and rushed to get my name out while she was still vulnerable. "I'm Cash Braddock."

She snatched her hand back. "Braddock? That drug dealer who framed my boy?"

"I assure you I didn't frame Henry. The same cop who came after him came after me." I gave her a whisper of a smile and tried my best to look honest as I lied.

"That fascist woman and her FBI team?"

I indulged myself in the image of Laurel parked a couple of acres away in a cheap rental car listening to this separatist hippie calling her a fascist. I couldn't help it. I laughed. "Yes, ma'am."

She glared. "Don't ma'am me. You set my boy up."

"You're right. I made a lot of mistakes. But I want to fix them. That's why I'm here. Please just hear me out."

She crossed her arms and stared at me. I waited for her to speak. She waited for me. I broke first.

"I was in a relationship with the fascist cop," I said.

"And you were fine with her being a fascist when you were dating her?"

"I never really thought of her as a fascist until you said it, but I like the description. That's definitely how I'm describing her from now on." I grinned and hoped it was charming. "I think if I report the relationship, it will cause enough doubt to get them to drop the allegations against Henry."

Melody stared some more. And then she smiled. "Okay. I'll hear you out." She led me into the house. "Would you like some tea?"

"I'd love some."

"Sit down. I'll bring it out."

There was an overstuffed striped sofa and a set of wooden rocking chairs. I opted for one of the chairs that offered a direct sightline into the kitchen. A hallway led from the living room to the back of the house. Sunlight from the open back door illuminated most of the hallway. The dogs Laurel had mentioned started barking. Melody whistled sharply and they stopped.

"Effective," I said.

"They drive me crazy, but they're trained well enough." She handed me a glass of iced tea.

"Thank you."

"You're welcome." She sat on the fluffy couch, tucked one of her feet under her, and took a sip of tea. "Now explain to me how exactly you plan to absolve Henry of the crimes your girlfriend accused him of."

"I believe I said I wanted to fix my mistakes. I didn't claim any sort of absolution," I said. She gave me a look that wasn't very friendly. "Kallen and I were together for about six months. For the entirety of that relationship, I was her CI. I think Henry and I can use that to undermine every professional decision she made during that time. Including the veracity of her version of the night he allegedly tried to kill her."

Melody smiled and I experienced a whisper of the fear Laurel had told me about. "Now we're getting somewhere."

"But I need to talk to Henry. And I think you can make that happen."

"Why do you think that?"

I shrugged. "He's a mama's boy, but I think his mom is real mad that he sullied the family name. You're the next in line. Plus, Kallen said they were never able to interview you because you were uncooperative. I'm finding a certain affection for people Kallen finds uncooperative."

"That'll do," Melody said.

There was a creak on the front porch. That was my only warning before Henry opened the door.

"Hey, Braddock." He smiled at me like we were buddies who saw each other last week instead of one of us stalking the other for a year.

Or at least, I thought he was smiling. He had a good start on a beard that obscured the lower half of his face. His blond hair was slicked back so tight it looked shaved. Between that and the short-sleeve plaid shirt buttoned all the way up, he looked like every Brooklyn white boy hipster. Leave it to Henry to manage to look trendy and also like everything wrong with cis men while he was on the run.

I could see the damage Laurel had inflicted on him. There was a small laceration on the bridge of his nose. Purple bruises branched off his nose and curved under his eyes. They weren't black all over like hers, but she had definitely broken his nose. His left pinkie and ring finger were buddy taped together. Bruises and scratches mottled his arms. Laurel was a goddamn hellion. I was so proud of her.

"Oh fuck." I stared at him for a minute before remembering that Laurel was listening in. If she hadn't figured out what was happening, I needed her to know like right now. "Henry. What the hell are you doing here?"

"You asked for me. I came." He walked to the couch and leaned forward to kiss Melody's cheek. "Hey, Nana."

"Have you eaten, baby boy? I can make you some lunch."

"Do you have any of that lemon vinaigrette left?"

"I believe I still have some of those lemons you brought. I'll fix it up."

"You're the best." He held out his right hand and helped her to her feet. She went into the kitchen and Henry leaned against the doorway leading to the hall. "So you're finally ready to admit that I should have killed that cunt?"

I took a deep breath and nodded. "Yeah. I want revenge on that bitch too. But for the record, your plan was a hot mess." I wondered how long it would take Laurel to contact the local sheriff's office. Maybe we should have run this scheme by her buddy at the FBI. I would have felt a lot better knowing an armed team of FBI agents were closing in on this house. Then again, neither of us expected Henry to show up in person.

He made a noise of disagreement. "It would have worked if it weren't for you meddling kids."

"She had half the Sac PD following her."

"Okay, maybe it was impetuous."

"You think?" Normally, I could get Henry to ramble. He was resisting that impulse.

"It's not like you were any help, dickwad."

"Well, I'm here to help now. But don't go rogue on me. I hate when you force my hand," I said.

"Fine. What do you have in mind?" Henry asked.

"Henry, did I put mint in the vinaigrette last time?" Melody asked.

"Yeah. And feel free to be liberal with it," he called.

"Do you want to wait until after lunch?" I asked pointedly.

"No, because you're not invited to lunch. What's your plan? It'll take her about ten minutes to put together a salad. After that, I boot your ass."

"Whatever." I took a leisurely drink of my tea. "I'm thinking I go on record with my sexual and romantic relationship with Kallen. We talk to a lawyer. Create doubt surrounding your case. Honestly, it shouldn't be hard to discredit her. She was fucking a CI. Who knows what other laws she broke."

Henry nodded. "It's a good start."

Jesus fucking Christ. Of course he wanted more. Where the fuck was Laurel? "What else do you have in mind?"

"I think you need to retract any statements you made to the cops about me."

"Well, yeah, of course."

"This is why I told you not to join that institution." Melody didn't shout, but her voice carried just fine.

"Your brother was a cop. Your son was a cop. Did you really expect your grandson to do anything different?" Henry made a face and rolled his eyes. He was being cute with his grandma. And he was letting me see it. More than anything, that convinced me he had bought my story.

"Yes. Your mama and I taught you to think for yourself. We taught you to care for others. And you let your dad and Uncle Dale convince you to join that damned department."

"She's right, you know. Cops are fascists," I said.

Melody stopped chopping herbs and pointed at me with her knife. "I like her. She can stay for lunch."

And that was the moment I caught sight of Laurel stealthily coming down the hallway behind Henry. She pressed a gun to the back of his head.

"Don't move," she said.

Henry stiffened but didn't shift his weight. He looked at me with pure hatred. "You fucking cunt."

"Oh, Laurel. Were you following me? I had no idea." I tried to feign innocence, but it mostly just came out deadpan. Laurel tried not to smile. It didn't work out for her.

"I'm going to kill you bitches. You do know that, right?" Henry said. It would have been chilling, but things weren't looking great for him.

"Put your hands on the back of your head," Laurel said.

"What the hell is going on out here?" Melody stuck her head out of the kitchen and swore. "Detective Kallen, I don't remember granting you permission to come on my property."

"Hello, Mrs. Brewer. Sit on the couch for me."

"You have no right to be here."

"Didn't your darling grandson tell you?" Laurel patted Henry down with one hand. "I quit the force. I'm a private citizen."

"Then you're trespassing."

"Okay. Sue me." Laurel removed a gun from Henry's waistband. She tucked it into her own at the small of her back.

"Get out of my house," Melody shouted.

"Sit on the damn couch and be quiet or I'll shoot Henry." Laurel took a knife out of Henry's pocket and slid it into her own.

"You did this." Melody pointed at me. Her knuckles were knobby with age, but her hand was steady. At least she didn't bring the knife out of the kitchen. She sat on the couch and glared.

We all heard the cars pull up the drive. From the sound of spitting gravel, it was quite a few.

Henry was holding completely still, but his eyes darted around the room. I couldn't see his jaw because of the beard, but the skin around his ears pulled like he was clenching his teeth.

I was so focused on the sound of cruisers and SUVs parking outside, the sound of a shotgun ratcheting was a terrifying surprise.

I jerked my gaze away from Laurel and Henry and found Melody pointing a twelve gauge directly at me.

"Fuck," I said. Henry laughed.

"Detective, put your gun down and give Henry his back," Melody said. We could hear boots crunching across the gravel. Melody stepped closer so the double barrels were just touching my chest. "Now, Detective."

Laurel lowered her gun. She reached behind her back and carefully extended Henry's to him. He took it and shoved Laurel aside to run down the hall. Laurel caught herself against the wall. Melody started to turn the shotgun in Laurel's direction. I grabbed the barrel and shoved it toward the ceiling. I was aware of heat on my hands and noise as it went off. I held tight to the barrel as Melody and I hit the ground. The door burst open and shouts of "Sheriff's Department" rang out.

"Cash, are you hit?" Laurel crouched over me, her eyes wide in fear.

I shook my head. "I'm good."

"Good." She sprinted down the hallway before I could ask if she was okay.

I was hauled to my feet and hustled outside. A young woman in a khaki uniform with a very serious ponytail sat me on the edge of the porch.

"Are you okay, Ms. Braddock?" She didn't make eye contact when she asked. Just looked at either side of my head, my arms, my legs.

I nodded. "I'm fine. Laurel wasn't hit, was she?"

"I don't know."

"How can you not know? Shotgun went boom. Was there blood everywhere or plaster everywhere? It's one of the two." I tried to stand, but she clamped her hand on my thigh and made me sit back down.

"Plaster, ma'am. There's no obvious sign that Ms. Kallen was hit. Our deputies are following her right now."

"Following her?" Either I was dense or this chick was speaking in riddles.

"She ran after Brewer."

Of course she did. I groaned. "That dumbass."

"Don't worry, ma'am. We'll catch him. We're setting up roadblocks as we speak."

"He's not the dumbass I'm worried about."

There was a commotion behind us. I turned in time to see Melody Brewer being bodily carried from the house. Her arms were restrained behind her and she was cursing a fucking storm. The deputies set her down as if she was going to walk. They made it two steps before she yanked out of their grip and launched herself at me. She got a solid kick to my jaw before they tackled her again.

"Dammit, Frank," Deputy Ponytail yelled. She helped me to my feet and walked me to the open back of an SUV. "I'm so sorry. Are you okay?"

I moved my jaw around. It was working just fine. "Yeah." I touched the side of my face. It was tender. "Don't take it out on Frank. Melody Brewer is a real pistol."

"Deputy Frank outweighs that pistol by about a hundred and fifty pounds."

I laughed. "Fair enough. Is there ice in any of these cars?"

"I'm sure there is. Hang tight."

A minute later, a different very serious looking sheriff's deputy came up. He was manipulating an ice pack to get it cold. "Hi there. I'm Deputy Ness. Deputy Harris asked me to take a look at you."

"Harris?"

"Brunette. Her hair is very slicked." Ness motioned like he was smoothing the sides of his head.

"Serious ponytail."

He laughed. "Yeah, serious ponytail." He held up the ice pack. "Do you mind if I check out your jaw?"

"Have at it." I tipped my chin up.

Ness walked his fingers over my cheek and across my jaw. It was unpleasant, but he was very precise, delicate. "Well, it looks like you're going to have an excellent bruise. I'd recommend a doctor visit so we can add details to the arrest report."

"I'll get right on that."

"I think you're being a bit sarcastic with me."

"Don't take it personally. I don't know how to express genuine emotion so I default to sarcasm," I said.

"Right."

"My former business partner tried to kill me and my ex-girlfriend a whole bunch of times. His grandma just took up the mantle. It's best for all of us if I don't process that immediately."

He nodded all wide-eyed. "So here's your ice pack."

"Thank you, Deputy Ness."

Chapter Fourteen

Cash Braddock, I'd hoped we were done," Michelson said. I dropped the ice pack. "Agent Michelson, same."

He grinned. "You want to fill me in on this little scheme?"

"I would, but I don't want to." I did my best to look cool and unaffected with my bruised jaw, sitting in the open back of an El Dorado County Sheriff SUV.

"Okay. Why don't I tell you what I know and you can fill in details if you like?" he asked.

"As soon as you update me on Laurel's whereabouts."

"That I can do." He pointed at the empty space next to me. I nodded. He unbuttoned his suit jacket and sat. "She chased Brewer about two miles into the forest. He had a quad stashed that he took off on. She pursued on foot, but quickly lost him. As soon as the sheriff deputies caught up to her, they took over tracking the vehicle."

"So where is she now? Is she okay?"

"She should be back here any minute. One of my agents is waiting to interview her and then you can see each other."

So they were planning on interviewing us separately. That was probably a good sign. No way this was going to go sideways.

"Are you sure she's okay? Brewer's grandmother got off a shot with her shotgun."

"I know she wasn't hit or otherwise seriously injured. The deputies escorting her back would have asked for medical assistance if she was. I assure you she's walking under her own power."

"Good. Okay. Proceed with your little interview."

"How did you, Kallen, and Henry Brewer come to be at Melody Brewer's house?"

"I don't know."

"You don't know how you got here?" he asked.

"I drove, silly."

"And Kallen and Brewer?"

"Yeah, they probably drove too. I guess they could have walked. Who's to say?"

"You are a very frustrating person."

"Thank you." I smiled.

He scowled. "Would you mind giving me some actual information?"

"I came here to lie," I said. Michelson closed his notebook and sighed. "No, not to you. To Brewer. I came to tell Grandma a story that would make Henry come out of hiding. It worked a lot better and faster than I expected."

"And Kallen?"

"You'll have to ask her that."

"Great," Michelson said. He looked like he was having a rough day. But in the karmic balance of who was having a worse day, I was going to nominate me so Michelson could suck it. "What was your plan if Henry showed up?"

"Well, he did. So," I waved my hand to indicate the house, the yard crawling with two different law enforcement agencies.

"What if he had tried to hurt you? There's a rapidly growing body of evidence that suggests he would like to."

"Not really. He had plenty of time and a gun. He didn't even try. Your growing body is bunk, pal."

"But what if he did?" He sounded exasperated.

I dug the stun gun out of my pocket. "Buzz buzz, motherfucker."

"You're going to be the death of me." He stood and shook his head before walking away muttering what sounded like "buzz buzz, motherfucker."

"Does this mean the interview is over?" I called.

He kept walking. But he was laughing. I could feel it.

A few minutes later, Laurel emerged from the trees. She was flanked by two deputies. Michelson was right. She was walking just fine. I watched the feds close in on her to direct her to the other side of a waiting FBI vehicle. She let them as she scanned the yard, but as soon as our eyes met, she stopped. A couple of burly dudes tried to block her, but she dodged them. We collided in the middle of the driveway. I wrapped my arms around her waist and held her close. Her arms were hard and soft and familiar around my shoulders. I could feel the breath rushing in and out of her chest. She smelled like sweat and crisp wood and it made everything okay for a brief moment.

"Are you okay?" she asked.

"I am. I'm fine. You?"

"Of course. You sure you're okay?"

"Swear. Grandma Brewer kicked my face, but that's it."

Laurel pulled back to study my face. "How the hell did you let a seventy-year-old lady kick you in the face?"

"Hey, I'm donating my time to the local senior community and I don't appreciate you undermining the seriousness of my work."

She started laughing and couldn't stop. The FBI and sheriff's department slowly gathered around us. Michelson tried to get Laurel's attention. He tried to order her away from me. She just dropped her forehead to my shoulder and laughed more. When he tried to get me to step back, I started laughing too. The tension around us grew, which just made it funnier. The cops were standing there in their uniforms of the patriarchy and they were powerless to stop us from giggling.

Michelson lost his patience. He waved off the officers and agents. When they dispersed, he gripped Laurel's elbow and pulled her away from me.

"Jesus Christ, Daniel. Calm down." She jerked her arm out of his grasp. She was still grinning like a dumbass.

"It's a miracle you didn't get yourself killed today. And you nearly got a civilian killed too." He tried to grab her again, but she spun out of his range. He visibly restrained himself and put his hands in his pockets. "Not to mention how many goddamn laws you broke." He clenched his fists, which pulled his trousers tight.

"I didn't break any laws. I just did some dumb shit. I'm a civilian now too, Agent Michelson. If I want to be an idiot, that is my constitutional right."

"Goddammit, Kallen." He turned and walked two steps away. After a count to ten, he turned back. "I am doing everything in my power to keep you safe. In part, that is because it is my job. But I'm also doing it because I respect you as a former colleague and as a friend. You don't need to participate in your own protection, but I would appreciate it if you didn't actively work against it."

Laurel stopped grinning. "I get why it looks that way, but I promise I don't have a death wish. We thought this would get us closer to him. We had no idea he would show up."

Michelson looked at me. "Can we have this discussion in private?"

Laurel laughed. "Why? You already know I was sleeping with her for months."

"Well, yeah." He seemed uncomfortable. "But that doesn't mean she should be privy to private discussions."

"She's going to tell me whatever you say anyway, but I can go over there if you'll be more comfortable." I nodded at my perch in the SUV. "Hell, I can take off." I glanced at my vehicle. It was surrounded by sheriff's cruisers. Maybe not.

"You can't leave until we've squared away accommodations for sequestering you."

"Fuck that," I said.

"We already told Reyes we're not hiding," Laurel said.

Michelson did another count to ten. "This guy has tried to kill you three times. He stalked you for a year. And you just showed up at his grandmother's house to see if you could force him out of the woodwork. And, shocker, he did show up. You just poured gasoline on this entire situation. He is not going to stop coming after the two of you." He said it all slow as if that would help us understand.

"He only tried to kill me twice. This time, he just announced his intention to kill me."

"That's the same thing," Michelson shouted.

"It's really not. You want to listen to the recording? Braddock is wearing a mic." Laurel was so accommodating.

"You wired her?" He nodded to himself. "You wired her. Great. Very helpful. This whole thing was worth it for a recording that won't even be admissible."

"Chill out. Today doesn't change anything," Laurel said.

"Actually, it changes things a little," I said. Laurel shot me a glare. "Well, it does. Before he wasn't sure where I stood. Now he knows we're in cahoots."

"Cahoots?" Michelson asked.

"Cahoots."

"She does this," Laurel said.

"I do what?"

"Say shit like 'in cahoots' in normal conversation."

Michelson took a moment then said, "She did say my theory was 'bunk' earlier."

We all turned at the sound of another vehicle crossing the rickety bridge. It was another unmarked police car. They parked and Reyes and Duarte climbed out. They hustled toward us. Reyes hugged Laurel. Duarte shook my hand. Then they switched.

"You guys okay?" Reyes asked. "Did they catch him?"

We all shook our heads. "The locals and my agents are tracking him through the woods," Michelson said.

Duarte nodded in the direction of the freeway. "They got the roadblock set up quick."

"They better." Michelson glared at Laurel. "Maybe you two can talk some sense into her. She still won't go to a safe house."

"Sure she will. We had an agreement." Reyes spoke like Laurel wasn't present. "Any escalation and they both promised we could sequester them."

"Well, actually—" Laurel said.

"Technically—" I said.

"Go ahead," she said to me.

"No, you."

"I'm sorry, did you both simultaneously white man 'well, actually' me and then apologize to each other for interrupting?" Reyes asked.

"The patriarchy is wild, man," I said.

Duarte pressed his lips together and clenched his jaw to keep from laughing.

"We said we would go into a safe house if Brewer escalated. He didn't escalate, we did," Laurel said.

"This looks a lot like he escalated." Reyes looked around the yard. "And I'm told he shot at you with a shotgun."

"That's incorrect," Laurel said.

"Yeah, it was his grandmother who popped the shotgun," I said.

"His grandmother?" Reyes looked at Michelson. "His grand-mother?" Michelson nodded. "What?" When no one immediately answered, he shouted, "What?"

"There's not much more to explain. Brewer ran, I chased him, Grandma shot at me, Cash tackled Grandma so she only shot the ceiling. It sounds like a big deal, but it really wasn't," Laurel said.

"Yeah. You guys are blowing this way out of proportion," I said. We were both lying. Without meaning to, we had shifted into our old dynamic. It was us against the world. Even though there was no us. It was rote, compulsory.

Reyes stomped back to his car and got in. Duarte started to follow, then hesitated and turned back. He hovered halfway between us and the car, waiting for direction.

"So can we go?" I asked.

Michelson blew out a dramatic breath. "Fine. But I'm going to step up patrols. I'm going to ask Sac PD to have the uniform watching your house do a walkthrough every hour. Kallen, you going back to Reyes's place?"

"I guess so. He's going to be real fussy."

I tried not to laugh. "So fussy."

"You mind taking me back to my rental?" Laurel asked me.

"Sure."

"One of my agents can take you," Michelson said. "It's the silver Ford compact on the service road to the east, right?"

"It's fine. Finish your scene here."

"He is still out there." Michelson pointed at the woods.

"I doubt he's waiting at my car," Laurel said.

"According to the rules of every movie, he's definitely waiting at your car now," I said.

Laurel laughed. "Okay, can one of the agents escort us to my vehicle?"

"Yeah, they can follow us to the freeway and scowl and write down license plates and time stamp things. It will be very official," I said.

Michelson waved over a sheriff and one of his agents. He got the sheriff to coordinate shifting cruisers away from my car while he briefed his agent. "Okay, you guys are clear to go. Agent Wilson will escort you to the rental vehicle and follow you back to Sac County. As soon as you arrive at your respective residences, check in with me."

"Is Wilson going to write down plenty of license plates?" I asked.

"Yes, and he will scowl." Michelson kept it deadpan, but I appreciated the callback. "If you see anything suspicious at any time, let me know."

"Yes, sir." I saluted.

"Don't be an ass." Laurel grabbed my arm and stopped me from saluting.

"Anything," Michelson said.

"We got it." Laurel grabbed my arm and pulled me toward the car.

We didn't say anything until we were over the bridge and back on the county road. Laurel directed me to the fire lane where her car was.

"You really okay?" I asked.

"Yeah. You got more physical than I did."

"I'd argue with you because you ran two miles and that sounds like a lot, but my jaw hurts where that bitch kicked me. So we can call it even."

She started laughing again. Not as hard as before, but still. "You still haven't explained how that happened."

"One of the sheriffs pulled me outside while they were arresting her. The sheriff sat me on the edge of the porch to check me over, make sure I wasn't injured or whatever. Then they marched Grandma Brewer out and she broke away from them and kicked me in the face."

Laurel found that hilarious. "I guess they weren't expecting an old lady to resist arrest?"

"She'd been resisting arrest the entire time. I think they might be incompetent." I said it conspiratorially. This was surely new information.

"There's merit to that suggestion."

I pulled up behind Laurel's parked car. Agent Wilson drove past us. He waved for Laurel to stay put. He parked diagonal across the lane. He jumped out and walked the perimeter of the car. Then he checked underneath it. After a look at the surrounding tree line, he motioned for Laurel to get out.

"That seemed super necessary," I said.

"You're the one who said Brewer was definitely waiting at my car."

"Good point." I rolled down my window. "Agent Wilson? Should you check the interior of the car as well?"

"I hate you," Laurel said quiet enough so Wilson couldn't hear her.

"Yes, ma'am." Wilson walked briskly to my window. "Ms. Kallen, would you mind giving me your key fob?"

Laurel dug the key out of her pocket and handed it over me. "Thanks, Wilson. Couldn't do this without you."

"No problem, ma'am." He clearly wasn't picking up on her sarcasm. He popped the trunk and checked inside. Then he opened the driver's door and stuck his head in. After a minute, he closed the door. "All clear."

Laurel got out and took the keys from him. "Wilson, I know you're escorting us back to Sac County, but could you follow Cash all the way home? There's a uniform stationed there, but I think it would be better to have you check the house. She's a little nervous after today."

"Yes, of course." Wilson nodded very seriously at me. "Nothing to worry about, Ms. Braddock."

"Thanks, Laurel," I shouted.

"You're welcome, honey. Be safe." Laurel blew a kiss at me and climbed in her car. She was the worst. I was definitely still in love with her.

CHAPTER FIFTEEN

I woke up to Nickels jumping on my bed. It felt late. The city outside was quiet like it was just before dawn. Nickels was sitting too close to the edge of the mattress so her weight pulled it down too much. I turned on my side and snuggled back into my pillows and my cat. But then I realized the fuzzy purring cat was very much not on the side where my bed was currently dipping down.

"Fuck." I sat up and opened my eyes.

"Hey, Braddock." Henry pushed me back down.

"Get the fuck out of my house."

"Now, now." He looked down long enough to draw my eyes to the gun in his hand. The room was dark, but the ambient streetlight was enough to clearly outline the shape.

"What are you doing here?" I asked.

"We didn't get to finish our conversation."

"That doesn't really justify waking me up in the middle of the night. You're disturbing my cat." We both looked at Nickels. She stretched and went back to sleep.

"When else are we going to talk? You have cops outside twenty-four seven."

"It obviously didn't stop you." Not that I was freaking out or anything.

"Chill, man. I'm here to tell you how you can make this all up to me."

I managed to not laugh or punch him, which I thought showed real growth. "Do tell. I'm on the edge of my fucking seat."

"You owe me, bitch."

"Whatever." I wondered if he was planning on killing me. It seemed likely that he would try at some point, but I was getting distinctive "wanna chat" vibes. So maybe not tonight? My gut was feeling more annoyed than scared. I decided to lean into that.

"I saw that little gallery you opened. It's perfect," he said.

"For what?"

"Everything. You can launder money through it fucking easy. We can massively scale up shipments. We're going to be party drug central. Definitely doing molly and K. Maybe GHB. Shrooms and acid for sure. And your old standards, of course. Xanax and codeine and shit."

"Yeah, sure. And we can just change the signage out front to say 'massive drug operation.'" I put my hands up and gestured to indicate a big sign. "Oh, and 'DEA, FBI, Sac PD welcome. If you have a badge, come on in.'" I called it like I was at a carnival.

"Keep your voice down."

"Please. It's not like the uniform out front can hear me. He's obviously not very competent." I nodded at Henry.

"If you're not going to take this seriously, I can just go with my original plan. Kill you and move to Mexico. I don't need you. I'd rather clear my name, but it's no sweat off my sack to shoot you in the head."

"Vivid imagery. Thanks for that."

"So this is what you're going to do. Call your lawyer in the morning. Start preparing a statement to hang Kallen and retract anything negative you said about me." The shadows behind Henry shifted. I forced myself to keep eye contact with him. "Once we square that mess, I've lined up suppliers. As soon as I give the go-ahead, we can be operational in a week." The shadow took shape. It was Lane. This was not good. "I'm not an idiot. I know we can't actively deal from the gallery. Not at first. Let Nate know he's not taking any jobs out of state. We need him here for distribution."

Henry had given this a lot of thought. I didn't like it.

"No," I said.

"No?" He wasn't expecting that.

"No. You're fucking delusional."

"Fine." He raised the gun. "Get up. We're going for a ride." He gestured toward the street with his gun.

Lane swung something at his head. It connected with a dull thud. Henry slumped and fell to the floor.

"Come on." Lane grabbed my arm and yanked me out of bed. Nickels hissed and darted away. Lane and I sprinted down the hall. She threw open the front door and we ran. Halfway through the yard, the uniform was out of his cruiser. "Inside. Bedroom at the end of the hall." Lane pointed. He ran inside.

We stopped and leaned against the cop car, gasping. Within a few seconds, we could hear sirens start a few blocks away.

"Jesus fucking Christ, dude," I said.

"You're welcome."

"You're my goddamn hero." I put my arm around her. She threaded her arms around my waist. We were still breathing hard from our sprint. "Should I go wake up Robin and Andy?"

"Yeah. Let's." Lane took my hand and we approached the porch. I watched our open front door for any movement while Lane rang the Wards' bell and pounded on the door. "Robin, Andy," she called.

Three cruisers pulled up from opposite directions and more cops ran in my side of the duplex. It was nice to have police on my side for once. And all I had to do was befriend half the detectives and find a worse criminal for them to focus on.

Robin opened the door. She was wearing short-shorts and a tank top. "What's going on?"

"Grab Andy. Henry Brewer just broke into our place," Lane said.

Robin turned and ran to Andy's room. A minute later, they joined us on the sidewalk.

"Sorry, pals," I said.

Robin leaned into my side. "We're all safe. It's okay."

"Yeah. It's all good." Lane put her head on my shoulder and reached across me to squeeze Robin's hand.

"Thanks," I said.

Andy leaned in front of us and took a selfie. She started tapping the screen. Robin snatched the phone. "Hey," Andy said.

"Do not post that."

"Why?" Andy tried to take back her phone.

"Because I'd rather not end up on social media in my pajamas."

"Fine," Andy said. Robin handed her the phone and she tucked it in the pocket of her gym shorts. "So what's going on? Why are we out here?"

"Henry Brewer broke into our place," I said.

"Shit." Andy leaned forward as if she could see what was happening through the walls. "How'd he get in? I thought the cop was watching for him. How'd you get out? Are you guys okay?"

I shrugged. "Lane came up behind him and smacked him in the head." I looked at Lane. "What did you hit him with?"

She grinned. "Fluid mechanics textbook. I bitched all semester that I couldn't get it in ebook, but who's complaining now, motherfucker?" She tucked her hands in the pockets of her yummy sushi pajama pants and leaned against the police car at the curb.

"I see you put on pants before saving me."

"I wasn't going to chase down a soon-to-be felon in my bikinis, thank you very much."

"What if he had killed me?" I asked.

"You're just mad that you're out here in your underwear." Lane looked pointedly at my boxer briefs. They were trunks. Very short trunks.

I tugged at the hem of my T-shirt. "I don't love it."

"Calm down. We're all barefoot and sleepy and feeling exposed and shit." Andy craned her neck to look in my open front door.

"Don't get all observant on me, punk."

Robin squeezed my arm. "They're coming back out."

Two of the officers emerged and came toward us. I met the cops in the middle of the yard.

"Did you get him?" I asked.

"No, ma'am. Not yet. I'm sorry," the taller cop said. "Vogt saw him going out the back. He chased him, but we lost him over on H Street."

"Are you for real?"

"Yes, ma'am."

If this dude ma'amed me once more, I was going to hit him. "He's not Michael Myers. How hard is it to catch one guy?"

"We're still looking."

The other cop nodded very seriously. "Detective Duarte is on his way. Dispatch is still trying to reach Detective Reyes."

I took a deep breath and tried to remind myself that they were doing their best. But I was still a little confused how their best led to Henry getting away again. "Can I go inside for my phone? I'd like to call him and Kallen."

"Sorry, ma'am. We need the all clear from our captain before letting you back in the house."

"Right. Got it." My cat was probably terrified, I had no pants, and Henry was still missing. This was fine. I went back to Lane, Robin, and Andy. "They didn't get him."

"Are you fucking kidding me?" Lane looked around as if Henry was going to come up behind us. A couple of the neighbors were looking out their windows, but the red and blue lights were keeping them indoors.

"Andy, can I use your phone?" I asked.

"Sure." She unlocked it and handed it to me. I scrolled through her contacts to Laurel and hit call. It rang for a while before she picked up.

"Andy? Are you okay?" Was how Laurel answered.

"It's me. We're fine."

"Shit. You scared me," she said.

I heard rustling. I imagined her sitting up in bed. "Sorry." Hearing her voice made me feel so much better and I hated myself for it.

"It's cool. I just wasn't expecting a call from Andy at three in the morning. What happened?"

"Henry decided he wanted to do a slumber party."

"Fuck. Seriously?"

"I know. We didn't have any snacks prepared and I'm not even wearing cute pj's, but it's fine."

"Cash."

"Everyone is fine. We're out here with Andy and Robin. The cops are looking for Henry and we are hanging out in the street barefoot."

"What about Lane?"

"She knocked Henry out with a very large textbook. Probably saved my life or whatever," I said. Lane chuckled and bumped me with her shoulder.

"Shit. Okay. I'm coming over right now."

"Bring Reyes. Dispatch is trying to reach him, but—" I stopped when I heard a deep voice in the background behind her.

"Just a sec, Cash." Laurel muffled the phone to have a conversation with Reyes. "Okay, I'm back. Ionescu just called Reyes. We're heading over."

"Cool. See you soon."

I should have asked her to bring me pants, but I assumed the cops would let me into the house long before they arrived. When Duarte got there five minutes later, I was getting frustrated. Ten minutes after that, Reyes and Laurel arrived and I was seriously displeased.

Laurel hugged Lane, then looked me up and down. She started to smile.

"Don't start," I said.

"I wasn't going to say anything." She put her hands up defensively.

"Can you get them to let us in?" Robin asked.

"I can try, but I don't have much sway anymore." Laurel squeezed Andy's shoulder and nodded at all of us before going to talk to Reyes and Duarte.

"Where's Nickels?" Andy asked.

"Probably on the top shelf of my closet. That's her current favorite hiding spot."

Reyes and Laurel came back. "You guys are clear to go back inside," Reyes said.

We collectively sighed and headed for the porch. "We're not going to get to go back to bed, are we?" Robin asked.

"You're free to do whatever you want. But I would like to talk to you about some security concerns," Reyes said.

"That's a no," I said.

"Yeah, I got that." Robin opened her front door. Andy went inside.

"I'll make coffee," I said. "Reyes, you want to head out back? We can meet you out there in a sec."

"Sure thing." He clapped a hand on Duarte's shoulder and led him through my house to the backyard.

"Any cops in here?" I called. Two uniforms emerged from the hallway leading to my bedroom. "You guys mind giving us a minute?"

They looked at me and Lane and Laurel like we were going to turn into Henry at any moment. Laurel nodded and they dropped the glare.

"Yes, ma'am." They went out the front door.

I went straight to my closet and checked the top shelf. Nickels was exactly where I thought she would be. "Hey, Nick." She meowed at me. "Yeah, I'm sorry. You did real good." She meowed again.

"Nickels okay?" Laurel asked from the threshold of my bedroom. She was giving the doorway a good two feet of space lest she be sucked in.

"Yeah, she's good." I stuck my head out of the closet. "We're going to be put in a safe house, aren't we?"

"Yep. We can say no again, but I don't think it's wise."

"Shit." I ducked back into the closet to change my T-shirt to one I hadn't been sleeping in. "Any idea how long?" I spoke up so she could hear me.

"Until they catch him or the threat is managed."

"So no fucking clue."

"Yeah, no fucking clue."

I pulled on a pair of jeans and looked around for a baseball hat. "Is my Massey Ferguson cap out there?"

"On the dresser."

I glanced out and found Laurel pointing at one of my dressers from her perch outside the door. "Thanks." I crossed the room and grabbed the hat.

"I'm sorry."

"What for?" I picked up a pair of Converse, but shoes suddenly seemed like too much. I tossed them back toward the closet.

"I thought you were safe. I never would have suggested yesterday's plan if I thought he could break into your house," Laurel said.

"I never would have gone along with it if I thought he could break into my house. This isn't on you." I couldn't handle her hovering anymore, and it didn't seem like she was going to come in. "You mind starting coffee? You know where everything is."

"Yeah. Sure. I can do that." She turned, hesitated, then continued down the hall. Insecure Laurel was strange.

Chapter Sixteen

As far as apartments went, it was big. As far as living spaces to share with your ex-girlfriend for an undetermined amount of time went, it was laughably small. There was a living room and a dining room, but it didn't appear we would ever get to use those considering the number of FBI agents and Sac PD lounging about.

Okay, it was like two agents, Reyes, and Duarte. But Reyes was doing some serious mothering and it was overwhelming.

"Do not under any circumstances go out on the balcony." Reyes pulled Laurel back from the glass doors leading to the deck. He closed the gauzy curtain so we could only see the faint outline of greenery and the shimmer of water from the pool below.

"You've got to be kidding me," Laurel said.

"The whole point of this is to keep you safe. I'm not going to blow it so you can look at a pool and some generic landscaping."

"You think he's going to be disguised as a groundskeeper? I'll watch out for anyone with a mustache wearing coveralls and clean boots." Laurel rolled her eyes.

"You're so good at this. You should be a detective," I said.

"The clean boots are always a giveaway," she whispered to me.

"Sorry if I don't trust your judgement or your discretion right now." Reyes yanked heavy light-blocking curtains across the window and the room fell into semi-darkness. "Last time I let you go off unmonitored you got shot at by an old lady, chased a fugitive through the woods, and Cash woke up with the murderous bastard sitting in her bedroom."

"Well, when you put it that way." Laurel dropped onto the couch.

"It's not putting it any specific way. Those are just facts."

There was a knock at the door. "It's Agent Malone."

Reyes nodded at Duarte, then at one of the bedrooms. Reyes took up a position by the front door. Duarte ushered me and Laurel into one of the bedrooms and closed us in.

"This is absurd," Laurel said.

I was finding it difficult to disagree with her. Just getting here had required three vehicles, a parking garage, two bridges, and a number of back roads in order to confirm we weren't being followed. We had been in this apartment for all of ten minutes and I was ready to take my chances back home.

Reyes knocked on the bedroom door before opening it. "All clear. It was Malone." As if we were confused when Malone had announced himself.

We filed back into the common room. There was a shorter black dude in a suit cut to accentuate the formidable size of his arms. He shook our hands. "I'm Richard Malone. I'll be running this operation." He pulled out a chair at the table in the center of the condo and nodded for us to join him. "Boyd will be up shortly with our supplies and equipment. We'll set up our command center here." He knocked on the large dining room table.

"So we're all just staying in this apartment indefinitely?" I asked.

"Well, until we catch Brewer," Duarte said.

"And we're only staying until Michelson can get two more agents assigned." Reyes nodded at Duarte.

"I'll be here for the duration though," Malone said.

"Are you a footie pajama man? Because Braddock and I have very strict rules about nighttime wear," Laurel said.

"Dude, don't be a dick," I said to her. She gave me a look. "It's okay if he's not wearing a onesie as long as he's whimsical. He seems like a superhero type. Maybe something in the Marvel or DC canon." We laughed. The guys did not.

There was another knock at the door. "That will be Boyd." Malone stood. He looked pointedly at the bedroom. These FBI guys were clearly going to be a riot.

Laurel sighed heavily but allowed Duarte to lead us back to the bedroom. We stood around silently until Reyes let us back out a minute later. Malone and a white dude were moving equipment cases from the small entryway to the center of the common room. A small living room jutted out opposite the kitchen. The forbidden balcony was off of that. Looked like we were going to be confined to the pockets of space around the FBI.

"Laurel Kallen, Cash Braddock, this is Agent Matt Boyd," Malone said.

"Agent Boyd." Laurel nodded and shook his hand.

"Matt is fine, ma'am." Boyd was Johnny Bravo shaped. All shoulders and torso. He shook my hand after shaking Laurel's. His grip was firm, if not a little timid, like he was afraid of crushing my hand.

"Boyd, what are your feelings on whimsy?" I asked.

Boyd looked at Malone who shook his head. "I don't know that I've ever examined my feelings on whimsy."

I shrugged at Laurel. "Better than outright rejection."

"There's got to be a line somewhere, I guess," she said. "Do you guys need anything from me or am I good to unpack?"

"Go ahead," Reyes said.

"Does it matter which room I'm in?" she asked.

Malone looked around. "You and Braddock are in those two rooms." He pointed at two doors on the far side of the common room. There was another pair of doors on the other side of the kitchen.

"Thanks." Laurel disappeared into one of the bedrooms with her bag.

Malone and Boyd continued unpacking equipment. In addition to laptops and a very necessary printer, they had a fuckload of surveillance equipment. I stood there watching awkwardly for a minute.

"Braddock, do you mind going into one of the bedrooms again? We need to install cameras outside and we can't have you visible when we open the doors," Malone said.

"Sure."

Boyd gathered a stack of cameras. Duarte stuffed his back pockets with hardware and various tools. Clearly, jeans were the way to go for safe house duty. Boyd already looked conspicuous enough with his muscles and his suit. Putting up cameras while wearing that was just too much. It would have been easier to put a sign outside announcing it was an FBI safe house.

"Cash," Duarte said.

I realized he and Boyd were standing at the front door waiting for me to disappear. "Oh, sorry." This was going to be a long couple of days. Hopefully, it wouldn't be a long couple of weeks. I ducked into the room Laurel had chosen.

She looked up from the open drawer she was setting T-shirts in. "Hey."

"You're actually unpacking," I said.

"Yeah. That's what I said I was going to do." She refolded a couple of pairs of chinos as she pulled them out of her bag.

"I just thought it was an excuse to leave the room." I leaned against the small desk in the corner.

She shrugged. "I've been living out of a suitcase for the better part of a year. I learned it's easier to settle in if you unpack even if you don't plan on staying long." She put the chinos away.

"Right."

"This is going to be weird, isn't it?" she asked.

"Naw, it's exactly what I wanted to do this week." I suddenly remembered my lunch date with Marjorie. "Shit. Except I have a lunch today."

She gave me a look. "You have a lunch today?"

"Yeah."

"Who the fuck are you?"

"It's not as weird as it sounds. Actually, it's way more weird than it sounds. I'm supposed to have lunch with my mom."

Laurel stopped arranging clothes to stare at me. "I thought your mom was dead."

"I kind of assumed so too."

"So you're having lunch. How long have you been in contact?"

"She showed up on my doorstep the day you showed up at the gallery."

"Shit," she said.

"I guess."

"That's like heavy, dude."

"It is," I said.

"So you've got to cancel your lunch?"

"Yeah. That seems difficult."

"How is that difficult?" she asked.

"I don't know. I've got to call her and, you know, talk."

"You could text her."

"Yeah, okay. I could do that." I pulled out my phone.

"Wow. How have you made it this far in life?"

"Pure luck," I said.

I'm sorry to do this at the last minute, but I have to cancel lunch today. That seemed reasonable.

Marjorie wrote back immediately. *Sure. Are you okay?*

Yeah, fine now. I've been put into an FBI safe house. Apparently they are real strict about coming and going all willy-nilly.

I imagine so. Maybe I could call you later?

"How's it going over there?" Laurel asked.

I sighed. "She's being all understanding and shit. And now she wants to maybe call me later." I waited too long to respond so she wrote again.

Unless that's not allowed. I don't want to endanger you.

Well, if she was going to be all rational about it, I couldn't very well blow her off. *Yeah, sure. That would be fine.*

Great!

Laurel crossed the small room to look over my shoulder. "Aww, you have a phone date. That's sweet," she said all saccharine-like.

"Shut up." I pushed off the desk. "I'm going to unpack too. I heard it really helps you settle in."

"Good luck with that." She went back to the bed and pulled a Dopp kit out of her bag. Of course she had a fancy little kit. My toiletries were in a Ziploc, which was a perfectly acceptable mode of transport for one's toiletries.

One of the guys had set my duffel just inside the doorway of the bedroom next to Laurel's. I picked up the bag and set it on the bed. Unpacking seemed difficult. I texted Kyra instead.

So I've been put in a safe house.

I unzipped my bag and dumped the contents out. Thankfully, Kyra wrote back before I had to start putting things away.

Shit. Are you okay? she asked.

Fine now. But you might want to cancel our studio visits this week. Or take Van.

I got bubbles but no response. I looked around at the space. It was a mirror of Laurel's room. A small desk was against our shared wall. Next to that was a dresser with a TV. There was a small closet and another door. The door opened and Laurel came out.

"How the fuck?" I asked.

"Shit," she said.

"How did you do that?"

"Our bathroom is connected."

"What?" I asked.

"Bathroom. Yours, mine. Connected. I believe they call it a Jack and Jill."

"Well, thanks for that little lesson on bathrooms."

"Okay, now can we admit this is going to be weird?" she asked.

"Absolutely."

By dinner time I had an entirely new understanding of weird. Duarte ordered pizza. Boyd gave me a soda like we were kids at a slumber party. No one seemed to find the prohibition approach to pizza strange. We ate in silence. Afterward, Laurel ditched me to get some work done. The agents went back to surveillance and somber typing on laptops. Boyd was real excited at the prospect of getting his paperwork done. Jodie Foster never got excited about her paperwork. Okay, maybe she did, but I still would have much preferred to be sequestered with Clarice Starling. Boyd was nice and all, but he lacked certain attributes.

I tried watching TV, but the air was too still. It made the volume too loud. Until I turned it down and it became too quiet. There was no in between. I had never been so idle in my life. And I was good at being idle. I'd made the majority of my choices in life around the concept of leisure. And yet I found myself watching FBI agents, Sac PD detectives, and a police consultant fill out reports rather than literally anything else. Just watching Boyd do paperwork was putting me to sleep. Watching Laurel do the same was barely more interesting.

Turned out watching someone I was sexually attracted to do a boring task was still boring, just with boobs. She also had a propensity to push her hair out of her face. And a new tic where she chewed on her pen. Who knew I found pen chewing sexy? Not me.

I finally went into my bedroom and started reading. When I woke up the next morning, I found them all in the exact same places, but with coffee and different clothes. Apparently, I should have brought work with me. I just wasn't a bring work with me type of person. I was generally an avoid any work type of person. It was kind of why I became a drug dealer. And obviously there were no downsides to that.

Chapter Seventeen

It was good Marjorie had given me a heads-up she wanted to chat on the phone. Otherwise I would have been seriously thrown off when it rang. As it was I was only mildly thrown off. I tossed the book I was reading onto the bed and answered.

"Hello?"

"Hello, Cash? It's Marjorie."

"Hey, how's it going?"

"Good, great. How are you?" she asked.

"Okay. Pretty bored. Turns out hanging around a safe house is kinda boring."

"Better than being in danger, though."

"There's that, yeah," I said.

"Are you there alone?"

I wished. "No. Laurel—my ex—is here. And a whole mess of cops."

"Oh." There was silence as she found an appropriate response to that. "That must be uncomfortable."

"It could be more comfortable."

"So what are you doing?"

"There was some pretty exciting unpacking. And a thrilling lecture about not looking out the windows. So reading, mostly," I said.

"No kidding. I spend all my spare time reading too."

I scooted up the bed and shoved some pillows between my back and the headboard. This was looking to be an actual conversation. "Yeah, I mean, I thought everyone did. Until I was trapped in a small ass condo for two days with five other adults, none of whom are reading."

"I never understood that. When I finally got clean, that was what saved me."

"Really?"

"You sound surprised."

"Well, it's not a narrative you hear a lot. Reading saved me from heroin." I tried to envision it, but I didn't know her well enough to see beyond a junkie clinging to a mass market paperback.

She laughed. Like really laughed. Not meeting her daughter for the first time in twenty years and trying to make it feel normal type of laugh. "You make a good point."

"I dig it. It's just unique."

"It was the only thing that distracted me. Some people go for Jolly Ranchers, I went for Ernest Hemingway."

"Wait. You like Ernest Hemingway?" That was just unacceptable.

"Oh, yeah. When I was about fourteen, I became fascinated with Hemingway and Gertrude Stein and it just snowballed into a Lost Generation obsession."

"When you were fourteen?"

"Yeah. I was a strange kid," she said.

"How so?"

"I'm not sure how much you know about your grandparents. But Dad was a real prick. Some alcoholic fathers are absent. Ours was present and he wanted you to know it."

"Clive wouldn't let me spend much time with them, but I got the same impression," I said.

"He didn't tell you about them?" She sounded surprised.

"He sort of did, but it was mostly basic facts. He wanted me to form my own opinions. My opinion was Grandpa was a dick and Grandma was sentient wallpaper."

She chuckled. "Yes. That sounds about right."

"How exactly does Hemingway connect with Grandpa?" I asked.

"Hemingway was an escape. Reading had always been my way out, but Hemingway was different. I read a story from *In Our Time* in ninth grade English. There was something so simple and straightforward about it. That was it for me."

"I fucking hate Hemingway," I said.

She laughed again. "No!"

"Yes, but I think it's just because his misogyny oozes from the page. I probably shouldn't have read so much background before reading him."

"See, I know all that, but it doesn't erase the comfort. The rhythm of his stories is my chicken soup. When everything is out of control, I can always go fishing with ol' Ernest."

"I gotta tell you, that's weird," I said very seriously.

"Oh, I know," she said. "So what are you reading?"

I flipped my book over to stare at the cover even though I already knew the answer. "*Fingersmith*. It's like a Victorian era queer crime thriller."

"That sounds fun."

"It is. I had to pack quickly so I went for thick books, which means Sarah Waters. Plus, her books always make me feel better about my own crimes. I almost never impersonate an heiress or a ghost in order to steal large sums of money," I said.

"Almost never? That's good of you."

"What can I say? I'm kindhearted." There was a knock on my bedroom door. "Just a sec. Someone is knocking." I muffled the phone against my chest and called, "Come in."

Reyes opened the door. "Dinner's here."

"Thanks, Dad. I'll be out in a sec."

He shook his head. "You're intolerable." He closed the door, but I caught his grin.

"I've got to go. Apparently, we do family style dinners in the safe house," I said.

"Of course. Thanks for talking to me. I've really enjoyed it," Marjorie said.

"Yeah, so have I." I was surprised to realize I wasn't just being polite.

"Maybe we can talk again soon?"

"Totally."

"Great. Good night, Cash."

"'Night."

When I got out to the kitchen, Boyd handed me a heavy ceramic plate with an unopened takeout container in the center. I turned to the dining room table in the middle of the room, but it was covered with laptops and various equipment cases.

Laurel was sitting at the bar on the other side of the kitchen. "Here, Cash." She nudged out the stool next to her.

"Thanks." I wove through the guys grabbing plates from Boyd and sat with her. "Is it me or is this apartment a little small for six adults?" I asked quietly.

"Technically, I'm pretty sure it was only intended for four adults. Reyes and Duarte are here unofficially." She opened her takeout container and dumped drunken noodles onto her plate.

"Right. That's not overkill or anything."

"It's not like there would be an abundance of space without them. There are only two other bedrooms." She was right. The issue was with the open floor plan with not enough floor.

"I don't suppose they have bunk beds in there." I dumped my own drunken noodles onto my plate.

"I'm reasonably certain they do not."

"So we should feel lucky they decided to give us our own rooms with our own beds?"

"I'm not going to write them a love letter or anything. The feds must have hundreds of places like this across the country. This was a choice. Probably based on money."

I looked at my pile of noodles. "I don't suppose beer was in the budget?"

Laurel laughed. "Not likely."

"I got you, buddy," Duarte said from behind us.

"Dude. Personal space," I said.

"Sorry." He skirted the bar and opened the fridge. He pulled out two bottles of Singha and set them in front of us triumphantly.

"Okay, I forgive you," I said.

"As long as there are more in there," Laurel said.

"Don't worry. I got a six-pack. And we're working so it's all you," Duarte said.

Laurel tapped the neck of her beer against mine. "So what have you been up to all day?"

"Reading *Fingersmith*. And I just got off the phone with Marjorie."

"Marjorie?"

"My mom."

"Oh. Weird. How'd that go?"

"I'm not sure." I twirled a fat noodle and ate it slowly. "I think I like her."

"What do you mean?"

"I mean, I guess she's an enjoyable person to talk to. It was just easy."

"That's kind of cool, right?" she asked.

I thought about that a minute. The whole conversation was too fresh to process. "Yeah, I think it is."

"I assume you didn't talk about like why she left you as a kid or anything?"

I grinned. "No, nothing quite so substantial. Just books we like and shit."

"She likes to read. Of course she likes to read. Is she a poetry aficionado like you?"

I shrugged. "Don't know. She likes Hemingway."

Laurel groaned. "Oh no. Don't you loathe Hemingway?" She shoved a forkful of noodles into her mouth.

"Indeed I do." I took my own bite of noodles.

The guys were all lounging around. Boyd and Reyes had gone back to their laptops at the dining room table. They'd barely cleared off enough room for their plates. Duarte and Malone were sitting at the bar on the opposite side of the kitchen. There was another laptop between them. Duarte used his fork to point at something on the screen. Malone nodded and made a note.

"Hey, Laurel?" I said quietly.

"Yeah?"

"Why the fuck haven't they caught Henry?"

"I don't know, honestly. As far as I can tell, he's been a lot harder to track than they expected. He's surprisingly good at hiding," she said.

"That's what's throwing me. He's not that smart." I'd been thinking about it for a few days. Henry wasn't built to keep such a low profile.

"He's been pretty sophisticated. He's smarter than you think he is."

"I promise you, he's not. We went to high school together. Dude is an idiot." I took a drink of my beer and glanced around. The guys were all absorbed in their own tasks. No one was listening to our conversation. "He only got as far as he did in school and the sheriff's department because he seems really nice and he doesn't have any qualms about breaking the rules."

"So he just cheated his way through?"

"Yeah. He usually found a girl who wasn't quite pretty and had her take his notes. He bought his essays. I'm certain he did the same thing in college. Even at the sheriff's academy, he was doing the bare minimum."

"He outran me. I'm thinking he didn't cheat on the physical portion," she said.

"I'll give you that. Maybe I'm wrong. This just doesn't feel like something Henry excels at."

"Then how is he doing this?"

"He's got to have help. The Henry I know wouldn't have the skills," I said.

"If someone is helping him, the feds missed it in their sweep."

"That's probably bad."

"Yeah, just a little bit. I'll talk to Reyes. See what he thinks."

Two beers later, I wanted to blame said beer for my decision-making process, but I was tragically sober. I should have gone to my room and read some Victorian high jinks, but Laurel was watching *Alien* and Sigourney Weaver was hot.

It was easier to watch television in the condo with someone. The night before, I felt like I was disturbing everyone's work. Which I was, but who did paperwork at eight p.m.? With Laurel controlling the remote, the decision had been taken from me.

Our third beers slowly approached room temperature as we nursed them. I scooted down the couch and put my bare feet on the coffee table. Ripley's arms were sexy. So were Laurel's, but I definitely wasn't thinking about that. Laurel slid down and put her feet up next to mine. She was wearing canvas deck shoes. One of them was coming untied. When the alien burst from Kane's chest, Laurel twitched. Her shoelace brushed my ankle. I became very invested in that shoelace brushing my ankle. Sweaty Ripley couldn't even distract me. And sweaty Ripley was pretty distracting. Laurel crossed her ankles and the shoelace shifted to the top of my foot.

As she watched, she unconsciously drew her thumb back and forth in the condensation on her beer bottle. The corner of the label came loose. She smoothed it down and switched the bottle to her other hand. Her now empty hand dropped to the couch between us. I felt like I could sense the slow tick of her watch inches from my arm. I couldn't, but that didn't quiet the imagined rhythmic tick.

She kicked off her shoes and put her foot up on the couch. I'd almost forgotten how she tended to take up space while sitting. The shift put us inches from each other. Too close for propriety, but far enough that we could pretend it was okay. As long as we weren't touching it was fine. It didn't matter that I could feel the heat off her bicep or the whisper of her T-shirt sleeve brushing my bare arm. I could smell the musky bite of her hair product, the warmth of her sweat. I knew how her skin would taste. I knew it would be salty and smooth from the summer heat. I knew how the remnants of the light beer would taste on her tongue.

I didn't want her. I couldn't.

Except, of course, I did. Watching a movie with her while surrounded by law enforcement agents in a cramped condo was somehow the most erotic thing I'd experienced in the seven months since she'd left. Maybe I should have tried getting laid. But I knew now what I'd known all along: no one would compare. That was my albatross. I couldn't control falling in love with her. That was beyond me. But I'd forgiven far too many sins. Each time I let her in, I'd fused some part of myself with her. It was impetuous and constant and I could no longer function without her. She was me. And I didn't trust either of us. So I sat and watched Sigourney Weaver stalk a monster.

CHAPTER EIGHTEEN

I woke up to a handful of photos of Andy and Nickels snuggling and a text from Robin. *Someone misses you.*

I looked through the pictures. Andy was curled up in the fetal position. Nickels was sprawled on the pillow next to her with her head tucked under Andy's chin and her butt pressed against Andy's forehead. It looked uncomfortable, but Andy and Nickels seemed good with it.

I hope it's your mom. Is it your mom who misses me? I asked.

Yeah, Cash. It's my mom.

Robin had assured me when we all packed up that I didn't need to feel guilty, but I still felt guilty. I'd scattered everyone I loved to protect them. It was exactly what Henry wanted. We were hiding and we were scared. Well, maybe pissed off more than scared. I thought of the dark bruise stretched across Laurel's throat. Okay, a little scared.

There was a knock at my bathroom door. I sat up. "Come in."

Laurel opened the door. "Hey, sorry to intrude," she said quietly.

"What's up?" I tossed my phone on the bed.

"Michelson is on his way over here to give us an update. Well, he's going to give them an update." She nodded in the direction of the living room. "But we're going to participate whether they want us to or not."

"Excellent. I love crashing FBI briefings." My phone vibrated. I glanced and saw it was Robin again.

"I didn't mean to interrupt. I can wait if you need to respond," Laurel said.

"It's cool. It's just Robin."

"How're she and Andy doing?"

"Fine. They like Robin's mom so it's just a mini vacation at Grandma's," I said.

"She lives out in Jackson, right?"

"Just outside of town. Andy can walk to the creek. Robin can walk to the main street. Grandma can walk to the wine tasting room. Nickels can look out the window at the birds. Robin says it's pretty great."

"I haven't been there since we did gold mining tours in elementary school."

"That sounds way more fun than Old Hangtown."

She grimaced. "That's morbid."

I shrugged. "I never gave it much thought. You know there's a bar where the hanging tree used to be. They have a fake body hanging from a noose."

"What?" She sounded incredulous.

"Yeah, it's on Main Street," I said. Her confusion confused me. The body hanging on Main Street had always been a quirk of my hometown. I suddenly saw it through her eyes. She was right. It was morbid.

"You're not serious."

"Serious as a hanging tree." I grinned.

"Cash."

"Honestly, I never gave it much thought until right now. Isn't it strange how they indoctrinate us with violence? The gold rush was horrific and lawless. We decimated the landscape and the people. And now they send school children to tour the carnage."

"Wow."

"What?" I asked.

"I forgot you just wake up like this. No coffee, no morning stretches. Just, boom, systemic power structures."

I was formulating a snarky response when Reyes knocked on my door. "Cash, you up?"

Laurel ducked back into the bathroom and closed the door partially.

"Yeah, come in."

"I just wanted to give you a heads-up that Michelson is on his way over. He's going to update us on Brewer. Afterward, I'll sit down with you and Kallen to tell you what's going on."

"It's cool. We can just sit in on the Michelson briefing," I said.

"Uh, no. You can't."

"Yeah, that seems like the best move."

"No."

"Hey, Laurel," I called.

She waited a couple seconds before pushing the door back open. "What's up? Oh, hey, Lucas."

"Reyes was just telling me Michelson is coming to brief them on the Brewer situation. I told him we would sit in on it."

"Great. That works for me," she said.

"No, that doesn't work. You two aren't law enforcement officers. You can't sit in on an FBI briefing," Reyes said.

"Sure we can. There's no reason we can't. Plus it's more effective. We might catch something you all missed. And I have the training. So does Cash from her time as a CI. It's prefect," she said.

Reyes stared at Laurel. She stared back. He sighed. "Fine." He closed the door.

"Well done," I said.

"I think it was a solid tag team effort."

Twenty minutes later, I went into the living room. Reyes, Malone, and Laurel were all discussing our participation in the briefing.

"Hey, pals, I thought we already figured this out," I said.

"I'm sorry. I can't have civilians sitting in on briefings," Malone said.

"Buzzkill, man," I said.

Michelson knocked on the door. Malone nodded at our bedroom doors.

"Yeah, yeah." Laurel and I went in and closed the door. A second later, Reyes opened it again. We went back out to the living area. Michelson and another agent were getting comfortable at the dining table. The other agent looked familiar. His dark hair was slicked back and his tailored suit couldn't hide how fit he was. I'd definitely met him before. "Alec." Laurel shook his hand vigorously.

"How the hell are you?" When he grinned wide, I recognized him. He was with Michelson in Marysville when the local sheriff decided to detain us. Turned out it was real convenient to have an FBI agent monitoring you when you went to piss on other people's territory.

"I'm so good. Really living the life." Laurel nodded at our cramped surroundings. "You remember Cash Braddock, right? Cash, this is Alec Orr."

"Yeah, we met up in Yuba County a while back," he said.

"Good to see you again." I shook his hand.

"What are you doing here? Reyes said it was just Michelson," Laurel said.

"Actually, why don't you all sit down. Agent Orr is the reason we're here," Michelson said.

"Oh, you want us to join the briefing?" I was aiming for a perfect blend of surprise and honor just to be asked. I nailed it.

"It will be a whole lot easier if we don't have to repeat information. And there's always the chance you'll catch something we missed," Michelson said.

"Wow. Yeah, great idea." Laurel turned to look at Malone and Reyes. "Don't you guys think that's a great idea?"

Malone grunted.

Reyes exaggeratedly rolled his eyes. "You know my doctor dramatically reduced my heart medication when Duarte became my partner."

Duarte looked up from his laptop. It looked like he was already taking notes on the meeting that hadn't started. "Really?"

Reyes sat next to him. "Yes, Jeff, really."

Duarte smiled and went back to typing. Boyd and Malone pulled up chairs at the far end of the table. Laurel and I sat opposite them.

"I think everyone here knows each other, right?" Michelson asked. We all nodded. "Good. Okay." He flipped open a leather portfolio and turned a few pages. "We found where Brewer was staying for the last two months or so. We weren't able to get anything from the room he was renting. It was cleared out. But we did manage to get his internet history for the last ten days."

"How do you know he was staying there?" Reyes asked.

"We have video of him coming and going. The bed and breakfast only keeps video footage for two weeks before it deletes. And they only have two cameras: one in the lobby, and one on the front porch. Orr interviewed the proprietor."

Orr was ready with his iPad of notes. "Their records show check in and out dates. The owners are an older guy and his daughter. Both of them remembered Brewer."

Laurel slowly went still the longer they talked. Her breathing was shallow and rapid. "Which B&B?"

Orr looked down at his notes, but it looked like he was stalling. "Shaw House."

She took a long, deep breath. "Which room?"

"Across the hall from yours," Orr said.

"That motherfucker."

"I take it that's where you were staying?" Duarte asked.

"Yep." Laurel was holding the edge of the table. The scar on her hand turned white as her grip tightened.

"So he's gone? Again?" I asked.

The agents and detectives all studied their laptops and notepads and said nothing.

"When did he check out?" Laurel asked.

"Two days ago," Orr said.

"The day we were moved into the safe house?" she asked.

"Yep." Orr nodded once.

"The same day I asked you to pack my stuff at Shaw House and check out for me?" she asked.

"Yep." He nodded again

"Okay, so someone tipped him off." I looked around. "We're all getting that, right?"

Boyd and Duarte nodded. Michelson hesitated before joining in. "We're doing a full review of everyone involved in the investigation. I personally did the background on Orr, Boyd, and Malone. That's why they're on this detail. I intended to bring in a few more agents, but we're going to keep it to this core group for now."

"What about you?" I asked Michelson. Maybe I was being a dick, but I didn't care.

"Actually, I did Michelson's background," Reyes said.

Michelson nodded, then grinned ever so slightly. "Which he didn't inform me of until afterward."

"Did he have surveillance in my room?" Laurel asked. Her voice was subdued. She was clearly terrified of the answer, but I was sure not knowing would have been worse.

"No," Orr said definitively. "I did a full sweep. There was nothing in the room."

"But there was something?" she asked.

He nodded. "A pressure plate under the carpet outside your room. He must have installed it at night when no one else was in the hallway. It would have taken too much time to install during the day."

"Why?" I asked. Granted, I didn't know what a pressure plate was, but I felt pretty certain it was a plate that detected changes in pressure. Seemed like you could probably just set it down and presto, it was installed.

"He took up the carpet in the hallway and put it underneath."

Yeah, okay that seemed time consuming. "So he probably wouldn't have done all that if he could get into her room."

"Exactly. And if he didn't have time to grab that when he left, he didn't have time to break into her room and take out any surveillance equipment." Orr made meaningful eye contact with Laurel. "I swear. There was nothing else."

She nodded a few times compulsively. "Thanks."

"You said you got his search history?" Duarte asked.

Michelson shook his head. "Better. His entire browser history."

"How?" Laurel asked.

"He started using the B&B Wi-Fi. Their system logged all of it."

"Why didn't he use it before?" Duarte asked.

"He was probably using his phone as a hot spot. He lost it when he attacked Kallen," Michelson said.

"So he's already being careless?" Duarte was somehow a combination of very sincere and eager puppy. On anyone else it would have annoyed the hell out of me.

Michelson exhaled loudly. "Christ, I hope so."

"When can we take a look at the internet history?" Reyes asked.

Orr tapped his iPad a few times. "It's shared with all of you. It's a big data dump so it might take a sec to show up."

Duarte started reloading his screen compulsively.

"Maybe you'll find something we missed." Michelson closed his portfolio. Digital data was not his jam apparently. "We've hardly started processing the information. Boyd, Orr, I want you two running background on our tech guys. They will be able to work through this much faster, but I want everyone screened before we bring them in." Both Boyd and Orr made notes. "Start with Jalen, then Sanford if we need him."

"I assume I can start combing through this?" Duarte asked.

"Yes. Malone, Reyes, do the same, but let Duarte take the lead. You understand internet culture the best. You showed that with the Sac State Rape Organization. I'd like you to parse out what needs the most immediate attention. Assign Reyes and Malone as you see fit." Malone and Reyes nodded at Michelson.

"What about us?" Laurel asked.

"You're civilians. If there's anything Duarte thinks you can help with, then he will let you know. But we're going to treat you like a civilian contractor because that's what you are."

"Jesus Christ. Not you too," Laurel said.

"Me too what?" Michelson asked.

"Reyes is on a whole 'you make poor decisions' kick too."

"This isn't that." Michelson put his hand up. "Make all the poor decisions you want. Our job is to keep you safe. You and Braddock have very specific knowledge. If we need that specific knowledge, we will ask. But otherwise, we just need you to follow directions and not take unnecessary risks."

"Where does laser tag land on the necessary risk scale?" I asked.

"It's not on the scale at all."

"At all? Seems like your list might have some gaps, man."

"Yeah, that's on me," Michelson said very seriously.

"So I guess laser tag is out for this afternoon?" I said. Duarte tried not to smile. Malone and Reyes shook their heads. Michelson laughed. "What? I thought it would be a fun team building activity."

"I still call dibs on Kallen's team," Duarte said.

CHAPTER NINETEEN

Boyd's printer came in handy when Duarte started printing reams of Henry's internet history. Laurel and I were given pages of WhatsApp messages to see if we could glean any information. We weren't making much progress.

"How can he be so boring? He's a former LEO. He was a dirty cop. He's been on the run for a year. And yet his texts are complete garbage." Laurel flipped the page in her packet with a bit more vim than necessary.

"I told you he wasn't that interesting."

"What conversation do you have?" she asked.

"Toy Story Cowboy." Seriously. That was the name. Not Woody, but Toy Story Cowboy. "What do you have?"

"Raphael."

Henry's screen name was Iron Man, which was severely uninspired. We also had Professor Utonium. The Professor Utonium conversation was the shortest. It was only six messages. They consisted of Henry explaining that he had a new burner, a confirmation of said burner, a question about whether or not a line was secure, and a confirmation of the security of the line. There was also a solo message with a purple heart and another with a rocket ship. Not the most illuminating of emojis.

Toy Story Cowboy alternated between sharing his exploits boning an allegedly freaky girl and various sheriff movements. He was providing vehicle placements, air surveillance, and locations of raids. He never seemed to have much detail, just that things were happening. We'd decided he was clearly EDSO, but the information was fairly easy to come by. Any sheriff in the county could access it. Hell, anyone with a keen ear and a police scanner app could figure out most of it. There was nothing to narrow down who he was.

"Ugh." Laurel was lying on the couch with her knees bent. I was definitely not thinking about how nice it would be to join her on the couch. She leaned over and tossed her packet on the coffee table between us. I was sitting in a wingback with my feet on the table. The packet hit the bottom of my foot and bounced back toward her. "You said the Professor one was even shorter?"

"Yeah." I grabbed the sheet with the Professor Utonium messages and held it out. She took it. I traded Toy Story Cowboy for Raphael. It was a quick read. More messages, but with a code that was impossible to decipher. It was all *E36-APV 1400* and *PFV-8CA5 0900*, which was extremely unhelpful. There were also discussions about speedboats and Jet Skis. Henry's responses suggested he didn't actually know much about various watercraft, but he didn't want Raphael to know that. He did, however, have a lot of opinions about color.

"How's the reading going?" Reyes asked. He sat next to Laurel on the couch. She moved her feet to make more room for him.

"It's not. This is gibberish," Laurel said.

"And these guys are dumb," I said.

"How so?"

"Who would opt for a navy blue Jet Ski when lime green with purple accents is an option? Come on. That's a no-brainer." I shook my head.

Reyes looked at Laurel and she shrugged. "She's right. That is a no-brainer," she said.

"What about you?" I asked.

Reyes shook his head. "I'm reading the most recent entries to the cloud account where he documented you two. It's creepy."

"Oh, I didn't know we had access to that," I said.

"Yep. It's all the same stuff we had access to previously, but it picks up where the other left off."

"Neat."

"If it's the same shit as before, where are all his other WhatsApp messages?" Laurel pushed herself into a sitting position.

"We don't have them. They were encrypted?" Reyes made it a question as if we would know the answer. But Laurel and I weren't big on the digital encryption knowledge. "With this burner, he apparently didn't think to change the privacy settings. Or he thought the settings would transfer over. I don't know. Either way, the texts are decrypted when they're backed up on his cloud account so that's how we can read them."

"What a dipshit," I said with the full confidence of someone who would have made the exact same mistake.

"Is there anything illuminating on the internet history?" Laurel asked.

"No." He nodded at Malone. "Malone is looking through the browser history, but it's mostly porn. Unimaginative porn."

"Right. I'll stop bitching about boring text messages then." I had no desire to look into whatever it was Henry got off to.

There was a knock at the front door.

"That'll be Duarte. We're going to review what we've learned over dinner. You guys in?"

"Yeah."

"Sure."

"Wanna pop into your rooms so we can let him in?" Reyes asked.

We rolled our eyes and huffed a little, but we did it. Ten minutes later, we were all set up around the dining room table with burgers and fries. Duarte had come through with another six-pack for me and Laurel. When Boyd did dinner runs, he never remembered beer.

Duarte did a quick review of each chunk of data we were looking at before turning to Malone. "What have you found in the internet history?" Duarte asked.

"Aside from porn, he looked up Jet Ski specs. He also googled 'cool cities in Mexico' before looking up real estate, hiking, and nightlife in each city on the list," Malone said.

I laughed. They all looked at me. "What? That's hilarious. Cool cities in Mexico? It's so uninspired."

"What would be inspired?" Boyd finally asked.

"Well, you'd look at like Mexico City or Guadalajara. Because everyone knows they are cool places."

"Right, sure. Everyone," Reyes said.

I glared at him. "And then you would look at which areas have activities or environment you're into. I'd look for beaches. Laurel would look for trails to run." Duarte and Laurel appeared to agree with me. The rest of the guys looked confused. "Jeez. It's like none of you are former drug dealers who had to check out international cities to live in." I shook my head and sipped my beer.

Reyes grinned. "Fair point. I've never given fleeing much thought."

"So what else did he look up?" Duarte asked.

Malone flipped through his notes. "New grips for his gun. He opted for a neon blue that's responsive to black light for a Glock and silver tooled sacred heart for a Smith & Wesson revolver."

"Oh, good. He's armed to the teeth," Reyes said.

"And he spent three hours one night looking at different beard styles and conditioning products," Malone said.

"Wow. That's…" Duarte looked at me. I shrugged at him. He grinned. "Embarrassing, honestly."

Reyes and Laurel laughed. "Is there anything else?" Reyes asked.

"Nothing," Malone said.

"What did you two find in the texts?" Duarte asked me and Laurel.

"Nothing. The important stuff is all coded. The remainder is just gross. Hot chicks and speedboats," Laurel said.

"What kind of code?" Duarte asked.

I looked through the Raphael messages. "Shit like E36-APV 1400."

"E36? Does that mean anything to anyone?" Duarte looked around the table.

Boyd set down his burger and reached for the packet. "Can I see it?"

"Sure." I handed it over.

He read and nodded. "Airport codes. I'll double check, but I think they're all small airports."

"No shit," Duarte said.

"So the superhero gang is flying something out of small airports?" Reyes asked.

"Looks like." Boyd typed on his laptop. "It'll take me a bit, but I can figure out all these codes and translate them. Like, for example, PFV is Placerville."

"Technically, they're not superheroes," I said.

"Yes, that's the important part," Laurel said.

Duarte gave me a look. "Uhh, technically, they are."

"Woody is not a superhero," I said.

"Okay, but he's heroic. Close enough."

"What about Professor Utonium?" I pointed at him with a french fry.

"He's part of X-Men." Duarte looked at me like I was losing my grip on reality. "They're definitely superheroes."

I shook my head and swallowed. "Umm, no."

"X-Men are absolutely superheroes," Malone said.

I was quite tickled that we'd brought him into one of our idiotic discussions. But he was still wrong. "X-Men are totally superheroes, but Professor Utonium isn't one of the X-Men."

Malone sighed. "Okay, he's the leader of the X-Men. A mentor still counts as a superhero."

"He's right," Boyd said. "Nick Fury is a superhero."

"I'm not disagreeing with any of that. But Professor Xavier is who you're thinking of," I said.

"Oh," Malone said.

"Oh," Duarte said.

"Who's Professor Utonium?" Boyd asked.

"He's the scientist who created the Powerpuff Girls. Obviously."

"Obviously," Laurel said. I shot her a look. "What? I knew that."

"Name the Powerpuff Girls," I said.

"Blue, red, and green," she said.

I rolled my eyes. "Those aren't their names."

"Okay, you name them."

"Blossom, Bubbles, and Buttercup. Boom, motherfucker," I said.

"How? How do you know shit like that?" Laurel asked.

I smirked. "Not just a pretty face."

"You're a jackass," Reyes said.

"Fine." I sighed. "I went to school with a kid who was obsessed with the Powerpuff Girls. It started in second grade and it lasted well into high school. He was my lab partner in bio." I turned to Laurel. "And also I remember weird shit."

"That doesn't exactly explain why you remember their names."
Duarte grimaced. "Unless it was you. Are you secretly obsessed with
the Powerpuff Girls?"

"No, but I'm terrible at biology. I memorized Powerpuff facts,
Curtis got me through bio. It was a solid partnership."

"Not to be a downer, but I think we're a little sidetracked here,"
Boyd said.

"Good point. Reyes, anything useful in the Kallen-Braddock
stalking files?" Duarte asked.

"No, it's all just the same disturbing shit."

"Wait," I said. They all turned to look at me. "I'm sorry. Curtis,
the bio kid. He was in chem with Henry. They became friends. At the
time, I thought it was a pity move to get girls, but what if they're still
friends?" There was silence.

"Jesus fucking Christ," Reyes said.

"What's the last name?" Boyd asked.

I tried to come up with it, but there was nothing. "I don't
remember. Mill something. Miller? Milner?"

"You remember Professor Utonium, but not his last name?"
Duarte asked.

"Well, I don't remember any biology either," I said.

"How can we find out? Can we call the high school?" Laurel
asked.

"It might tip someone off. We still don't know who is helping
Brewer," Malone said.

"Yearbooks? Any chance you have one?" Reyes asked. "We
could send a uniform to your place to pick it up."

"No, they're in Clive's garage." I stood to get my phone out of my
pocket. "Give me a second." I hit Clive's name. It rang for a minute.

"Hello?"

"Hey. Listen, can you do me a favor?" I asked. I knew he would.
It didn't matter if we weren't speaking, he would show up when I
needed him. Being angry was a luxury, a privilege born out of an
excess of love.

"Yes, of course. What do you need?"

"There are a couple of tubs in the garage labeled 'Cash
Memories.' My yearbooks are in them. Can you pull them out?"

"Sure." He hesitated. "What do you want me to do with them?"

"For now, just let me know if you can find them." Just because I imagined I knew the location didn't mean it was the actual location.

"Okay. Does it need to be now?"

"Kind of, yeah."

"That's fine. I'll call you back in a minute." He hung up.

"Clive's checking," I said.

"Who is Clive?" Boyd asked.

"My uncle."

Ten minutes later, Clive called back. "I've got them. You didn't specify which so I grabbed first through twelfth grade."

"No shit. Okay. I need to find a specific kid I went to school with. His first name is Curtis. Last name starts with Mill, I think."

"Are you messing with me?" he asked.

"No, I swear."

"Okay, what years were you in school with him?"

"All of them, but start with ninth grade."

"I'm putting you on speaker," he said. I heard a tick when he tapped the screen. Then I heard the creak of a book spine opening. "How are you? Marjorie said you'd been put into a safe house?"

"I'm okay. I'd rather not be in a safe house, but it's not terrible."

"Millard," he said.

"What?"

"Curtis Millard. Could that be him?"

"Holy shit. Yeah, I think so. Can you send me a photo?"

"Just take a photo of the yearbook page?"

"Yeah. Quality doesn't matter. I just want to make sure it's him."

"Sure. Sure. Page forty-seven," he muttered. I heard the flop of heavy pages. "Okay. Photo is coming to you."

My phone vibrated. I pulled it away from my ear to look at the screen. It was little Curtis all right. "Yep. This is him. Thanks, Clive."

"Yeah, no problem. You sure you're okay?"

"I am. I swear."

"Okay, bye."

We hung up. Everyone at the table was staring at me intently. "Curtis Millard."

CHAPTER TWENTY

Over the next hour, Clive slowly sent me every single yearbook photo of Curtis. In third, fourth, and sixth grade he was wearing Powerpuff T-shirts. In seventh, he was wearing a Professor Utonium shirt. By eighth, he must have figured out it wasn't making him any friends. Of course, the bedazzled Ed Hardy shirt he'd worn instead was a whole different level of terrible. I wondered if his jeans were embroidered too. But I knew they were.

Malone contacted Michelson and Agent Jalen, the FBI tech who had only been cleared ninety minutes before we made the Professor Utonium connection. They were running background on Curtis, but the guy was a ghost. He'd bought a small house in Garden Valley about six months before, but they hadn't been able to find a job or social media or any digital footprint. He didn't even have utilities. Dude was off the grid.

Boyd was in a deep dive with small airports. He was trying to match flight plans with the airports and times, but we could only speculate on dates. It was a slog. But it was also our best bet at identifying Raphael.

Toy Story Cowboy was our main focus. He was clearly a sheriff, but beyond that we couldn't find anything to identify him. Laurel and I pored over the messages he'd sent Henry, hoping some detail would jump out. We'd started making notes about the girl he was sleeping with in the hope we could identify her. Thus far, nothing. And it was starting to feel skeevy.

Laurel readjusted her seat at the table and rolled her shoulders. She winced.

"You doing okay?" I asked quietly.

"Fine. My stitches are itchy."

"You have stitches?"

"Yeah, from where he got my shoulder." She pulled the neck of her shirt aside so I could see the white gauze again.

"Oh, yeah. Didn't you pull a stitch before?"

"Yep. Not pleasant."

"What about your thigh?" I glanced at the offending thigh but couldn't see anything aside from her chinos.

"Those itch too. It's all itchy. I mean, it's healing so that's a good thing, but it's super uncomfortable."

"Does anything help?"

She shrugged the non-injured shoulder. "When I clean it and change the bandage, it's a different kind of discomfort. I was supposed to get the stitches out yesterday, but you know, safe house."

"Isn't that like bad?"

"It's probably not good. I had Duarte get me supplies to remove the stitches, but I haven't had the courage to do it."

"That's dumb. Let's go yank those fuckers out," I said.

"Seriously?"

"Yeah. It sounds disgusting. I can't wait."

"Have you ever taken out stitches before?" she asked.

"Heck no. But give me five minutes with the internet and I'll be an expert."

"Yeah, okay."

"Cool. I'll meet you in the bathroom in five minutes," I said.

Behind me, Duarte laughed, then turned it into a cough. "I'm sure I only heard a small portion of that conversation, but just so you know, it sounded odd."

"Nope, we're arranging a tryst. We just need some surgical scissors, tweezers, and probably disinfectant," I said.

Duarte nodded. "Okay. Cool. Freakier than I thought you two were, but that's great. I support you."

"She's taking out my stitches," Laurel said.

"Yeah. That makes more sense. Want me to get the supplies I picked up for you?" he asked.

"Yes, please." Laurel pushed back from the table.

Seven minutes later, I let myself into the bathroom armed with knowledge gained from three websites and two YouTube videos. Laurel wasn't there yet. But there was a grocery bag on the counter. I emptied it. There was a pair of scissors and a pair of tweezers. Both were sealed in surgical packaging. There was also a box of gloves, a pack of Steri-Strips, sealed squares of gauze, rubbing alcohol, and cotton balls. According to my extensive internet searching, Duarte had done well on his shopping trip.

"Hey." Laurel let herself in. "I didn't know if I should, uh, leave my shirt on or not?"

"No. Take it off. It'll be easier to clean the whole area."

"Pants?"

"Umm, I guess lose those too."

"Right. Okay." She stripped off her T-shirt. She wasn't wearing a bra, which I wasn't expecting. Christ, she had excellent boobs. I focused on the square of gauze high on her chest, but my gaze kept getting pulled down. "Sorry," she said. "I haven't been wearing a bra. The strap just rubs my stitches."

"Yeah. Sure. Totally." I was being so cool about this.

She pushed off her chinos. Thankfully, she was wearing boxer briefs. I couldn't handle naked Laurel. "Where do you want me?'

"Uh."

"Seriously, Cash?"

"The counter. Just sit on the counter." I washed my hands thoroughly before pulling on gloves. And I didn't even look at her boobs while I was doing it.

I teased off the tape holding the gauze in place. Underneath was a neat red line almost two inches long. A line of perfect sutures intersected the healing wound. I wiped the whole area down with rubbing alcohol. The sting of the alcohol made my nose itch.

"Want me to open the scissors?" Laurel asked.

"No. They're sanitized. You'll contaminate them."

"Got it."

I unfolded a square of gauze before opening the scissors and tweezers and laying them on it. "Okay, I'm going to cut the first stitch and pull it out. It shouldn't hurt. It'll just be a tug."

"These aren't my first stitches. Not by a long shot."

"Oh. When else have you had stitches?" I pinched the knot of the first stitch and pulled it up. Then I slipped the tip of the scissors in and snipped the loop. I braced my pinkie, ring, and middle fingers against her chest to keep my hand steady. I gently tugged the knot and the suture pulled out. I looked up at her face. She was staring at the wall over my shoulder. This close to her, I could smell her in perfect layered detail. Her sweet deodorant, the salt of her sweat, the bitter almond and cedar of her skin. It was excruciating.

"The first time, I guess I was in third grade? I was playing basketball with Lance and he elbowed me in the face. Split my lip. Probably didn't need stitches, but my mom was worried about scarring."

"When else?" I gripped the next knot and pulled up to get the scissors under it.

"The summer before high school, I decided to take up whittling. Stabbed my hand after ten minutes," she said. I snipped out another suture. "You know that scar on my hand?"

"Yeah."

"That's from whittling. My dad was livid because he had just reviewed knife safety. And we were in a cabin two hours from civilization."

"Smooth."

"Oh, yeah."

"I've never had stitches," I said.

"Never?"

"No. I spent my childhood indoors reading. Or gardening with Clive."

"Hey, gardening is dangerous."

"It's really not." The suture I was pulling caught and tugged at the skin before coming out. "Sorry. Did that hurt?"

"No. It's fine."

"Have you ever had to get stitches for a gardening related injury?" I asked.

"No. But I probably should have. One summer Lance and Logan and I were up at my grandma's. Logan and I were wrestling in the shed and I cut the back of my thigh on a pair of garden shears. We knew we'd be in trouble for wrestling so Lance poured hydrogen peroxide on it, covered it in Band-Aids, and I wore long shorts all summer."

"How did any of you make it to adulthood?"

"I'm really not sure. We made a lot of bad decisions."

I pulled out the last suture and set it in my pile. "Last one."

"Do I get a lollipop now?"

"No. You still need Steri-Strips and we have to do the stitches on your leg."

She let out a big sigh. "Bummer."

"Don't move." Her breathing was fine, but exaggerated sighing was too much movement. I was having enough trouble concentrating. I peeled off the adhesive backing for a sheet of Steri-Strips. I used the tweezers to lay the first strip over the wound.

"Is that it?" Laurel asked.

"Yeah. That's it. One Steri-Strip for a two-inch laceration."

"So that's not it?"

"No. Dipshit." I placed three more strips. "Okay, now you're good." I prepped another cotton ball to wipe down her thigh. I knelt on the bath mat so I was eye level with her leg. The wound was perfectly centered on the top of her thigh. It looked a little thicker than the one on her shoulder. And it had a few more stitches. I covered the whole area with rubbing alcohol. Alcohol dripped out of the cotton ball and dribbled down her thigh.

She shivered. "That's cold."

"Sorry." I braced my hand with splayed fingers again and grabbed the first knot with the tweezers. I teased the scissors under the line and clipped it. The loop of plastic thread that came out was slightly longer, but it pulled out just as easy. I removed two more before I realized Laurel's breathing was a bit erratic. I glanced at her face to see if I was hurting her. She was biting her lip and staring at the ceiling. "Are you okay?"

"Yep. Fine." She didn't look at me.

"Because you kind of look not fine." I moved my hands away from her.

"Can you just finish?" she asked.

"Not if I'm hurting you. Pain can be a sign of infection. If that's the case, we need to get you to a doctor." The internet was very clear on that. And the internet never lied.

"It doesn't hurt."

"Then why do you look like it hurts?" I asked.

"Because you keep brushing the inside of my thigh. It's a lot of touching."

"Oh. Sorry."

"Stop apologizing and just finish," she snapped. "Shit. I didn't mean that. Not like that at least. It's just a really confusing combination of sensation with your hands and the stitches coming out and all."

"Totally. I'll try not to make it weird." I picked up the next knot while keeping my hand off her skin. I cut the suture and pulled it away. It was a bit shaky, but it came out okay. "Did that hurt at all? It tugged more."

"It wasn't bad. I could feel it more."

"Okay. I have to touch you, but I'll try not to make it sexy."

She started laughing. "Great. Thank you."

I pressed my fingertips to brace instead of my whole hand. And I did my best to not brush her with the back of my right hand. "Only five to go."

"Distract me. Tell me a story."

Right. Because I didn't already have enough happening in my head. "Sure. Uhh. What kind of story?"

"How are things with your mom?"

"Okay, I guess. I talked to her again this afternoon. She seems pretty chill."

"Wow. Calm down with all the details," Laurel said.

"Sorry."

"How's Andy? Did she get her license?"

"She did. She fucking loves Gracie-Ray." I pulled out another stitch.

"Who is Gracie-Ray?" she asked.

"That's what she named her truck. She and Lane are currently replacing the bed with wood slats."

"No way. That's just what I thought she should do."

"It looks amazing. They have it all sanded and stained and varnished. They were supposed to install them this week, but you know." Another suture slid out. Three left.

"Lane is living in the Tri Ep house and Andy is at Grandma's," Laurel said.

"Yep. But watching Nate try to help them was highly entertaining." I snipped another. "They brought him to the hardware store to use his masculine privilege and help load the wood, but then they tortured him the entire time they were de-constructing the bed." Two left.

"Aww, I bet he loved it."

"Of course he did," I said.

"What else? Is she doing okay driving and parking it?"

"Oh, yeah. You taught her well. She can parallel park that beast with her eyes closed. It's super fun on crowded streets. It almost got Robin a date." I tugged out one more.

"How did Andy parking get Robin a date?"

"This dude offered to park it for Andy on K. She smirked and rolled her eyes and parked. When they got out of the truck, the guy started hitting on Robin. Said she was an impressive teacher."

"What happened?"

"Robin said, 'I know,' and walked away."

Laurel laughed. "Nice."

I teased out the last stitch and held it up. "Boom." I peeled the adhesive off another sheet of Steri-Strips. "We're almost done." I placed the strip, careful not to pull at her skin. When the strips were all in place, I stood and stripped off my gloves. "Now you get a lollipop."

Laurel looked around. "I don't see any lollipops."

"Well, it's a metaphorical lollipop. I think you'll find not having stitches its own reward, much like a lollipop."

"That's a bullshit lollipop." She scooted off the counter. "Thanks, Doc." She put out her hand to shake.

I laughed and shook her hand. "Anytime."

Her hand felt good in mine. She was looking up at me. The bruising had mostly faded from around her eyes. I brushed my fingertips under eye. She didn't blink, didn't waver. I leaned forward and kissed her.

Chapter Twenty-one

Her lips were firm and warm. She tasted like beer and french fries and I wasn't aware of the aphrodisiac combination of those flavors until right then. She ran her tongue over my lip. I groaned. She twisted her hands in the back of my T-shirt. I pulled her tight against me. I spread my hands over the soft skin of her back. She was almost naked. And this was a bad idea.

I pulled away. We pressed our foreheads together. We were breathing heavily. The air between us still tasted like her.

"You're killing me." She opened her eyes and looked at me in pained accusation.

"I'm sorry," I said.

"Don't be sorry. Just keep kissing me."

"I can't. Fuck. I really can't." I took a step back. Her hands dropped away from me.

I retreated into my room and closed the door. I sat on the edge of the bed and took a couple of deep breaths. That was stupid. Really stupid. I reached for my phone to call Robin but stopped at the last moment. If I asked Robin for advice, I'd have to tell her what I needed advice about. I wasn't particularly in the mood to tell her I'd kissed Laurel. She would tell me it was stupid and I already knew that. Or she would tell me it wasn't stupid and I couldn't handle that.

It took me ten minutes to get my breathing to even out. I could feel the heat slowly draining from me. My energy went with it. My hands were still shaking, but less so. I went back into the common room. Laurel was leaning over Boyd's shoulder at the table. She was asking questions, but I could hear in her tone that her heart wasn't in it. I picked up the Toy Story Cowboy packet and dropped into the wingback chair in the living room. Duarte was stretched out on the couch reading his own information packet.

The cowboy mentioned that his paramour had an allegedly sexy flower tattoo on her left breast. Well, he didn't phrase it quite like that. I added it to the list of identifying features. Not that a flower tattoo was helpful in identifying anyone. It wasn't exactly distinctive. It might have been if there were any details, but alas the cowboy had only said "hot flower," which was less than helpful.

I heard Laurel's voice go up. I didn't hear what she said, but I heard the excitement.

"Where?" Boyd asked.

"There. Zoom in. Can you click on that picture?"

He clicked. "I don't get it. What am I looking at?"

"Cash, Duarte, come look at this," Laurel said.

Duarte and I looked at each other. He shrugged and pushed himself off the couch. I followed him to the table.

"What's up?" Duarte asked.

"Look at this picture. Does anything stand out to you?" Laurel pointed at a photo that took up most of Boyd's laptop screen.

It was a whole bunch of planes lined up on the tarmac of an airport. Two or three lines of them. There were snow tipped mountains in the background. The amount of melt put it somewhere in late summer. Evergreen trees filled the middle ground of the photo.

"What are we looking at?" Duarte asked.

"The planes," she said.

I focused on the planes. There were a lot. Some were sleek and aerodynamic looking. Jets, I guess. Some looked like they came out of an adventure film about the thirties. I knew nothing about planes. But some of them were painted real pretty.

"Motherfucker," Duarte whispered. He leaned in close. "Damn, you're good." He straightened and lightly punched Laurel in the shoulder.

"You see it too?" she asked.

"Yes, I fucking see it."

"Anyone want to fill me in?" Boyd asked.

"Yeah, same," I said.

"The plane back there with the red on the tail?" Duarte pointed at a plane in the back row. "It's Raphael's ninja mask."

"Bullshit." I leaned close and squinted. They were right. Maybe. "That might be Raphael's mask."

"Fuck off. That's for sure his mask," Laurel said.

Boyd turned his head and grunted. "Oh. There. I see it." He looked around at all of us. "That could be a ninja turtle mask."

"I'd say I'm ninety-nine percent sure," Duarte said.

"Naw. I'd say like 82.36 percent," I said.

"You're the worst," Laurel said.

"I know." I made eye contact with her and smiled. Then we both remembered what we were doing twenty minutes before and looked away. "Where are Malone and Reyes?" I asked.

"Malone went to meet Agent Jalen. Reyes is on the phone." Duarte nodded at the closed bedroom door.

"Go get him. We need a tiebreaker," I said.

"What airport is that?" Laurel asked.

"Placerville," Boyd said.

"Can we confirm it's still there?" I asked.

"Yeah, but I need to call Michelson and Malone before making a move. They will decide the best approach."

Duarte came back to the table with Reyes in tow.

"What's going on?" Reyes asked.

"We think we found a small plane with a red eye mask reminiscent of the Teenage Mutant Ninja Turtles painted on the tail," Boyd said.

"What?"

"There's a plane with a ninja mask painted on it. A red ninja mask. Like Raphael," Laurel said.

"No shit. Let me see." Reyes stepped closer to the laptop. I backed up. Boyd leaned out of the space in front of the screen. "That could be a face mask."

"Right?" Laurel leaned over Reyes so she could see. As if she hadn't already looked.

"Do we have any other photos?" Reyes asked Boyd.

"No. This is a promotional shot on the airport's website," Boyd said.

Reyes stepped back and sat next to Boyd. "So the plane might not even be there?"

"No way of telling yet."

"Still. This feels big, right?" I asked.

"Oh, it's big," Laurel said. Then she checked herself. "Maybe."

"It's a start. It's something to investigate," Reyes said.

"Call Malone. And Michelson. Find out how they want us to proceed," Duarte said to Boyd.

Boyd reached for his phone. We stared at him. "Are you all planning on watching me call Malone?"

Laurel and I looked at each other and shrugged. "Yeah, basically," she said.

Duarte nodded. "Yes."

"Yep," Reyes said.

"Nope." Boyd stood and went into the room Reyes had just come out of.

"Jeez. Touchy," Laurel said.

"So we just wait?" I asked.

"Yeah. What were you hoping for? Rushing in guns blazing?" Reyes asked.

"A little," I said.

"So you're anti-cop until it's inconvenient for you and then you want guns blazing?" he asked.

"It's El Dorado County. There aren't any Black people for you guys to accidentally shoot or blame shit on."

"That's fucking rich," he said.

"Christ. Calm down. My issue is with systemic police violence and power." My issue was also with people who participated in that power structure, but I thought it was probably a bad idea to announce that in a safe house filled with cops.

"Okay. No. We're not doing this. We know where you both stand." Laurel stepped between us. As if we were going to come to blows. Or maybe she just wanted to interrupt our flow. "Cash, you want another beer?"

That was a tough call. Debate where I was surrounded by the dudes I would be disparaging or a beer. "Yeah, sure."

She grabbed two bottles from the fridge and popped the tops off. She handed one to me. "Settle in, pals. It's going to be a long night."

❖

By midmorning we were all groggy from staying up half the night. Michelson was getting a warrant to search the Placerville Airport and its hangars. I was bored out of my damn mind. If I wasn't sequestered, I would have dragged Nate up to the airport and started checking planes myself. Of course, Henry's accomplices likely knew exactly what Nate and I looked like so it was possible that was a bad idea.

Laurel was avoiding me, which I didn't blame her for. But she was also hot, which I found extremely unfair. She had spent most of the morning helping Boyd wade through flight manifests to find flights that could match up with the locations and times we'd pulled from Raphael's texts. Her competence and confidence were just as they had always been. She was straightforward and quick. And she had the location of every piece of paper on the table memorized, which was just unnecessarily capable. She was wearing cutoff chinos and a baggy V-neck. Her feet were bare. She looked casual and summery and completely unconcerned with how attractive she was.

Also I'd checked and she still wasn't wearing a bra.

"You want to get off?" Duarte tugged at my shorts.

"Huh? What?" I looked at him in surprise.

He pulled at the iPad tucked under my leg so it wouldn't fall off the couch. "Get off the iPad, dude."

"Oh. Right. Sorry." I lifted my leg so he could pull the iPad out.

"I take it you haven't found anything new?" he asked.

"Nope. I even checked the internet history. Malone was right. There was a lot of porn."

He grimaced. "Yeah. He tried to warn you."

"Don't victim blame me."

"Right, of course. You didn't willingly look at a browser history entirely made up of PornHub links only to be shocked that it was all porn or anything."

"Exactly." We grinned at each other. "I'm all for people getting off however they want, but that was abnormal, right?" I asked.

"It's not like addicted to porn levels, but it was a lot. That said, he was doing a ton of solo surveillance and it's certainly one way to pass the time." He shrugged. "Maybe it's a cis straight dude thing?" As if he wasn't a cis straight dude.

"Maybe. I don't spend time with many cis dudes. Just Nate, really. And we don't talk about our masturbation habits."

"And you think Cash and I have strange conversations," Laurel said.

Duarte and I turned our heads in unison. I was sure it looked quite comical. "We're discussing Henry Brewer, thank you very much," I said.

"Yeah." She scrunched up her face. "I'm not sure if that makes it better or worse."

I shrugged because I didn't know either. "What's up?"

"I just wanted to give you guys a heads-up that Jalen and Michelson are headed over here."

Duarte sat up straighter. "Do they have an update?"

"Not yet. We're waiting on the warrant to come through. But since Jalen is the only one who is cleared to work on this, Michelson was afraid someone at headquarters might be spying or something. He's getting paranoid."

"Or it's totally rational," I said.

"Yeah, it just seems a little over-the-top. I'm sure half the agents are secretive and weird about what they are working on. No one would notice if Jalen did the same thing. Anyway, they will be here soon."

Duarte leaned forward to see where Reyes, Malone, and Boyd were. "Are they sleeping here?" he asked quietly. "Because we're already cramped."

"Honestly, I have no clue," she said.

He shook his head and unlocked the iPad. "If they are, I'm bunking with you, Braddock."

"Why me?"

"You seem less squirmy than Kallen," he said without looking up from his iPad.

"Naw, she's not squirmy. But she does like a good snuggle."

"Hey," Laurel said.

Duarte laughed. "I forgot you two were, uhh, never mind."

"If you can't say it, you probably shouldn't do it," I said.

"And if my Catholic grandmother ever asks, you tell her I never have," he said.

"You got it." I grinned. "Grandmothers love me."

Laurel sat in the wingback next to us. "Most of the time grandmothers love you. But remember when you let that grandmother kick you in the face?"

Duarte whipped around to see my reaction.

"One time. You get kicked in the face by a grandmother one time and suddenly it's your whole brand."

"Your life is so much cooler than mine," Duarte said reverently.

CHAPTER TWENTY-TWO

Here was the thing about Agent Randy Jalen. She was hot. I was expecting a geeky tech dude, but turned out she was not a dude. And also she was smoking. Sure, she was still a geeky tech dude, but with more hot chick happening.

Her brunette hair was pulled back in a messy bun. She was wearing jeans and a starched blue dress shirt. Her shoulder holster was barely covered by a boxy blazer. A briefcase strap diagonally bisected her chest. She was wearing aviator style eyeglasses that were clearly stolen from a seventies kidnapper. None of it should have been attractive and yet it was.

"Agent Jalen, this is Detective Lucas Reyes from Sac PD. That's Jeff Duarte." Michelson pointed at each of them in turn. "Detectives, this is Miranda Jalen."

"Randy, please." Jalen leaned forward and shook their hands.

"Good to meet you," Reyes said.

"Glad to put a face to the name." Duarte grinned. She smiled back.

"I believe you know Laurel Kallen." Both Laurel and Jalen nodded. "And this is Cash Braddock." He nodded at me.

I shook her hand. "Nice to meet you."

"Do we have a warrant yet?" Reyes asked.

Michelson shook his head. "I already pissed off the judge by calling too many times. But Jalen is making progress with tracking the flight records so maybe that will turn up something."

"On that note, you mind?" Jalen pointed to the less crowded end of the dining table.

"Go ahead," Michelson said.

She nodded and set her briefcase on the table. It was a beat-up leather and canvas number. She unpacked a laptop and an iPad with a keyboard. She shrugged out of the blazer and hung it on the back of her chair. It immediately drooped to one side. She sat, opened the laptop, and started clicking. One-track mind, that woman.

"Want me to walk you through what we have?" Duarte asked.

"Yeah, that would be great. Where's Malone?" Michelson looked around.

"He should be back shortly. He's on a grocery run." As Laurel said it, there was a knock on the door. "That'll be him." She looked at me and nodded toward our bedrooms.

I followed her in. Five minutes before when Jalen and Michelson showed up, I'd been in my room. Presumably, Laurel had gone into her own room. This time, it would have been weird to go into separate rooms, which was how I ended up in a bedroom with my ex who I'd recently kissed.

"So." I looked around. Not at the bed though. Definitely not there.

"So you're just going to avoid me?"

"Well, not if you're going to just call it out like that."

"When did you become a coward?" she asked.

"I've been an emotional coward my entire life, thank you."

She sighed. "Yeah. Me too."

There was a knock on the door. "Oh, thank God." I opened it.

"You two are clear," Duarte said.

Malone and Reyes were unloading groceries. There was a grace in their movements around each other. I walked to the bags on the counter waiting to be unpacked and glanced in.

"I didn't get you beer, but I did get those kettle chips you asked for," Malone said.

I pulled the bag of chips out. "I'll forgive you then."

Duarte leaned past me. "Malone, when you're done, I want to give Michelson an update."

Reyes paused with his hands full of romaine. "Go ahead. I can finish here."

"Okay, thanks." Malone finished unloading apples into a bowl on the counter, then followed Duarte to the end of the table opposite Jalen.

"How's it hanging?" I opened my bag of chips and sat at the bar to watch Reyes.

"Great. Are you planning on eating and watching me instead of helping?" he asked.

"See?" I pointed at him with my chip. "Phrases like that are why we call you a dad."

"It's a perfectly reasonable question."

"Well, to answer your perfectly reasonable question, yeah, I am planning on sitting here and eating and watching you," I said.

"Okay. Are you planning on letting Laurel off the hook anytime soon? Or are you just going to let her twist?"

I crunched a chip and froze. "Uh."

"Because she knows she screwed up." He opened the fridge and put away a gallon of milk and a half gallon of soy milk. "Either let her in or let her go."

I finally swallowed my very dry mouthful of chips. "I thought you two didn't talk about me and her."

"We didn't. Now we do. You want to sit there and not help, this is what we're discussing." He handed me a cold La Croix.

"I feel for your kid. How old is she?" I opened the can and took a swig.

"She's exactly not the point years old."

"You know other people can hear us, right?" I asked.

"Jalen is in her own world." He nodded at Jalen who was completely enraptured by her laptop. Her blazer had fallen off the back of her chair and was pooled at her feet. "Michelson, Duarte, Kallen, and Malone are briefing and not paying attention to us." He looked around. "And I'm pretty sure Boyd is finally getting some sleep."

"Right. Great. Super."

"So what's the issue?"

"I don't know if I can trust her," I said.

"Why?"

"You know damn well why. For the first month of our relationship, I thought her name was Laurel Collins. Oh, and she was an undercover detective investigating me," I said. He stopped putting shit away and faced me fully. "That's kind of a big deal."

"Nope." He turned and started folding grocery bags. "Already resolved and moved past that one. You don't get to bring it up now."

"You don't get to dictate what I can or cannot bring up. And also, when you consider the larger narrative of her quitting the department, leaving me, and moving out of town, then it becomes just a little more relevant again."

"I'll grant you that. But also, it wasn't about you." He tucked the folded bags into an empty cabinet.

"Maybe not, but it hurt me just the same."

"So you're just going to torture her indefinitely? That's a dick move, even for you," he said.

"I'm not trying to torture her. I didn't mean to kiss her. And I apologized."

"What?" he whisper-shouted. It was possible she hadn't told him about the kiss.

"Nothing. I—Nothing."

He crossed the kitchen so he was standing a foot away from me. "You kissed her?" he whispered.

"A little."

"When?"

"Last night?"

He stared me down. "You crazy kids need to work this shit out. I can't take it."

"Calm down. Worst-case scenario, your doctor ups your heart medication again. It can't be that expensive."

Behind me, all the voices stopped suddenly. I turned around and saw Michelson on the phone.

Reyes came around the counter. On his way to the living room he said, "You better hope not. I'm sending you the bill."

"Whatever." I followed him to the living room where we all waited quietly for Michelson to hang up.

Michelson was giving one-word answers that were more grunts than they were actual syllables. He seemed displeased. He finally hung up. "Fuck. That stupid bureaucratic fuck."

"I take it the warrant went through with flying colors?" Laurel asked.

Michelson glared at her.

"What's the issue?" Malone asked.

"The magistrate feels we don't have a compelling enough reason to search the rental hangars."

"Wait. So you're saying a red smudge painted on a plane in the background of an undated promotional photo isn't solid evidence of a connection to TMNT?" Laurel asked.

"Weird," Duarte said.

"It's 82.36," I said.

"What?" Michelson asked.

"That's the percentage I was sure it was Raphael's face mask. Did you tell the judge about the 82.36 percent?" I asked.

The bedroom door opened and Boyd came out. He was looking more casual than I'd seen him thus far. He was wearing jeans and a crisp button-up, similar to Jalen's, actually. Except his shirt was painted on. The dude was seriously cut.

"You're just in time," Malone said to him.

"For what?" Boyd asked.

"The bad news. Our warrant was denied," Michelson said.

Boyd grunted. "Damn. So no records?"

"And no hangar search," Michelson said.

Boyd leaned against the wall. "Yeah, but that's only the indoor ones. Most of their rental space is on the tarmac."

Michelson stared at him. We all did. "You never told me that," Michelson said.

Boyd looked confused. "I'm pretty sure I emailed you." He went to the dining room table and opened his laptop. After a minute, he read aloud, "The rental hangars at PVF are both indoor and on the tarmac. Most of the rental spaces are located outdoors."

"Jesus Christ. Okay, so are they only public space?" Michelson asked.

Boyd shrugged his Johnny Bravo shoulders. "It's all public, but the tarmac is restricted for safety reasons. But if someone wanted to rent a space, they would probably give them a guided tour."

"Why didn't you tell me all this before?" Michelson asked.

Boyd sighed and picked up the laptop to read again.

"Never mind." Michelson put his hands up. "Never mind. That's on me."

"I also said in the email that a warrant would gain us greater access." Boyd half-shrugged.

"So we're sending Boyd to do a tour, right?" Laurel asked.

"Obviously," Duarte said.

"No. What? No, no, no," Boyd said.

"Why not?" Laurel asked.

"I'm not good at subterfuge. I'm good at paperwork. And research. I'm a bad liar."

"How?" Laurel asked.

"Not everyone is good at undercover work, Kallen," Michelson said. He looked at Boyd. "And that's okay."

"Fine, but we're all recognizable." Laurel pointed at Reyes and Duarte. "Brewer knows us so his accomplices also know us. And you were at Melody Brewer's place so you're blown too." She nodded at Michelson.

"I'm not bringing in anyone else unless we have to. Intensive background isn't feasible right now," Michelson said.

"I'd do it, but I'm Black and it's El Dorado county. I don't fit the right profile," Malone said.

"What about Alec?" Laurel asked.

"He might be blown too after clearing your room at the B&B," Malone said.

"He might, but have you ever seen him out of his fed suit?" Laurel asked.

Malone shook his head. Boyd and Michelson joined in. "He looks completely different. Mess up his hair and put him in some khakis and he's unrecognizable."

"Bullshit," Duarte said.

"Trust me," she said.

"She's right," Jalen said. We turned in surprise. "Orr and I jog together. Once he loses the hair gel, he looks completely different."

"He still doesn't have the knowledge to feign being a pilot," Boyd said.

"Would you do reconnaissance if you had Orr with you?" Laurel asked.

"What?" Boyd appeared shocked at this turn in conversation. "Why?"

"Because it's a good skill for you to have." Said the woman who made a career out of undercover.

"Did you call it reconnaissance so I wouldn't get freaked out by the term undercover?" Boyd asked.

"Yes."

Boyd nodded very seriously. "Okay. I'll go with Orr. But you have to give me tips on going undercover," he said to Laurel.

"Sure. I can do that," she said.

"I'll call Orr," Michelson said.

Agent Orr showed up an hour later. His dark hair was still wet from the shower, but instead of slicking it per his usual, it was falling in a dashing tumble of curls onto his forehead. He had on round frame tortoiseshell eyeglasses. He wore a striped pocket-T, khaki shorts, and sneakers. His confidence had softened. It was still present, but it seemed to be held up with a smile rather than a gun.

"Told you," Laurel said.

"This is wild, man." Boyd walked around Orr. "Are the glasses real?"

"Yeah. I wear contacts normally. My eyesight isn't bad, but I don't like to miss anything," Orr said.

"What do you think?" Laurel asked Michelson.

"Let's send them in." He waved Orr to the makeshift conference table. "Boyd, go ahead and call the airport to set up an appointment. Then we will teach you the basics of reconnaissance."

"And I'd like a crash course in aviation," Orr said.

Boyd nodded. He took Orr's phone to call the airport. As if the rinky-dink Placerville Airport would notice. Or have caller ID for that matter. Still, the attention to detail was cute.

CHAPTER TWENTY-THREE

Orr and Boyd spent half the night practicing aviator lingo and how to lie. I wouldn't have minded, but my room shared a wall with the common area and I really didn't need to memorize what FBO stood for and I already knew how to lie.

The next morning, Boyd and Orr headed up to Placerville for their tour. We were all quite invested for the first half hour of the drive, but by the time they arrived we were pretty uninterested. Duarte and Jalen were bonding over data entry. Such was the glamorous life of a law enforcement officer, apparently. Michelson and Malone monitored Orr and Boyd's location. Laurel and Reyes were making lunch for all of us, which was adorably domestic. Against my better judgement, I sat at the counter and watched them.

"Whatcha making?" I asked.

"Green salad and grilled chicken breasts," Reyes said.

"Are you letting Laurel out on the patio? Because that's super unfair. I want to go outside too."

"What? No," he said.

"How the hell are you grilling inside? That's some bullshit right there."

"That's what I told him," Laurel said.

"Grilling chicken on the stovetop is just fine," Reyes said.

"Lucas, it's not," Laurel said.

"Yeah, I'm with her," I said.

"Shit," Malone said quietly. He tapped his phone screen and sighed.

"No. Dammit." Michelson angrily stood and put his hands on his hips. "Dammit." I was certain any bad guys in the vicinity were running in terror at his stance.

"Not the plane, guys," Malone said.

"What? No. No way." Laurel came around the bar. Reyes and I followed her to the living room.

"Yeah. I know." Malone held up the phone so we could see the photo Orr had just sent.

Duarte and Jalen got up from the dining table to look. We all crowded around Malone. The plane in question did have a figure painted on the tail, but it wasn't Raphael. It wasn't any of the Ninja Turtles. It was an old school aviator with chunky goggles and a red scarf flying behind them. Which was, in retrospect, much more logical. I would have found it funny if it didn't mean my time stuck in this stagnant safe house would surely be extended.

"Fuck." Laurel gripped the back of the empty wingback. Her knuckles turned white. "I thought we had him for sure."

"Same, dude. Hard same," Duarte said.

"What happens now?" I asked.

"Boyd and Orr will document as many planes as possible and we will look at the owners. See if anyone jumps out," Michelson said.

"More research. Super," I said.

"I told you police work was all reading documents," Laurel said.

I nodded. "Yeah, I know, but I didn't believe you."

She shook her head. "That's on you."

"If you're willing, we'll need you to look at the owners and let us know if you recognize anyone," Michelson said to me.

"I can do that," I said. Anything to pass this time. "This blows."

Duarte clapped his hand on my shoulder. "It certainly does blow." He grinned. I rolled my eyes at him.

"Lunch will be ready in ten." Reyes went back to the kitchen.

Laurel followed him. "But don't get excited. It was grilled indoors."

❖

I finally gave in and called Robin. So of course she didn't pick up. I flopped dramatically on my bed and the power of being overly dramatic paid off when my phone started ringing. I answered without looking. "Hey, pal."

"Cash?" Marjorie asked.

"Oh shit." I looked at the screen. It was, in fact, Marjorie. "Sorry. Hey."

"Expecting someone else?"

"Sort of. I just called my buddy for some advice so I assumed it was her calling back."

"Oh. Well, maybe I can give you some advice. What's going on?" she asked.

I didn't see that coming. "Umm." I wasn't prepared to chat with my mother about a woman I'd kissed and also was madly in love with but also very angry at.

"Sorry. That was forward of me. You don't trust me yet."

"No, it's not that."

"I don't blame you. I did abandon you, after all," she said.

"You left. You didn't abandon me. There's a difference." Apparently, we were going to have that discussion. I sat up. This wasn't a lying down conversation.

"I'm not sure I understand the distinction, but I still understand why you might not trust me," she said.

"No, it's not that I don't trust you. It's just that I don't know you." I still didn't know what I wanted from her or what I owed her, but I could at least be honest. And I honestly didn't know her. She liked Hemingway and sparkling water. Not exactly the basis for a relationship.

"I get that. Really, I do. I'd like to change that. I wish I could have been there when you were growing up, but that wasn't an option."

"I know," I said.

"You do?" She sounded surprised.

"Yes, of course. Even as a kid, I knew you were an addict. And I knew Clive wouldn't let you have access to me if you weren't clean."

Her voice went up half an octave. "He told you that when you were six?"

"God, no. He said you were sick and you couldn't be around us because someone could get hurt. When I got older and we talked about it more, he told me he essentially gave you an ultimatum."

"Right. That makes more sense. Christ, he was always so good with you. Even if I wasn't an addict, I never would have been that good." She laughed wryly. "Which was why he was so strict in telling me I couldn't be a part-time parent. It was the right thing to do."

"He was an awesome parent." Even when I was mad at him—which I definitely still was—I knew he'd been a good parent.

"I know. I just wished it could have been me. But it couldn't. I tried. And now you're an adult and you don't know me. I hate that. Sorry. I was hoping we could have this conversation in person. I'm rambling again. We don't need to discuss this."

"It's fine. You know I don't expect anything from you, right?" I asked.

"You probably should."

"I don't. I've got a good life." I didn't need anything from her, but it seemed rude to tell her that. "I had a great childhood."

"I know you did. He always sent photos and art projects you'd made. He gave me regular updates until you turned eighteen. That was our agreement. I feel like I know you even though I'm quite aware I don't actually."

I finally asked the question we'd been talking around for the last twenty minutes. Hell, for the last two weeks. "Is that why you showed up?"

"Ultimately, yes. But I've been trying to build up the courage for a long time. I'd hoped Clive or you would take the initiative, but I realized that wasn't going to happen. It couldn't."

"Why not?"

"You probably thought I was dead or as good as," she said.

"You're not wrong."

"And Clive always told me I had to come back on my own. He wouldn't help me. He was never angry at me for blowing up his life, but I don't think he'll ever forgive me for blowing up yours."

"It sounds like you two have some shit to work out. I'm not sure it has anything to do with me."

She laughed. "You sound like Lloyd."

"Lloyd?"

"Sorry. My husband. When I announced my intention to come back here, he gently suggested I try to separate my guilt toward you from my guilt toward Clive."

"I think I like this Lloyd." His name was Lloyd, but that wasn't his fault. I mean, if my name was Lloyd, I'd tell everyone my name was Bob, but then my name was Cash so maybe I couldn't judge.

"I think you will, yeah." She sounded hopeful at the possibility.

"So why now?

"Why what now?"

"You said you announced your intention to come back to Lloyd. What made you decide to do it now? What changed?" I was expecting cancer or the birth of someone's child. Even if she wasn't here for my kidney, she'd clearly been struck by something.

She sighed. "I was sitting on our deck having my morning coffee. We can see a sliver of the beach from the deck. There was this couple doing a wedding photo shoot. That's not unique. We see it all the time. But I realized you were of an age where you might be getting married. Or maybe you already were. Either way, there were important things happening in your life that I wanted to be there for."

"Because you saw someone getting wedding photos taken?" I tried to keep the disbelief out of my voice, but a little slid through.

"Yes. There was this couple doing such a mundane thing, but for them it was probably a grand moment and I knew I had to try. I didn't want to miss out on any more of your grand moments. Even though I knew showing up could have hurt you. I was terrified of causing you pain."

"But you decided to risk it?"

"It was a gamble and it was selfish, but I couldn't wonder anymore. I traded the possibility of pain for the possibility of a fuller life."

"Well, shit." That was a really good reason to blow up your life.

"Shit?" she asked.

"I generally make a habit of avoiding deep thoughts about emotional states and you're making that kind of hard."

"You don't strike me as the type who avoids deep thoughts."

"Heck no. Deep thoughts about poetry or philosophy I'm all for. Give me all the Lorde and Foucault. But talking about feelings isn't really my jam."

"Are you sure?"

"I promise. You've known me for about two weeks. I'm big on avoiding uncomfortable conversations."

"That may be, but we've had a total of four conversations and one of them was a deep feelings, weight of history, expectations of family and parents sort of discussion."

"Damn. Yeah. We're going to need to talk about some really frivolous stuff to wipe that slate clean."

"Yes, of course." She sounded completely sincere.

"What are your feelings on pop music?" I asked.

"I feel like you're going to judge me, but big fan."

"Excellent answer."

"Why's that?"

"Well, it's honest. I'm into honesty when it's convenient for me. And also I, too, am a big fan," I said.

"No. You seem like you'd be into something really random and cool. Like punk, but only from 1978. Or underground rap from the Bay."

"I don't dislike punk or underground rap, but I'd argue being into pop is totally random and cool."

"But it's not serious, which I value, but I guess I didn't expect you to value it," she said.

"Why? Because we denigrate vapidity as a society?"

"I'm trying here, Cash, but I don't think you're as good at frivolous conversations as you hoped."

"Hmm. You might be right."

Someone knocked on my door. "Hey, Cash, I'm about ready to start sorting photos of planes, if you want to join," Boyd called.

"Yeah. Give me a minute," I called back.

"I take it you need to go?" Marjorie asked.

"I do. I'm helping one of the agents sort through a list of small plane owners."

"Do you need to help them? Isn't this their job?"

"It is, but since I'm connected to the case, I might recognize a name they won't. The more I help, the faster we get out of here," I said.

"Then, by all means, go help. Good night, Cash."

"Good night."

Boyd was sitting at one end of the table. Duarte and Jalen had officially claimed residence at the other end. No one else was around.

"If you want to go through the photos and read the numbers to me, I'll plug it in and give you the owner's name," Boyd said.

"Yeah, sure. Sounds like a hoot."

"It sure is."

"Where is everyone else?"

Boyd looked around. "I think they all went to bed."

"It's only eleven."

He shrugged. "I guess sitting around here all day is hard work."

"Look at you making jokes."

"I'm a scream, ma'am."

Chapter Twenty-four

I was sitting with Boyd, reading him N-numbers from the planes he and Orr had photographed that afternoon. He'd retrieve the owner's name from the FAA database. I'd tell him if I recognized them. I never did. We were halfway through the list and I'd dozed off with my chin on my fist twice. Boyd was not impressed with my stamina. I glanced at the time. Just after eleven thirty. I wasn't impressed with my stamina either.

"Do you want to take a break?" he asked.

"No, but I need coffee." I stood.

He nodded and turned the laptop I was using so he could see the next number. I went into the kitchen and put together the coffee machine. Last time we had to research a bunch of people we knew nothing about, Duarte and I had used social media. I wondered if these people were on socials. Probably Facebook this time instead of Twitter and Insta. Thus far, they were all middle-aged white people. So, yeah, Facebook.

"Hey, Duarte," I said.

He looked up from his end of the table with Jalen. "Yeah."

"These guys who keep their planes at the airport, you think they're on socials?"

"Shit." He half closed his laptop. "Yeah. I bet they are."

"You still have your dummy accounts activated?"

He shrugged. "I think so. I never bothered deleting them."

"Do you have a dummy Facebook?"

"No, but it'll take us two seconds to set a couple up."

"Make sure you include photos of planes," Boyd said.

"Why?" Duarte asked.

"If you're looking at all these people, the Facebook algorithm will suggest to them that they should friend request you. If you have a bunch of planes and aviation paraphernalia, then they won't think it's odd," Boyd said.

"He's right," Jalen said. It made me wonder how often she was listening when she was working. Probably all the time.

"Give me a minute and we'll get started." I held up the bag of coffee I was measuring out.

"You know there's a Keurig in there, right?" Duarte asked.

I cringed. "I'm morally opposed to Keurigs."

"Of course you are," Duarte said.

"They make terrible coffee," I said.

"Your moral opposition is based on flavor?" Jalen asked.

"And, you know, the environment." I shrugged.

"But mostly the flavor," Duarte said.

"And aesthetics."

"So flavor, then aesthetics, then environment?" Duarte asked.

"I'd prefer not to rank my reasoning," I said.

"You're a strange person," Jalen said.

"Aww, shucks. Thanks." I poured water in the machine.

"Is she always like this?" Jalen asked Duarte.

"Pretty much yeah. She also rails against the white supremacist cishetero patriarchy a lot."

I glanced up. "Duarte." He looked at me in question. "You remembered to include cishetero in the power structures. That makes me so happy."

"Heck yeah I did. Gender is a construct. Heteronormativity is a prison."

"You do listen when I talk," I said.

"With the important stuff yeah."

Boyd cleared his throat. "How do you know when it's important? She talks a lot."

"Wow. Rude," I said.

Duarte laughed. "The man makes a point, Braddock."

Boyd sputtered. "I'm sorry. That's not what I meant. I just meant you talk about a lot of different subjects."

"It's cool, man. I do talk a lot." I sat back at the table.

"So what's cishetero?" Boyd asked.

"Cis as in gender. Hetero as in sexual," Duarte said.

"Nailed it." I half stood to high five him. He smacked my hand.

"I don't know what those words mean," Boyd said.

Jalen finally looked up from her computer. "Cisgender is someone whose gender matches what they were assigned at birth. Heterosexual like straight. So including the combination cishetero in the white supremacist patriarchy highlights that being queer or trans is outside the existing power structure."

Duarte made eye contact with me and mouthed "Wow." I mouthed "Hot" back at him.

"Okay, so this is an extension of the privilege I experience as a white guy?" Boyd asked.

"Basically, yeah. Because you are presumably straight and cis." I realized I'd just assigned him a sexuality and a gender marker so I added. "Which I only assume because you hadn't heard the terms and a queer person in your situation likely would have," I said.

"Hmm. Okay." He made a very serious face. After a minute he nodded. "I'll think about that."

I waited to see if he needed to share any of those thoughts, but he just kept plugging in numbers.

Duarte brought his laptop to my side of the table. "What's your fake Facebook name going to be?"

"Brash Caddock."

"Dude."

"So that's not a good name?" I feigned ignorance.

"It is not," he said with vehemence.

"Okay. We're aiming for bland white guy?" I asked.

"Affirmative."

"Will," I said. He nodded in encouragement. "Williamson. Will Williamson."

"You're not taking this seriously."

"Well, no." Though he should have expected as much from me. "But I'll try. What's your name going to be?"

"Justin Dieter," he said.

"You came up with that really fast."

"It's the name I use for undercover work."

"Okay, no fair."

"When you're done debating names, let me know what sort of planes each of you want. I'll send you a couple of photos to use," Boyd said.

"Will Williamson totally flies an old plane. Like those crop dusters. What are they called? Biplanes?" I asked.

"Yep, biplanes. And Duarte is right. That's a dumb name," Boyd said.

"Fine. What do you think my last name should be?"

"Jameson." He didn't even think about it, which was very annoying.

"Great. Whatever. Will Jameson flies an old biplane."

"Justin Dieter has something fast," Duarte said.

"Like part ownership of a jet?"

"Yeah. A jet. Justin Dieter likes fast sleek shit."

Twenty minutes later, Will and Justin had Facebook accounts. Duarte embellished whatever details were visible on private accounts. I started searching the Twitter and Instagram for the names on Boyd's list. The coffee kept me from dozing off, but it couldn't combat the utter boredom of typing in names and getting absolutely no viable hits. Literally. I went through the entire list without finding a Twitter or an Instagram account. When I was finished, I went back to reading N-numbers to Boyd. Once he got a name, I'd punch it into socials. In total, there were nearly fifty planes. Not one hit.

"You finished with those accounts?" I asked Duarte.

"Yeah, sure. Is it time to start searching with them? I can be done."

"What are you doing?" I leaned over to look at the accounts up on his screen.

"Well, I gave Will some hints of white supremacy," he said matter-of-factly.

"What the fuck, dude?"

"I wanted him to fit in."

"So Justin isn't racist?" I asked.

"No, but Justin is misogynistic. And he's cool with the gays— capital T, capital G—The Gays—but he's pretty transphobic. I figure the misogyny feeds into his transphobia."

"We are a delightful pair."

"We certainly are. We followed the local EAA chapter Facebook page, which super fun fact, has a noose in the logo. I love that for us," he said.

"What's an EAA chapter?"

"You know, Will, I tried to find that out, but their website was less than helpful. I'm thinking one of the As stands for aviation."

"Hmm. Good reconnaissance, JD." I nudged him with my shoulder.

"JD?"

"Yeah. I figure you go by JD."

"Totally. Of course I do."

Boyd's printer came to life. He grabbed the sheet and handed it to me. "When you two are done with the circle jerk, here's the list of plane owners."

"Is it technically a circle jerk if there are only two people?" I asked.

"I think technically it's just mutual masturbation." Duarte hit the "technically" just right to imitate my usage. I turned around to check the room. Laurel was in her bedroom. We were still alone. "What are you doing?" he asked.

"Laurel already gave us shit for discussing masturbation. If it happens again, she'll never let it go. But we're clear."

"Yeah, she would be insufferable." Duarte looked around.

"Paranoid?" I whispered.

"Aren't you? She's everywhere," he whispered back.

"Focus, you two," Boyd said.

"Yes, sir." I saluted Boyd.

We split the list. I started at the bottom and Duarte started at the top. Five in and I had seen enough footage of small planes on big horizons for a lifetime. Every single name on the list had a Facebook account. And every single one of them had posted a video or a photo album in the last month. These were the people fueling Facebook. It was depressing as shit. In my first ten names, I found one woman, one Black dude, but seven significant mustaches. Which tracked for both my assumptions about Placerville and small plane owners.

By one in the morning, Duarte and I were closing in on the middle of the list. I'd started drawing mustaches on the list next to the names when I found particularly distinctive facial hair. Duarte misunderstood my poor drawings and his first five had little planes drawn next to them. "I thought the planes meant you were crossing them off the list," he'd said. For all our searching, we weren't finding anything. Too many of the accounts were private. We couldn't get any real information. Plus, we didn't really know what we were looking for.

"Done," Jalen said quietly.

"With what?" Boyd asked.

"Cross-referencing the Raphael messages with FAA registered flight plans."

The three of us stopped what we were doing and looked at her.

"So do you have the pilot?" Duarte asked.

"Gavin Frank," she said.

"No shit?" I said.

"No shit." She nodded with authority. "Gavin Frank is the only pilot who could have conceivably made the runs referenced in the text messages."

"Frank comma Gavin. Motherfucker is on the list." Duarte pointed to a name near the top of the list. "I went right past him. Nothing stood out."

Duarte and I typed the name into the search. Gavin Frank's account was mostly private. His banner looked like the majority of the other accounts. It was two-thirds Photoshopped violet sky and one-third plane. We could see a few years' worth of cover photo changes. We scrolled through them. In December two years previous, Gavin's cover photo was him and another dude who looked like him kissing opposite sides of an old woman's face. She had to be their grandmother. I kept scrolling, then went back and stared.

"What's up?" Duarte leaned over to look at my screen even though his showed the same information.

"I know this guy." I pointed at the guy with Frank. "But I don't know where from."

"Looks like they're related. Brother or cousin, probably," Duarte said. "Does Frank have any brothers or cousins close in age?" he asked Boyd and Jalen.

"Give me a minute." Jalen typed and scrolled. "A brother, Travis Frank."

Duarte looked at me. I shook my head. It wasn't ringing any bells.

"Oh, shit," Boyd said.

"What?" Duarte asked.

"Fuck. Jesus Christ," Boyd said.

"What is it, man?" I asked.

"Travis Frank is an El Dorado County Sheriff."

I looked back at the photo. "That's it. That's the motherfucker who was arresting Melody Brewer and let her go so she could kick me in the face."

"Wait. Melody Brewer is the grandmother who kicked you in the face?" Duarte asked.

"I'm sorry. Isn't Melody Brewer Henry Brewer's grandmother?" Boyd asked.

"Yeah."

"How did a grandmother kick you in the face?" Jalen asked.

"You know what, Randy Jalen, grandmothers are capable of lots of things. Even kicking people in the face," I said.

Duarte put his hand on my forearm. "She's a little touchy about the subject," he said to Jalen.

"I am not. I'm just saying people write off grandmothers and they are exceedingly capable. Also, Henry Brewer's grandmother is a terrifying woman. The face kick was nothing. She also tried to shoot me and Laurel with a shotgun."

"I think I see why she's so touchy," Jalen said.

Chapter Twenty-five

The shouting woke me at the ungodly hour of eight. It was excited shouting though, so that was probably good. I brushed my teeth, glared at my hair, pulled on some shorts, and padded out to the common room.

"A fucking sheriff. I knew he had help," Michelson was saying.

"Well, actually," Laurel and I said simultaneously. She whipped around to look at me. We grinned.

"I hate when you 'well, actually' me," Michelson said.

"Wow. Yeah. That must be really annoying," I said.

Jalen laughed. She was still behind her laptop, but she wasn't pretending she wasn't listening anymore.

"They are the ones who said he had help," Duarte said.

Michelson sighed. "Yes, they did. But we all agreed that they were correct."

I smirked and poured myself a cup of coffee. I sat at the counter so I could participate in the conversation without actually participating. Laurel moved from the couch to sit next to me. We angled away from the counter so we could see the makeshift conference table. The move put Laurel in front of me. She was wearing a gray linen short-sleeve button-up. It looked textured and soft. I refrained from touching it to check.

Reyes and Duarte were at the table with all the FBI agents. Behind Boyd was a freestanding whiteboard. It was probably six feet wide. It was a new and not altogether welcome addition to the already crowded common room.

"What did you find out about the sheriff?" Malone asked.

Boyd scrolled through his notes on his laptop even though he didn't need them. "We don't have much to go on. His digital footprint is pretty shallow. We do know he was present at Melody Brewer's house when she was arrested."

"How do you know that? Did you contact EDSO?" Michelson asked. He didn't look happy at the prospect.

"No. He's the one who detained Mrs. Brewer and let her escape long enough to assault Cash. Cash remembers him," Boyd said.

"No way." Laurel turned to look at me.

"Yeah, I remember the sheriff who removed me from the house yelling at Frank when he let Grandma Brewer go," I said.

"Wait. What does he look like?" she asked.

Boyd flipped his laptop around. "Here." He had a photo of Travis Frank in uniform.

"Shit." Laurel reached for the laptop. "I know him too. Reyes, you see this?" She turned it so he could see.

He leaned back to look. "Oh, shit. That's the sheriff who helped us conduct interviews."

"Which interviews?" Michelson asked.

"All the EDSO interviews. He also escorted us around when we were interviewing Brewer's family and friends," Laurel said.

"So he's probably been obstructing all along. Or at least monitoring our investigation into Brewer," Malone said.

"Dammit." Michelson wrote some angry notes in his leather notebook. "Okay, what else do we know?"

Boyd read from his notes. "Both Frank brothers attended Union Mine High School. No connection to Millard or Brewer there. Travis went to Chico State. He was hired at EDSO soon after graduation."

"And the little brother?" Michelson asked.

"Gavin went directly into the Navy after high school. He attended community college for a few years when he got out. We can't find any connection to Brewer," Boyd said.

"So either we haven't found it yet or Brewer and Travis Frank became buds at EDSO. They were hired around the same time," Jalen said.

"Can we contact EDSO? Is there anyone we can trust there?" Duarte asked.

Michelson thought about that for a minute. "Not yet. Let's do a deeper dive into the Franks. Get me addresses. I'd like to set up surveillance at their residences."

"You think Brewer is living with one of them?" Malone asked.

"It's possible. Even if he's not, maybe one of them will lead us to him," Michelson said.

"Okay, I've got current addresses for both. Gavin has a condo in Cameron Park. Travis owns a small house in Diamond Springs." It had taken Jalen ninety seconds to find out where they lived.

"Are they in neighborhoods? How populated is the surrounding area?" Malone asked.

"Gavin's place is just off a golf course. He's in a small development with about ten other units. Older places built in the eighties, but still pretty pricey." Jalen passed her iPad down the table. I caught a glimpse of Google Street View.

"So that's unlikely if Brewer is trying not to be seen." Malone passed the iPad back.

"Travis is in a neighborhood. It's a bit more ramshackle but quite suburban overall. Same issue there." She handed the iPad down the table again.

"No garage?" Boyd asked.

"Doesn't look like it," she said. "But he could have come in at night."

"Yeah, but it looks like the neighbor across the street has security cameras." Boyd zoomed in on something and handed it back.

"If they still have them, it might be a deterrent," Michelson said.

I leaned forward and whispered to Laurel, "See, this is why I didn't want to go to a safe house. We could go stake out those fuckers in like two minutes."

She turned her head a little. "I know. You and Nate were always more effective at this shit."

"We also weren't bogged down by laws and warrants and shit."

She shrugged and laughed quietly. "Minor details."

"Has anyone considered what a geek, a pilot, and two sheriffs—one disgraced—are up to? Because their texts aren't illuminating, but they clearly are doing something," Jalen said.

"Exactly," Michelson said. "This is why I want surveillance on them yesterday."

"It's got to be drug distribution, right?" Duarte asked. He looked back at me for confirmation. "That's what he told you?"

"Yeah, totally. When he broke into my place, he said he had suppliers in place to get us up and running within a week," I said.

At a look from Michelson, Boyd stood and adjusted the whiteboard. He wrote the suspects' names and their aliases. "What do we know?" Boyd asked.

"Frank—Raphael—is flying something all over the state," Malone said.

Boyd wrote it on the list. "And into Nevada and Oregon. There were a few airports across the state lines."

"Brewer has drug suppliers," Duarte said.

"Frank, cowboy variety, is the inside man. He's providing information on local law enforcement," Reyes said.

"Both for whatever drug ring they're developing and to keep Brewer from getting caught," Duarte said.

"Brewer's got to be managing this whole thing," Malone said.

"Why else would Gavin be telling Brewer his flight plans?" Jalen asked.

"That's what I'm thinking," Malone said.

There was a lull as everyone stared at the board. Curtis Millard had a whole lot of nothing under his name.

"So, aside from a childhood obsession that I happen to remember about Curtis, is there any reason to think he's included here?" I asked.

"Well, no," Boyd said.

"Yes," Jalen said. We stared at her and waited. "I used Will Jameson's account and sent a friend request to Gavin. He accepted. I went on a deep dive and found this." She handed the iPad down the table again.

It got to Boyd and I nudged Laurel. She sighed and got up to grab it. We looked at the photo, then looked at everyone around the table. They also looked confused.

"Smoke meth and hail Satan?" Laurel asked.

"Yep. That is a photo from two months ago of Curtis Millard wearing a T-shirt that says 'Smoke meth and hail Satan' with his arm around Gavin Frank." Jalen stood to take the iPad back from Laurel.

"Hmm." Boyd nodded and wrote *Meth?* under Curtis Millard's name.

"Well, this took a turn," I said.

"It certainly did," Laurel said.

"Okay. Hypothetically, let's say Millard is making meth. Gavin is flying it out. Travis is greasing the wheels. And Brewer is managing them," Malone said.

"There are a lot of questions there." Michelson was not sold on any of it.

"Absolutely. What are they?" Boyd held his dry-erase pen at the ready.

"Meth is not Brewer's usual jam," Laurel said.

"But he's morally bankrupt and would have no problem distributing meth," I said.

"But if he wanted to use your contacts, which he clearly does, then meth isn't a viable product," Reyes said. "Your customer base was very specific."

"Yeah, that's true. I can't imagine any of your customers buying meth," Laurel said.

My phone started vibrating. I pulled it out and saw Robin's name. I held it up. "Sorry, I should take this." Laurel nodded. Everyone else seemed unconcerned. I swiped it and headed to my room. "Hey, pal."

"Hey yourself."

"Where have you been all my life?" I shut the door and flopped on my bed.

"Just pining for you, of course. Come rescue me from my mother."

"I thought you liked your mother?" I asked.

"I do, but I haven't lived with her in twenty years. She never stops making breakfast food. Everything smells like bacon. My hair, my clothes. My absurdly expensive face cream that used to ease me to sleep with the scent of jasmine and ylang-ylang smells like bacon."

"Robin Ward, my love, I will buy you more face cream that smells like jasmine and ylang-ylang. I will buy you a whole tub of face cream." I didn't know what ylang-ylang was, but I felt confident I could figure it out.

"Aww, you do love me."

"Did you doubt it?"

"Never." She sighed. "So, what's going on? We are missing prime summer grilling and drinking beer time. They need to wrap this up."

"Agreed. I haven't been outside in like six days." I missed sunshine and also air that wasn't shared with a bunch of smelly boys.

"That's horrible. How are you holding up?"

"Well, I kissed Laurel."

"No," she shouted.

"I had a talk with my mom about why she came back."

"Holy shit," she said.

"And I made a Facebook account."

"Okay, that's it. I'm on my way."

I laughed. "It was a dummy account. So we could Facebook stalk someone."

"Oh, thank God. I thought that was you giving a code that you'd been kidnapped."

"No, but good instincts," I said.

"You kissed Laurel?"

"Yes, I needed to talk about it, but I called you and you didn't pick up."

"Is that past tense? Do you no longer need to talk about it?" she asked.

"Heck no, man. I still absolutely need to talk about it."

She laughed. "Okay. How did the kissing come about?"

"I offered to take out her stitches."

"You did what?"

"Her stitches were annoying and she missed her appointment so I offered to remove them for her. I did so good."

"How does removing sutures lead to sexy kissing?"

"Honestly, no idea. She was topless and…" I tried to expand, but I couldn't think past topless. I couldn't be that stereotypical. There had to be more.

"And?"

"She smelled really good?"

"Yes, this seems like solid reasoning to make big decisions. Topless woman who smells good," she said.

"Aren't you glad you decided to let me be a role model for your kid?"

"Every day."

"Anyway, I realized she was naked and I was taking advantage, which led to me thinking maybe I wasn't making the best decisions so I stopped kissing her. And she was like, hey, let's not stop. And I was like, hey, we have to."

"That sounds very responsible of you. When you discussed it afterward, what did she say?" Robin asked.

"I'm sorry, you think we discussed it afterward? Have you met me?" My voice went a little high-pitched, but in my defense, I was pretty incredulous.

"Fair point. I know you didn't discuss it. It's kind of amazing that you called me to talk about it."

"I know. Look at me growing."

"I'm very proud," she said.

"We were alone for like two minutes the next day and she called me out on it."

"What did you say?"

"That I was an emotional coward and she admitted she was too and then someone else came in the room and I ran away." It seemed perfectly reasonable at the time.

"Awesome. Great decision-making. So what are you going to do?"

"I don't know. That's why I called you. Tell me what to do," I said.

"What do you want?"

I thought it was a difficult question, but apparently, I knew the answer immediately. "I want her, but I don't trust her."

"Yeah, that's kind of necessary."

"Only if we want a healthy relationship."

"And, presumably, you do," she said.

"Yeah, ideally."

"I'm not sure I can help you, pal. Trust is built over time. But you have to start the process at some point."

"Wow, yeah. Super unhelpful."

Chapter Twenty-six

When I went back out to the common room, everyone had dispersed. Jalen was still at her spot at the table. I'd yet to see her go farther than three feet from her seat, which was making me worry about her. Duarte was sitting with her and typing into his own set of laptops. Laurel was stretched out on the couch again. She had a cup of coffee balanced on her chest. I poured my own coffee and dropped into the wingback across from her.

"Where did everyone go?" I asked.

"Michelson's in one of the bedrooms calling the DEA office in Sac." She nodded at the closed bedroom door. Reyes was in the other bedroom having a phone conversation, if the pieces I could hear were any indication. "If they don't have an investigation open, he wants to bring them in. If they do have an investigation, he wants all their info."

"Nice. What are the chances they have an investigation open?"

She shrugged. "No clue. They clearly haven't come across any hints of Brewer because they would have contacted Michelson."

"They would?"

"You know law enforcement agencies talk to each other, right?"

"I guess. They never seem all that competent, honestly."

"Well, let's hope they are. Michelson's giving them Millard, assuming he's actually manufacturing or distributing drugs." She sat up a little so she could sip her coffee.

"What's that mean for us?"

"If we're lucky, they will start surveillance on him immediately. If we're really lucky, Brewer is hiding out at his off-grid house."

"I don't see why they don't just go knock on Millard's door and check for Henry? He's a fugitive," I said.

"Because it will tip Millard and Brewer off that we've connected them."

That was pretty logical. "Oh. Okay."

"Malone, Boyd, and Orr are trading off watching the Franks. Michelson will have a couple of agents join them as soon as Jalen finishes background checks."

"Why not have Duarte and Reyes help out?" I nodded at Duarte at the table.

"We apparently still need babysitters."

"I feel like we don't need babysitters." There was no way to say that without sounding petulant.

"Agreed. The point was hiding. Brewer doesn't know where we are."

"Boom. Hidden." I spread my arms to indicate the condo.

"Exactly."

"So they're off saving the world or whatever and we have to sit around here and twiddle our thumbs?" I asked.

"Yep. It's a bum deal."

"The bummest of deals."

"Is bummest a word?" she asked.

"All words have to be created before they become words."

"So it's not a word yet?"

"No, it's a word now. But it wasn't thirty seconds ago before I created it. You get it."

She looked at me like she absolutely did not get it. "Okay."

I sipped my coffee and felt like there was some connection between the creation of words and the creation of trust, but I couldn't quite figure it out. Laurel finished her coffee and set the mug on the coffee table. Robin said I had to start the process in order to build trust, but Robin didn't know I already trusted Laurel. There were some massive gaps, mercurial questions, but each day sitting in this stuffy condo seemed to fill in the edges just a little. Before we'd come to the safe house, I was afraid my attraction to her would cloud the issue, but it seemed to give my vision perfect clarity. It didn't matter that she was hot or smart or confident. It mattered that sitting next to her in silence healed parts of me. Even the parts she had broken.

"Hey, Laurel?"

She looked over at me. "Yeah?"

"I think I'm ready to have that conversation."

She sat upright instantly. "Are you sure?"

"Yes."

We glanced over. Duarte and Jalen had their heads buried. "Now?" she asked.

"Yes." I stood. Laurel followed me to my room. I closed the door. She stared at me.

"So what do you want to talk about?" She seemed nervous as fuck.

"Oh, I'd rather not talk." I stripped off my T-shirt and tossed it.

"Yeah, okay."

We both took a step forward and then we were kissing. She tried to pull her shirt off. I tried to help unbutton it. Neither of us were entirely successful. We couldn't stop kissing long enough. She tasted bitter like coffee, pure like her. She kissed down my neck, leaving a cool, damp trail. Her hands were at my waistband, wrestling with the button on my shorts. By the time we fell onto the bed, we'd managed to almost entirely strip. I was still tangled in my boxers and she had one sock on. Just one.

"Who wears socks in summer?" I asked as I tried to remove the sock with my big toe.

"My feet get cold." She pulled it off and tossed it.

"Weirdo." I rolled on top of her and slid my thigh between hers.

She gripped my hips and pulled me tighter against her. Her fingers twisted in the elastic of my underwear and pushed them down. I kicked them off. Her hands went to my ass, grabbing, kneading, pulling me tight against her. She groaned and looked down the joined length of our bodies. And then she started to smile, to laugh.

"I fucking missed you."

"Shut up." I kissed her and marveled at the feeling of her lips pressed against mine. The slope and arc of our lips slid together and apart in perfect, grasping unity. We kissed and kissed and kissed. It was coming home and relief and yet seemed like it always existed. No matter where we were in time, this perfect kiss was happening.

Her hands moved up, grasping my hips, my ribs. She traced the edges of my collarbones with her fingertips. She dug into the hint of muscle over my shoulders. I moved against her, trying to climb inside her skin. She slid her fingers around my wrist and pushed my hand between us. I slid into her. She arched against me. She gripped the back of my arm, holding me in place. I started to move. Slowly at first. She pulled my head down to kiss me again. She pressed her tongue inside my mouth, pulled it back. Her fingertips skated over the back of my head. She tugged my hair, held me closer. She traced the edge of my jaw, cupped my chin to hold me still. Her lips moved against mine and away. When I chased her, she held firm, then leaned up to kiss me again.

It was distracting as all hell. Not quite distracting enough to break my slow rhythm though. Her breath caught when I sped up. I braced my arm against the bed to hold myself steady. I started to fuck her hard, fast. She moaned and pulled my head to her uninjured shoulder. I sucked and bit. Her moans got louder and I pressed my free hand over her mouth. The vibrations cut through me and I nearly came just from listening to her. I pumped in and out of her. She wrapped her foot around my leg and arched hard off the bed. When she came, she went stiff. The sudden shift forced me to drop against her. She wrapped her arms tight around me. Her hands still grasping, tracing, feeling every inch of my skin.

"Told you I missed you," she said.

"Maybe you should miss me again in a minute." I grinned against her skin.

"You are the worst." She smiled. "I love you. You need to know that."

I stopped grinning like an idiot. "I know."

"Good." She kissed me sweetly, then thrust her hip up and flipped me onto my back.

"Show-off."

"Yeah." She dipped down for another sweet kiss. Her hands slid into mine and pinned them to the bed. The kiss shifted to decidedly not sweet. She bit my lip, then sucked it.

I squeezed her hands and tried to touch her, but she held firm. She stopped kissing me long enough to slide down my body. She kissed across my chest, sucking each nipple for not nearly long enough. I whimpered when she moved lower. She nipped at my ribs, dipped her tongue into my belly button, spent an obscene amount of time in the hollow of my hip before finally lowering her mouth. She started by licking the length of me. Her hair fell forward and tickled my thighs. She swirled her tongue over and around, never slowing, never touching my clit.

"Please." The word came out a choked cry. It had been so long since I last came. I simply hadn't cared to bother. Not if it wasn't going to be her. And suddenly we were here. She splayed me open, rendered my flesh valuable again.

She sucked my clit into her mouth. Her tongue built a rhythm designed to make me forget my own name. She was perfectly capable of making me wait. She knew exactly how to bleed me dry of everything except the desire for her. And yet, she didn't. Like she knew the depth of my need, knew making me want more was useless. I was already wanting.

I came hard and long. I was aware only of her and the pounding of my heart. I gasped for air as she crawled back up my body. She stopped when we were face-to-face. I reached up and pushed her hair back out of her face.

"I love you too."

"I thought you might." She smiled slowly and kissed me.

❖

It was dark, but barely when someone knocked on Laurel's door. "It's me," Reyes called.

Laurel looked at me in panic. I was certain my expression was about the same. I started to get out of bed, but I was hecka naked, the bathroom door was eight feet away, and Reyes was already opening the door. I dove back under the covers. Laurel pulled the blanket up.

"Jeez, Lucas. You're supposed to wait for acknowledgement after you knock."

"Oh, sorry." His voice hesitated. "I, uh, I always come in like that with you. I didn't realize it bothered you."

"It's fine. I'm just giving you shit."

"Cool. I just wanted to update you. We found a cabin in—why are you in bed? It's like eight thirty."

She tugged the blanket a little. I focused on taking shallow, quiet breaths. "I was taking a nap. We've been pulling weird hours."

"You're naked. Oh, fuck." He closed the door. "Is Cash under there?" he whispered.

"No." Laurel had entirely lost her ability to lie.

"Yeah." I sat up. Laurel looked at me in horror. "It's fucking hot. I couldn't breathe."

"Shit." Reyes turned toward the door. "I'm going to go. I'll check back later."

"Dude, you're fine. We just need clothes," Laurel said.

I leaned over and whispered, "My clothes are all next door in my room."

"Right." Laurel looked over the edge of the bed and checked the floor, but I was quite certain we had removed all our clothes twenty-five feet and a wall away. "Give us five minutes, okay?"

"Yeah. Sure. Five minutes." He nearly tripped trying to get out and shut the door behind himself.

"I think he took that well," Laurel said.

"Oh, yeah. The two of you were chill as fuck." I kissed her and climbed out of bed.

"I don't think I appreciate your tone." She also climbed out of bed. "Are all my clothes in your room too?" She spun in a circle to check the floor again.

"Unless I dozed off and you went to grab your clothes and bring them over here, yeah, they're where you left them." I walked through the bathroom to my room. I came across her shirt first and tossed it on the bed. She found my shorts and one of her socks. Her underwear and shorts were under the sheets we'd kicked onto the floor. My T-shirt was hanging off the edge of the dresser. My boxer briefs were under one of the pillows.

There was a knock next door. We gave up on the final sock and threw on our clothes. After a respectable ninety seconds, Reyes let himself into Laurel's room and loudly closed the door.

"Kallen? Braddock?"

"We're coming. Just a sec." Laurel rushed to button her shirt.

We filed back to her room and found Reyes leaning against the dresser, staring intently at the floor.

"You doing okay there, buddy?" I asked.

"I'm super." He kept his eyes on his feet.

"We're dressed now. You can look," Laurel said.

"Yeah, sure. I know that." He looked up, but still refused eye contact.

Laurel stepped into his line of vision. "Stop being weird."

He grinned. "I'm sorry. I just didn't see that coming. And I've never seen you in bed with someone."

"Well, yeah. If you had, that would be creepy."

"Yes. Okay. Good point."

"What did you come in to tell me before?" Laurel asked.

"Oh, that. Jalen found a cabin," Reyes said.

I sat on the edge of the bed. "Can we narrow that down? There are a lot of cabins in, you know, the world." Laurel sat next to me. I could feel the heat radiating off her.

"Listen, I'm so cool with this." Reyes pointed back and forth between me and Laurel. "Really. Just super cool." Laurel and I looked at each other. I raised an eyebrow and she smirked. He did not seem super cool. "But also this is strange for me. So if you could just kind of ease me in, that would be great."

"Which part is throwing you off?" I asked.

"The whole thing. I've never seen Kallen in a serious relationship."

I turned back to Laurel. "Never?" She shrugged.

"And, yes, the former criminal thing is throwing me off. But I think it's more than that. I spent so much time denying that you two were anything other than detective and CI and now you're actually in a relationship, but you're not detective and CI anymore. It's just weird for me, okay?"

"Shit," Laurel said.

"What?" he asked.

"I didn't think about that. You know when Gibson was making his allegations, we weren't actually in a relationship, right?"

"You weren't?" He was surprised and maybe a little relieved.

"No. I lied to you and I feel like a dick, but I wouldn't have let you lie for me."

He nodded. "Good. That's good."

"How long has he known about this?" I asked.

"Since he read Brewer's stalking notes," Laurel said.

"Fuck. Okay, so you two have some shit to work out?"

They both shook their heads, but then Laurel shrugged and started nodding. He joined her a second later. "I guess," she said.

"All right. Let's do this. Reyes, you've got ten minutes and then we want to know about this mystery cabin," I said.

"I really don't have questions. I just want her to be happy. You make her happy. Actually, I don't know if you do, but I know not being with you makes her miserable."

"Aww, I think he loves you." I nudged Laurel with my shoulder.

"Yeah, whatever." Laurel rolled her eyes. So Reyes rolled his.

"Okay. Mystery cabin. Spill."

"The Franks have a family cabin. It's in their maternal grandfather's name, which is why it took so long for Jalen to find. It's in the middle of fucking nowhere."

"You think Brewer is hiding out there?" Laurel asked.

"It's a possibility, yeah. We're pretty sure he's not staying with Gavin or Travis. We tailed them all day and saw no indication that he was there."

"What about Curtis?" I asked.

"The DEA had a team in place by noon. They're pretty sure no one is home."

"Isn't he in the middle of nowhere too? Can they even get close enough to see if he's there?" I asked.

"He's far from county maintained roads, but his house is right on the river. From there, they have a straight sightline into his house. Everything is battened down and locked up. Patio furniture, solar panels. Even his little fishing boat has been pulled up."

"So we're thinking he's with Brewer in this cabin?" Laurel asked.

"Yep. That's the hope at least."

"Can we get a warrant to go into the cabin?"

Reyes shook his head. "Magistrate thinks our case is flimsy. He's an asshat who always errs on the side of privacy and liberty and shit."

"Is this that dickwad we had during the Roth case a couple of years ago?"

"Yes." Reyes sounded stoked that she remembered.

"Ugh. He was the worst."

"Anyway, DEA is liaising with Malone. It sounds like they're going to shift surveillance from the Millard house to the Frank family cabin tomorrow."

"Excellent," I said.

"Okay. I think that's it." He gripped the edge of the dresser and started to push himself up. "I'm going to go because I'd rather support you two from outside the room you've been having sex in all day."

"We haven't been having sex in here all day," I said.

"Right."

"No, we had sex in my room and the shower and then the dresser in here and—"

"No." Reyes threw himself away from the dresser. "Come on. Please stop."

"Prude," Laurel said.

"I am not." He stomped to the door.

"This is payback for the two months you were sleeping with that uniform after your divorce," Laurel said.

He turned back. "That was maybe ill-advised, but in no way relates to this."

"I walked in on you two like five times." Laurel turned to me. "It was disgusting."

I nodded. "That sounds terrible."

"I saw his bare ass. I'll never unsee it."

"No wonder you needed so much therapy."

She shook her head sadly. "I don't think it helped. Some trauma you can't recover from."

I rubbed her back. "Yeah. You're probably right."

"Jackasses. Both of you." Reyes let himself out and closed the door hard.

We could still hear him grumbling as he walked away. We started laughing.

"That was fun," Laurel said.

I hooked my finger in her shirt and looked down. "You know what else is fun?"

"Talking about our feelings?"

"Okay. Who are you and where's Laurel?"

"I'm all for avoidance, but apparently, I didn't deal with a lot of shit before and it kind of fucked up a lot for me."

I sighed. And then genius struck me. "Fine. But we're playing strip share."

"I hesitate to ask, but what is strip share?"

"For every emotional truth I share, you take off an item of clothing. Strip share." I was quite pleased with myself.

"I'm only wearing three items," she said.

I grinned. "Guess it will be a short game."

"Okay. We can play. But for every flippant or avoidant answer you give, I put on an item of clothing."

"Hoo boy. Challenge accepted."

"Have you forgiven me for leaving?" she asked.

"I don't think it's a matter of forgiveness. I think it's a matter of understanding why. I still don't understand why, but I'm starting to."

She nodded. "I'm impressed."

I drew a circle in the air with my finger to tell her to get a move on. "Show how impressed you are by taking off your shirt."

She unbuttoned the shirt and let it drop off her shoulders. "Why now? Why were you finally ready today?"

"I talked to Marjorie and she told me she came to see me because the possibility of pain was worth the trade-off to have a fuller life."

Laurel cocked her head. "I like that."

"You know what I like?" I stared pointedly at her shorts.

"How can you be so flippant and so serious simultaneously? It's very strange."

"Was that your question?" I asked.

She laughed. "No." She stood and kicked off the shorts. Then she sat and stared at me for a long beat. "Why are you an emotional coward?"

"What?"

"You said it before, but I've been thinking about it since. You're quite comfortable with conflict and debate and anger, but anything with emotional resonance terrifies you."

"I just don't like talking about feelings."

"But that's not true. You will talk all day about feelings. And you'll tell me you love me. But you struggle to hear it when I tell you I love you."

"No?" I meant to deny it, but it came out a question. "I don't think that's true."

"The first time I told you I was in love with you was after you'd been released from County. Rather than hear it, you got out of the truck," she said. I opened my mouth to deny it, but she kept going. "I know it was because you were mad at me. You had every right to be. But then I said it again when we were on that stakeout in Davis. And, yes, there was a lot of shit happening, and yes, you told me you loved me a couple of days later, but there was this moment of panic. You just froze. Why are you so afraid of me loving you?"

I was very aware of breathing. It felt like I shouldn't be able to. My chest had just been cut into, after all. We stared at the truth she had spilled all over the bed.

"I've never let someone love me after they left me. I did it for the first six years of my life on constant repeat. I learned that once someone had hurt me—really truly hurt me—then it wasn't safe. And I've let you love me twice and both times you broke my heart."

She nodded. And nodded and nodded. "Yeah. Okay. That's fair."

"What are you going to do about it?"

"Stay. Every day. Even when we're sick of each other. Especially then. I'll talk to you. You'll talk to me."

"Sometimes it might really suck."

She gave me a wry smile. "I know."

"You know what I think?"

"What?"

"I think you owe me those underwear."

CHAPTER TWENTY-SEVEN

I poured myself into one of the dining room chairs next to Jalen and Duarte and sighed. They didn't respond. I took a deeper breath and sighed louder.

"What's up, Cash?" Duarte asked.

"I'm bored."

Laurel set a cup of coffee in front of me. "Cash, didn't I tell you not to bother Jeff this morning?"

"Maybe." I sighed again.

She sat next to me. "How goes the operation?"

"The DEA team is in place. They can't see much. No one has gone in or out of the property," Duarte said.

"Any sign of Brewer?" Laurel asked.

"Nope."

"Any sign of Millard?"

"Nope."

"Any indication they are on the right track?"

"Well, they're reasonably certain someone is living there. There's a clean truck under a recently built aluminum carport."

"Okay. A clean truck. What else?" Laurel asked.

Jalen shook her head. "Nothing. I promise to keep you two informed."

"This is not fun," I said.

Laurel squeezed my thigh under the table. "Patience."

"I don't have patience. I'm going to watch cartoons."

Laurel laughed and followed me to the couch. I pulled up Netflix and started the first Scooby-Doo show that popped up.

"Is this what you do in your downtime?" Laurel asked.

"I'm too amped up to read poetry. And I don't have my cat. And we've been inside for over a week. I've decided to become a vampire."

"A vampire, huh?"

"Yeah."

"Sounds scary," she said.

"Oh, it is."

"A Scooby-Doo watching vampire."

"There's a lot of sex appeal in Scooby-Doo. Velma is hot. Plus, drug usage? Fun."

"Okay." Laurel scooted down the couch and leaned her head against my shoulder.

"Are you sure that's okay?" I whispered.

She shrugged. "I don't care."

"Cool." I didn't know it until she said it, but I had given up on waiting for Laurel not to care what other people thought.

We settled in. She was touching me unthinkingly. Her knuckles rested gently against the outside of my thigh. Her hair tickled the edge of my jaw. It felt simple and unimportant and it was everything.

"Don't forget to call Lane today," I said.

"Shit. Yeah, thanks." She pressed a fast kiss into my shoulder, then went back to her investment in Scooby and the gang.

Two hours later, Jalen got a phone call. She'd gotten many in that time, but none seemed important. This one seemed important. "Both of them?" Jalen typed some shit on her keyboard. "No, stay in your vehicle. I'll loop Boyd in. Just a sec."

I nudged Laurel. "What's going on?" I nodded at Jalen.

"I'm not sure." She sat and leaned forward to hear better.

"Okay, you guys can both hear me?" Jalen waited. "Malone, stay with the vehicle. Boyd, it sounds like we're heading toward the freeway. Take a different road and wait there. We'll let you know if they get on going east or west."

"Let's go find out." Laurel stood and held out her hand to tug me to my feet.

We sat at the table. Duarte was watching Jalen intently. When we joined, he went and knocked on one of the bedroom doors. A minute later, Reyes came out and sat with us.

"You got that, Boyd? East. They are heading east. Stay on them. Malone, drop back so you can take over if he needs you. I'm muting, but I can hear you." Jalen tapped the mute on her phone and looked at us. "Gavin just went to Travis's. They left in Travis's truck and got on the freeway going east."

"Any idea where they are going?" Laurel asked.

"Could be the airport. Could be the cabin. Could be fucking Tahoe. There's no way to know," Duarte said.

"Well, we do live in California. So, you know, most everything is east," I said.

"We don't have to include you in these little meetings, you know?" Duarte said.

"Yeah, but you like me."

A few minutes later, Jalen announced they had passed the exit for the airport. Fifteen minutes after that, they got off in Pollock Pines.

"That's how you get to the family cabin, right?" Duarte asked.

"Yep," Reyes said.

Jalen switched from her call with Malone and Boyd to a call with the DEA agents. "Pierce? You have Gavin and Travis Frank headed your way. They're in one of Travis's vehicles. It's a navy 2010 Chevy Silverado."

We waited. I wondered if the gang would figure out what was going on with the pint-sized monsters in Crystal Cove. Velma would. She always came through.

Jalen switched back to Boyd. "Yes, I got you. Continue past the driveway. Agent Pierce will call and tell you two where to go." Jalen switched over. "Yeah, that was Boyd in the white Explorer." She listened for a moment. "Thanks." She hung up.

"The Frank brothers are at the cabin?" Duarte asked.

"Yeah. Pierce will keep me updated." Jalen typed out some notes.

"How do you do this headquarters shit? Sitting and waiting is hard," I said.

"It's not a task for everyone," Jalen said.

"Yeah. I'm getting that."

Jalen sat straighter. "Okay, here." She tapped her phone and iPad, then handed Duarte the iPad.

Laurel and I tried to see, but we couldn't. We went around the table to look over Duarte's shoulder. It was a photo taken from a telephoto. The quality wasn't ideal, but we could clearly see Curtis Millard hugging Gavin Frank.

"Swipe and you can see two more photos," she said.

Duarte did and we were treated to Millard shaking Travis Frank's hand. He swiped again and we saw them walking around the corner of the cabin.

"Thrilling," I said.

"Can you confirm that it is Curtis Millard?" Jalen asked.

"Oh, yeah. That's definitely him," I said.

"Good." She sent a text. "Now we wait and see what they're doing."

"Nope. Now I watch Velma be smarter than boys." I went back to the couch. Laurel stayed behind to be detectivey. I got through another episode before Laurel called me back to the table.

"We've got more photos coming in," Jalen said.

I looked for her iPad, but it was locked. Laurel touched my forearm and pointed to the midway point on the table. Someone had set up a computer monitor. Jalen typed and photos appeared on the monitor.

"That's much better," Duarte said.

Jalen half smiled. "I know."

The photos were of the Franks loading big dark garbage bags into the bed of the truck. Curtis was helping, but he only carried one or two bags, whereas the brothers looked like they were carrying four or five each. The final photo was the truck piled high enough to obstruct the rear view, but probably not high enough to blow off. Travis was tying it down.

"What the hell are they doing?" I asked.

"Not a damn clue. We need to get inside those bags and find out what they are transporting," Reyes said.

"Great idea. We'll just tell the DEA team to pull them over and ask for a look," Duarte said.

"While we're doing that, we should just ask them what the heck they are up to and have they seen that rascal Henry Brewer," Laurel said.

"You're so smart. I bet they know where he is, the scamp," I said.

We had another forty-five minutes of thumb twiddling before the brothers made a move. They got off the freeway in Folsom and headed south, where there was no town. The plot thickened. They turned onto White Rock Road, which led to even more nothing.

"What is even out there?" Duarte asked. He was zooming in and out on the map and finding nothing. "Cash?"

"How the hell should I know?"

"Didn't you grow up there?"

"No, I grew up outside of Placerville. Closer to where the cabin is than where they currently are."

"Oh. It all looks close together on this map." He turned the map digitally as if that would illuminate something.

"They're in a completely different county."

"Okay, well does anyone know what is out there?" Reyes asked.

Laurel looked over Duarte's shoulder again. "Elk Grove. That's the closest city."

"Yeah, Grant Line is the back road we used to take to get to Elk Grove," I said.

"So you do know where they are headed." Duarte tried to make it sound like an accusation, but fell short.

"We're in Elk Grove. They're probably coming to kill you two," Reyes said.

"Score. No more boring waiting," I said.

"Is there anything else there?" Laurel asked.

"No. Just the dump," I said. They all looked at me. "What?"

"That's clearly where they are going with a truck full of trash bags, you idiot," Duarte said.

"Oh. You think?"

"Yes, obviously," Laurel said. "Jeez, you're lucky you're hot."

Jalen opted to not berate me. She called Malone instead. "Hey. It looks like there's not much out where they are heading aside from the landfill." The excitement in his voice carried over the phone line even though I couldn't understand what he was saying. "I know. This could be a solid break for us."

I looked at Laurel in question. "How is the dump a solid break?"

"Shhh. Just a sec." Laurel waved me down.

"Yeah, I'll see if we can get someone out there." Jalen hung up.

"Do we have a team available that can meet them?" Reyes asked.

"I don't know yet." She punched a different number. "This is Agent Jalen. We need a recovery team out at the Kiefer Landfill ASAP. Yes, I can hold."

"How did she already figure out the name of the landfill?" I asked.

Jalen sighed and turned her laptop so I could see the screen. She'd already googled the location and brought up a map. "Still here," she said. "No, it's got to be now. The suspect's vehicle is ten miles out." She shook her head and listened. "Okay, I'll tell our guys to mark the area." She hung up.

"Are they sending someone?" Reyes asked.

"Nope." She hit another number. "What's your location?" She grinned at the response. "I need you to get back on Fifty and head west. Lights and sirens. Get off at Sunrise. I'll send you the rest of the directions from there. You're heading to the landfill. Make sure you get in line right after Frank's truck." She hung up and started typing again.

"Jalen," Duarte said.

"Wait." She typed some more before triumphantly hitting enter. "Okay. Boyd is on his way."

"Isn't Malone already following them?" Duarte asked.

"Yeah, but he's driving a sedan. It'll be super obvious waiting in line to enter a landfill. Boyd is in a landfill appropriate vehicle."

"You've got him driving to Sunrise to beat them to the dump?" I asked.

"Yep. Boyd was waiting in Folsom in case we needed another vehicle."

"Shit. No wonder you said lights and sirens."

"Is that a stretch?" Reyes asked.

I nodded. "But it might be doable with lights and depending on traffic. Grant Line is usually empty."

"I thought you didn't know the area at all," Duarte said.

"I don't, but I did learn to drive out there. So."

"Whatever." Duarte shook his head.

Seven minutes later, Jalen's phone rang. "Hello?"

We could hear Boyd shouting. "I fucking made it." We couldn't make out anything after that, just mumbling, but it was enough.

"Okay, once you get to the landfill, pull off like you're checking cargo. When you see Malone approaching, slide in. He will continue past."

"Sounds like we got 'em," Reyes said.

"Now will someone tell me why garbage is exciting?" I asked.

"Once garbage has been put curbside or, you know, dropped at a landfill, it's within our purview to search it, gather evidence, whatever our little hearts desire," Laurel said.

"I don't know about you guys, but my heart has no desire to dig through garbage," I said.

"We don't need to. We just need to see if there's meth making paraphernalia present in the bags," Laurel said.

"And there's probably plenty of other evidence to indicate how many people are living there, what they're doing if they're not making meth, that sort of thing," Reyes said.

"Wow. Law enforcement sure is glamorous," I said.

Jalen muted her phone again. "Okay, Boyd is in line to enter the landfill behind the Frank brothers."

"Woo hoo," I said flatly. Reyes and Duarte glared at me.

There was an absolutely thrilling three hours of a DEA team cataloguing the refuse bags from the Frank cabin. Early reporting was sparse, but the palpable excitement over literal garbage was enough to make me grab *Fingersmith* and check out of the conversation. I stretched out on the couch and immersed myself in con artists who were probably not clean either, but at least they were more interesting.

"You doing okay over there?" Duarte called to me.

I gave him a thumbs-up. "One hundred percent less discussion of garbage over here, pal."

"Excellent. You're doing great." He returned the thumbs-up.

Michelson and Malone showed up an hour later. Orr had followed the Franks back to the cabin. He and Boyd were now on standby in Pollock Pines while the DEA continued watching the cabin.

Laurel and I took up our spots at the counter again while everyone else gathered at the table. Michelson sat at the head of the table opposite Jalen. He was in jeans and a navy polo with FBI stenciled on the chest. His badge was hanging from a chain around his neck. Malone was wearing the same thing. They both had clearly showered, which was good considering they had been wading through garbage. But also I was hoping Malone hadn't been tailing criminals while wearing an FBI polo. Seemed a tad irresponsible.

"DEA is still sorting, but we have clear evidence that they are producing methamphetamine at the cabin," Michelson said.

"That's great," Reyes said. "Okay, not great. Great for our case."

Michelson grinned. "Agreed. They found vanilla and grape flavoring as well as powdered caffeine."

"Oh, shit," I said.

Everyone except Michelson looked at me in question. Michelson nodded. "Yeah."

"They're making yaba aren't they?" I asked.

"Bingo." Michelson pointed at me.

"Wait, I've heard of that," Laurel said. "From Southeast Asia. They're sort of like meth pills, right?"

"Well, they are pills with meth in them, but they're more like hallucinogenic ecstasy pills," I said.

"Ooh, that sounds fun," Duarte said.

"Heck, yeah. And also absurdly addictive, cheap to make, and easy to smuggle," I said.

Laurel looked back at me and smiled. "You know so many neat things."

"The DEA boys said they've seen a rise in yaba use in the last few years, especially among younger users."

Reyes locked eyes with me. "That would totally play into your customer base."

"It would, especially the college kids."

"And they're shipping them all over the West Coast."

"DEA seized twelve pounds of purple yaba in Vegas a week ago," Michelson said.

"Three weeks ago, Gavin Frank flew into a small airport outside of Vegas," Jalen said.

Malone flipped through his notes. "Bakersfield PD busted three dealers with purple yaba in the last month."

"He flew to Wasco four weeks ago," she said.

Malone started reading. "Palmdale, Santa Clarita—"

She cut him off. "Yes, all of those."

"Where else?" Michelson asked her.

"San Luis Obispo, Reno, Palm Springs, Fresno, Redding. Everywhere, boss."

Malone and Michelson compared notes. "Purple pills in Reno, Palm Springs, and Redding. Nothing in San Luis. Pink yaba in in Fresno. Could that be related?" Michelson asked.

"You said they had vanilla and grape. Pink might be vanilla flavor," I said.

Malone nodded. "Yep. And if we add pink yaba in, we get Eugene, Oregon."

"Which was six weeks ago," Jalen said.

"Okay. Can we call this in?" Reyes asked. "I'd call this an abundance of evidence."

"Yeah, if they won't give us warrants, then I'm investigating the judge," Duarte said.

Michelson nodded. "Yes. Jalen, send me your report. And dumb it down this time. Malone, type up the list the DEA gave us and match it with Jalen's report. Reyes, Duarte, make sure those two don't die." He pointed at me and Laurel.

"Solid plan, my man," Duarte said.

Laurel turned and squeezed my thigh. "This is going to take some time. I'm going to call Lane. You want in?"

"Heck yeah."

"Come on." She led me to her room. I flopped on the bed. "You know we're actually calling Lane, right?"

"Yeah, of course. But if you want to make out after, we can."

She rolled her eyes. "I'll think about it." She called Lane and put it on speakerphone.

"Hey, big sis."

"Hey, baby girl. You're on speaker with me and Cash." She set the phone on the bed and sat on the edge far away from me.

"Hey, Laney. Happy birthday."

"Yeah, happy birthday," Laurel said.

"Thanks, guys."

"So what's the bar crawl?" I asked.

"She's going on a bar crawl?" Laurel whispered. I waved her away.

"It's not so much a crawl. We're going to Old Sac. We'll probably end up in one of the places on the river."

"That sounds fun," Laurel said.

"Totally. Low key, but also celebratory," I said.

"Exactly. The sisters wanted to get a brew bike, but I managed to talk them out of it."

"Oh. Yeah. That would probably be too much."

"That was my thought. I don't want over-the-top. I wanted simple. And I know you said you'd be my protector, but I'm okay," Lane said.

"Huh?" Laurel said.

"I know. You're going to be fine," I said. "But you can still call me. And you've got Nate's number."

"Yeah. It's all good. I'm excited."

"I'm glad."

"I think I missed something," Laurel said.

"No. Cash just said she would be my backup because I was nervous about going out, but I'm good. It's going to be fun. I've got my sorority sisters. It'll be chill."

"It'll be great," I said.

"If you need a ride, call Lance. He's on duty tonight," Laurel said.

"Hell no. If I need a ride, I'm calling Seth. Lance will torture me."

"He will not."

"Yes, he will. He called an hour ago and said 'If you call me, I'll torture you.'"

I laughed. Laurel shook her head. "He's such a dick," Laurel said.

"Call us in the morning and tell us all about your night, okay?"

"I promise."

"Laurel." Reyes knocked on the open door.

"Just a sec. We're on the phone with Lane," Laurel said.

"Happy birthday, Lane," Reyes called.

"Is that Lucas? Thanks."

"Let me know when you guys are done," Reyes said.

We wrapped up and went back out to organized chaos. "Where's the fire?" I asked.

"At the Frank cabin," Reyes said. "Not literally. Our warrant went through. Jalen is staying here with us, but everyone else is heading up to the arrest party."

Chapter Twenty-eight

It was after midnight when my phone rang. I could hear the buzzing. I checked the nightstand, but the only phone was Laurel's. I followed the sound to my shorts on the floor and dug the phone out of my pocket.

"Hello?"

It was Lane. "Cash?"

"Yeah. What's up? Are you okay?"

"No." She sniffled. Her voice caught. "I'm scared."

"Where are you? What's going on?" I sat on the edge of the bed.

"I had a drink. It was really strong. There might have been something in it."

"Okay. I'm going to come get you." I looked around for my underwear. They had done a disappearing act.

"Am I just being paranoid? Maybe it was just strong."

"Either way I'm coming."

"But what if it's nothing?" she asked.

"It's not. You're uncomfortable. I'm on my way. It's that simple. Do you know where you are?"

"The bathroom." Excellent. Very helpful.

"Good. Do you know which bar you're in?" My boxer briefs were tangled in my shorts, which was why I hadn't been able to see them.

She sniffled again. "No. It's on the river."

"Okay. Is there anyone else in the bathroom?" I shook the shorts with one hand to get my underwear out.

"Yeah. One person."

"Does she seem nice?" I asked.

"Yeah, I guess."

"Can I talk to her for a sec?" I tried to get my boxer briefs on, but they were a little too tight to put on one-handed.

"Okay."

There was a muffled conversation. I took advantage and set the phone down long enough to pull up my underwear. I put the phone back to my ear just as an unfamiliar woman's voice came on the line. "Hello?"

"Hi. This is going to sound weird, but my friend thinks she was slipped something," I said.

"Shit." She sounded both concerned and horrified.

"Can you tell me the name of the bar you're in?"

"Yeah. It's the West End in Old Sac."

Oh, good. I actually knew that one. "Awesome. She's supposed to be there with her sorority sisters. They are Tri Eps. I'm on my way to pick her up, but if you could just see if there are any Tri Eps in the bar and direct them to her?"

"Totally. Of course. Are they wearing their colors or anything?"

"Probably not. It's not an official sorority outing."

"It's cool. I'll find them."

"Thank you so much."

"Sure thing."

There was another muffled conversation and Lane came back on the line. "Cash?"

"Yeah, Laney. I'm on my way okay?"

"Are you sure?"

"Yes, absolutely. The girl from the bathroom is going to find your sorority sisters, but you just stay put okay?"

"Like in the bathroom?"

"Yeah. That's a good place."

"Okay. Hurry."

"I will." I hung up and turned to find Laurel sitting up in bed, starting at me. "Oh, fuck." I jumped.

"Sorry. What's going on?"

I found my T-shirt and pulled it on. "Lane called. She's drunk and scared and thinks she might have been slipped something."

Laurel threw back the sheet. "How are we going to get past Reyes and Duarte? They're not going to want us to leave."

"We can just explain to them. I mean, Henry is in custody by now, right?"

"He's supposed to be, which means according to every movie and also your logic, he's definitely not." She had a point.

"They're never going to let us go."

"Nope."

"Then let's just be real quiet," I whispered.

"Yeah, okay," she whispered back.

We quickly, quietly got dressed. I darted back to my room to get shoes, but didn't put them on. When I got back to Laurel's room, she was holding her shoes and peeking out her door.

"Anyone out there?" I asked.

She shook her head. "Follow me." She tiptoed out. When I'd gotten through, she carefully closed it. We took two steps into the common room before she took my hand and squeezed. She nodded at the couch. Duarte was asleep on it. I nodded. She led me through the common area. She dug in the inside pocket of the blazer Reyes had left hanging by the door. She undid all three locks, which seemed like overkill, but what did I know? Outside, she closed the door. I pulled on my shoes while she locked the door with the keys she'd taken. She stepped into her shoes. We hustled down the stairs to the condo parking circle.

"I'm going to call a Lyft," I said.

"Don't bother." Laurel held up the keys. A car fob was hanging with them.

"You're fucking devious."

"I know." It only took us a minute to find the sedan Reyes was driving. In two minutes we were on the freeway headed back to Sac.

"Do you feel like a juvenile delinquent right now? Sneaking out. Taking Dad's car?" I asked.

"No." She smirked. "I sneaked out plenty as a kid. That was much more scary."

"You did?"

"Yeah. Didn't you?"

"Never," I said.

"Seriously? Cash Braddock, drug dealer, rule breaker extraordinaire, never sneaked out?"

"I didn't have to. Clive trusted me."

"Jesus. I bet you didn't have a curfew either, did you?" She merged onto 50.

"No. I just told him what time I'd be home. If it was unreasonably late, he'd ask why. I'd tell him."

Laurel shook her head. "My father would have lost his shit if I got home one minute after midnight. And, yes, before you ask, the boys had a one a.m. curfew."

"And Lane had midnight?" We got onto I-5.

"Of course."

"But not because of sexism?"

"No way. Definitely not. It was because they tried out the later curfew and it just didn't work. So they went back to the original."

"Right. Yeah. Logical."

She got off the freeway. We were on the main stretch of Old Sac. "Which bar?"

"She's at West End." I pointed. "Two blocks down. I don't see any parking though."

"Fuck it. We've got cop plates."

"You're so hot when you break rules."

"I know." She pulled up out front of the bar, yanked the brake up, and hopped out.

We stormed into the bar, ready to punch anyone who was hurting baby girl, and found Lane at a table with her sorority sisters. They were making her drink water. One of them was playing with her hair.

"Laney," I called.

She looked up. "Cash! You came." She saw Laurel behind me. "And you brought big sis."

"Yeah, of course." I leaned over and hugged her. Then I stepped aside so Laurel could hug her too. The sorority girls on either side of Lane scooted over a seat so we could sit. "How are you feeling?"

"Okay. Embarrassed. I might have overreacted."

I looked around the table. There were five women with Lane. The one sitting next to Laurel spoke up. "She didn't overreact. She hasn't had alcohol in months and she had a strong margarita. It hit her hard." She leaned over to squeeze Lane's hand. "There's nothing to be embarrassed about." The other women echoed her.

Lane nodded. "Thanks, guys."

"I take it you've been hydrating properly?" Laurel nodded at the nearly empty water glass in front of Lane.

"Yeah." Lane drew a line in the condensation.

"She's probably done drinking for the night, but I think some food might help," the woman directly across from Lane said.

"There's no better drunk food than Pieces," I said.

Three of the sorority sisters looked up in excitement. "Oh, we're so going."

"We need Pieces," one of the brunettes said.

"It's the only option." The other brunette who looked identical to the first nodded.

The woman next to Lane asked, "Is that the place you always talk about, Dakota?"

"Yeah. We have to go," Dakota said.

I squeezed Lane's shoulder. "What do you say? Are you up for pizza?"

She smiled. "Yeah. That sounds good."

Laurel looked around the table and counted. "I don't think everyone will fit in the car we took. We'll need to call a Lyft."

The woman next to Dakota raised her hand off the table. "It's cool. I'm DD."

"Great. Let's go."

We ended up with Lane and Emmy in the stolen cop sedan. Savannah, the DD, took Dakota, Karina, and Briana. I tried very hard to tell the brunettes Karina and Briana apart, but quickly decided it was an impossible task. Karina was wearing a teal top. Briana was wearing yellow. That was the only difference.

Laurel drove down Capitol and missed the turn on 3rd to get to N.

"Dude, where are you going? You're going to hit the Capitol."

"No, I'm not. Oh, shit. Yes, I am."

"That was quite the roller coaster." I laughed. "It was quite enjoyable."

"Holy shit. Oh, fuck. Jesus fucking Christ," Lane said.

I spun around. "What?"

"You two are back together." She squealed. "Why didn't you tell me? Happy birthday to me."

I shook my head and tried to look sad. "No, Lane. Didn't Laurel tell you? She's engaged to someone else."

"What? No. Who? Wait." She smacked my arm. "Jerk."

"You know better than to believe a thing she says, Lane," Laurel said.

"Except we are back together, yeah. That you can believe."

"Wait, so which of you is Lane's sister?" Emmy asked.

"That would be me." Laurel raised her hand.

"But you're the roommate?" Emmy asked.

"Yeah," I said.

"But you two are together?"

"They are very complicated," Lane said.

I was going to deny it, but she wasn't wrong. We were a little complicated.

"Cute," Emmy said. She was very chill. None of Lane's squealing.

Laurel found legal parking in front of Pieces Pizza. Savannah paralleled three spots behind us. I left Laurel to move two outdoor tables together and went inside to order for us and Lane. The sorority girls lined up with me. Those who hadn't been to Pieces looked around. It was a janky hole-in-the-wall. The furniture inside was all mismatched patio tables and chairs. It hadn't been updated in thirty years and it hadn't started with any sort of design. It was perfect.

After some debate, it was decided two pitchers of beer were needed. I was gearing up to order when Dakota took charge. It was a frankly sexy monologue.

"Two pesto pepperoni. One veggie with garlic. Two vegan, one with garlic, one without. Two pesto, feta, sun-dried tomato. One with olives added, but no garlic on either. And a mushroom and olive. An order of pesto sticks, two sides of ranch. Two pitchers of Arrogant Bastard and eight glasses, thanks."

The chick behind the counter nodded and nodded. Her white girl dreads swung back and forth. I was reasonably certain it was a requirement that at any given time, at least one employee working had to have dreads. "Righteous. Extra garlic on the pesto pepperoni?"

"Nope."

"And what about the mushroom and olive?"

"Nope."

"Got you. Anything else?"

Dakota looked down the line in question. Emmy and I shook our heads. Savannah and Briana were laughing at something and not paying attention. Karina had gone back outside to sit with Lane and Laurel. "No. I think we're good."

The chick called the order out to the guy on register. He checked IDs and filled two pitchers of Arrogant Bastard.

Dakota poured a cup of water. "Savannah, bring this to Lane."

"Sure." Savannah went outside with Lane's water.

Dakota started to collect cash from the other girls, but I stopped her. "I got this."

"Don't be silly. This is stupid expensive pizza."

"Seriously. Consider it a thank you for taking care of Lane."

She rolled her eyes. "We'd do that anyway."

"I know." I handed the register guy some cash and tucked a couple more bills in the tip jar filled with water.

"Thanks. You're sweet."

I shrugged. I wasn't. We carted the beer and glasses and stacks of napkins outside. Lane and Laurel were laughing at something Savannah said. Karina and Emmy had gotten up to inspect the sweater knitted onto the tree behind Laurel. Dakota and I poured a few beers. Laurel took one. Lane held up her thumb and index finger to indicate a small glass. I poured slowly.

"Tell me when," I said.

About halfway up she said, "Stop."

Dakota held up her glass and tapped it against Lane's. "Happy birthday, sweetie. We love you." The other women grabbed glasses and echoed the sentiment.

"You guys are the best." Lane turned to me and Laurel. "And you two. Is it safe for you to be out here?"

"It's fine," Laurel said.

"Wait. Why wouldn't it be safe?" Emmy asked.

I rolled my eyes. Laurel sighed.

"They're supposed to be in an FBI safe house right now," Lane said.

There was a chorus of exclamations ranging from "What?" to "What the fuck?" to "Huh?"

Laurel gave them a shortened version that culminated in the arrest teams leaving a few hours before.

"Is that why you have a black eye?" Dakota asked her.

"Two actually. But it's pretty dark so you probably can't see them," Laurel said. Which just made them all demand that she step into the light coming from the Pieces window.

"Oh, wow," Karina said.

"Is that a bruise across your throat too?" Briana asked.

Laurel shrugged. She was clearly not equipped for a sorority girl interrogation. I found her discomfort hilarious.

"She was stabbed too. You guys should see that," I said.

"I hate you," Laurel said.

"You wound me." I grinned.

"Well, let us see," Karina said.

Laurel sighed and pulled aside her shirt collar. A few of the Steri-Strips I'd put on had come off, but most were still there. The wound was an angry pink line. The dots from the stitches were faint, but the pattern was visible.

There were gasps of fascination and horror. Karina and Savannah leaned close to look. Briana averted her gaze. Emmy was indifferent.

"Pizza's up," Dakota said.

"Thank God." Laurel stood. She, Dakota, and Emmy went inside to retrieve it.

When they came back out, Dakota directed them to each of us. "The birthday girl is mushroom and olive. Me and Savannah are the pepperoni. Emmy, you have the veggie. The sun-dried tomato with olives is Cash. The one without is Laurel. And the twins have the ones without cheese. You two will have to figure out which one has extra garlic."

"So you two are actually twins?" I asked.

Karina and Briana nodded. "Yeah, that's why we're identical," Karina said.

"Right."

"You couldn't tell?" Savannah asked.

"Sometimes I can't tell straight girls apart." I shrugged. "I thought it was just that."

"She's not joking. It's an actual problem she has," Lane said.

They all found that delightful. Very little is worse than a bunch of sorority girls laughing at you because you can't tell them apart.

CHAPTER TWENTY-NINE

We poured into the house around three in the morning. I didn't have my keys, but luckily Lane had hers. It took a few attempts to get the door unlocked because we had ordered another pitcher of Arrogant Bastard. And then we ordered another. The cop sedan and Savannah's car were back on 21st Street awaiting tickets. And I had a line of sorority girls who needed beds.

Lane went around opening windows. The air inside was stagnant from being closed up for a week. I kept looking for Nickels before remembering she was with Andy and Robin. Two minutes later, I'd look for her again and remember again.

I pulled out blankets and pillows, which was probably useless considering how warm it was. Savannah called dibs on the living room couch. Emmy, Dakota, and Lane all insisted they could fit in Lane's bed. Laurel and I knew Lane starfished when she slept, but that was an issue for them to work out. The twins piled the remaining blankets on the living room rug and looked like happy campers.

"Did you have a good birthday, lil Lane?" Dakota asked.

"The best. You guys are the best." She sighed at how much they were the best. "I need ice cream."

Dakota groaned. "Oh my God. We do need ice cream."

"Cash, is there ice cream?" Lane asked.

"Laney, you know damn well there's no ice cream."

Lane sighed. "Okay."

"I'll go raid Robin's freezer. She will have ice cream," I said.

That earned me a cheer from the sorority girls. Laurel shook her head at me and laughed.

"Cash is the best dad," Savannah said to Lane.

"Oh, I know," Lane said.

"Laurel, you're in charge of bowls and spoons. And I've got a jar of that gross dark chocolate sauce Lane likes in the pantry."

Laurel saluted me. "I won't let you down."

I grabbed Robin's keys and let myself in the back door. I flipped on the kitchen light and opened the freezer. Six varieties of ice cream. The woman had a serious problem. I grabbed a canvas grocery bag and loaded up. I was so going to owe her. I turned the light back off. I was still a little drunk so I almost tripped twice on my way to the back door. I let myself back out onto the deck. I was locking the back door when I heard him.

"That's right. Keep it quiet and slow," Henry said.

"What do you want, Henry?" I asked.

"I want you to set down the bag, put your hands on your head nice and easy. No sudden movements. No loud sounds. If you make loud sounds, I'll shoot you, then go in and shoot your girlfriend and her sister and all her little friends."

"I'm not sure you're a killer, man." I turned to look at him.

He was sitting in one of the Adirondacks on Robin's porch. His face and torso were in shadow, but his hands and gun were in a perfect streak of moonlight. He'd put on the neon blue handgrips. They looked cool. Also terrifying. "I didn't say I'd kill them. There are lots of places to shoot someone without killing them."

"Okay." I set the bag down. "I'd like to avoid that." I was sobering up real quick.

"I know you would. They don't need to get hurt. Me and you are going to take a walk. We're going through the gate at the back of your fence." Dammit. Laurel was right. I should have nailed it shut.

"Sounds fun."

"Start walking. Nice and easy."

We walked through the yard. It was difficult to keep my balance with my hands on my head. My sobriety was short lived. Trees from the neighbor's yard blocked most of the moonlight, which made it difficult to see. It would take Laurel five minutes tops to realize I was gone. I could walk slow, but not that slow. I very much didn't want to let Henry take me to a different location. I read books. I watched movies. It was never good to let them take you to a second location.

The back gate led to a narrow alley. Safety lights were installed at random intervals, but most of them were to my right. I opted to sprint to the left. I took two steps before I fell. Every muscle seized. When I could move again, I took a deep breath, thankful for the grit under my cheek. Any sensation other than what I'd been feeling. It took me a minute to realize he'd tased me.

Henry knelt next to me. "Hold still or this is going to hurt more than it needs to."

He spread his hand on my right shoulder and pulled the prong out. It wasn't bad. When he moved his hand to my ribs on the left, I decided to make another move. He yanked the second barb. I rolled and slugged him. He fell away from me and I got to my knees before he hit me with a face full of pepper spray. I got to my feet and took three steps before I went down again.

It burned everywhere. I couldn't see and honestly didn't care. My eyeballs were on fire. I blinked and blinked and each time it just made it worse, but I couldn't stop. I gasped for air and each breath was torture.

Henry was next to me again. I could sense him even though I couldn't open my eyes. "Take your time with it. Just breathe through the pain. I know it hurts." My nose dripped, which mixed with my drool. I went to swipe at my face, but he stopped me. "I wouldn't recommend touching your face. It will make it worse."

I hacked and spit instead. I fucking hated him. "Fucking asshole." Saying that much caused me to start wheezing and coughing.

"Yeah. I know. I can make it hurt less, but you need to stand up and walk with me."

"Fuck you. I'm not going anywhere with you." Jesus fucking Christ, it hurt. I focused on breathing, but there was so much fluid in my nose and mouth it felt like I couldn't get air into my lungs.

"Okay, that's your call. But I'll just spray you again and stuff you in my car. Either way you're coming with me. It's up to you how that happens."

I spit at him. I couldn't open my eyes, but I could hear him well enough to hit him.

"Cunt." He backhanded me.

I tasted blood, which was a nice break from the heat of the pepper spray on my lips, but then he sprayed me in the face again. I dropped to the ground, blind and in overwhelming, blistering pain again. I knew from the first time that the initial shock would wear off, but breathing through it was a bitch. I tried to tell him I was going to kill him, but all that came out was hacking and mucous.

He yanked me to my feet and shoved me in the back seat of a car. I kicked out so he couldn't close the door. He grabbed my feet, hauled me out of the car, and punched me in the face. I heard a strip of duct tape being pulled off a roll. He gripped my ankle so I kicked out again. He kicked me in the ribs. I curled up and he was able to tape my ankles together. Another kick in the stomach and he got my hands together behind my back.

"You are making this way harder than it needs to be. I was going to be nice and wash your eyes out. I was going to let you drive. But no, you just had to be difficult."

"Yeah, I know." I spit some blood and mucous onto the pavement. "I'm always such an asshole when people try to kidnap me."

"I tried to be your friend, bro. You're the one who fucked me over, remember?" He slugged me in the face again. When I was reeling, he hauled me up and shoved me in the car. He slammed the door. Yep, I was fucked.

He got in the driver's seat and drove out of the alley at a nice sedate pace. I tried kicking the back window.

"Knock yourself out. The windows are tinted and it's after three in the morning. No one is going to help you."

"It doesn't matter." I spit a stream of mucous onto the floorboard. "Laurel is realizing I'm not coming back with ice cream. She'll call her FBI buddies. It won't take them long to find you."

Henry laughed and turned the radio to a deafening level. The noise was annoying, but in a way it was pleasant to have a different sense assaulted. After a few minutes, I was able to get my eyes open. My vision was smudged like Vaseline on a camera lens. I couldn't see much out the windows since I was lying across the back seat, but I tried to track where we were going. I gave up pretty quickly. Everything was a light-smeared blur. With my hands behind me I couldn't get enough leverage to sit up. I tried to get the duct tape off, but twisting and pulling wasn't enough and I didn't have the brute strength to tear it. The combination of booze and pepper spray was also a bit debilitating.

I could feel the shift in speed when we got on the freeway. I rolled to my side to take the pressure off my hands. It also helped with breathing. I had a steady stream running from my nose and eyes. It was pretty disgusting. When I readjusted, I realized it was my phone digging into my thigh, not the seat belt like I originally thought. My elation quickly died. It hadn't vibrated, which suggested Laurel hadn't noticed I was gone. She should have. Something was off. Maybe the battery had died. Even if it wasn't dead, and Laurel did call, Henry would hear the vibrations and probably toss it out the window.

We stayed on the freeway for at least forty-five minutes, maybe an hour. My ability to judge time wasn't great when I was unable to see anything. I was tired, but too afraid to sleep. By the time we got off the freeway, my vision had sort of cleared. I could see towering evergreens. We were back in the foothills. Great. We turned and the road shifted to gravel. We went over a rickety bridge. I wondered if he could possibly be dumb enough to take me to his grandmother's house. That hope quickly faded. The road we were on was much longer than Grandma Brewer's driveway.

He finally stopped driving. He took the keys out and turned around. "How you feeling, bro?"

"Homicidal."

He grinned. "I'm going to take you inside now. Are you going to make it easy or hard?"

"I don't know. Guess it'll be a fun surprise for you."

"Yeah, I thought that might be the case." He got out and came around to the side of the car my head was on. He opened the door. Before I could do anything, he punched me. I saw stars again and he pulled a hood over my head. He grabbed under my armpits and hauled me out of the car.

I started screaming the second I was out of the car. Henry laughed and dragged me. I squirmed and fought, but he was too strong. The ground under my heels was rough and uneven, then it shifted to something smooth like concrete. He hoisted me into a chair.

"Keep screaming if you want. No one can hear and you're just going to wear yourself out," he said from behind me. I stopped screaming.

I heard duct tape again. I threw myself off the chair and wriggled about six inches. Very effective. I heard a loud crackle, then felt like I was kicked in the chest. This pain was different than before. It was more focused pressure. Brighter, sharper. When he stopped, I felt winded. He put me back in the chair and held me in place with his hip as he taped me to it.

He cut the tape on my ankles and I immediately tried to kick him. He just laughed and dodged it. I listened and when he came close again, I kicked him.

"You are a tricky bitch, aren't you?" he said.

And then he shocked me again. The noise made me tense up a second before he touched me and then the pain started to radiate. When he stopped, I didn't have the energy to kick him again. He secured both my ankles to the chair. He pulled the hood off my head. We were in an old shed of some sort. It was about fifteen feet by twenty. Shop lights were hung from the low ceiling. He tossed the stun gun onto a workbench.

"What's your plan here? You've got a couple hours at the most before the feds track us down," I said.

He smirked. "You mean because they've been so successful with that for the past year?"

"You're such a dipshit, man. You only made it this long without getting caught because of Travis Frank. He's sitting in federal lockup right now. You're fucked. Can't copy Deputy Frank's answers anymore."

"Shut the fuck up." He pointed at me with his canister of pepper spray.

"Oh, did I hit a nerve? Who's going to be the brains and let you pretend to be in charge?"

"I'm in fucking charge," he shouted.

"Are you? Curtis cooks the meth and makes the yaba. Gavin flies it everywhere. Travis protects all of you. What do you do? Just get all your friends arrested."

"It was my fucking plan. Curtis would still be a backwoods tweaker if it wasn't for me. I saved him from crackhead obscurity."

"And now he's going to prison. I'm sure the thank you card is in the mail."

He took a step toward me, then stopped himself. "Yeah, fine. I'm the asshole who gets my friends arrested. But at least I do shit, okay? You would have gotten old selling Xanax to suburban housewives. What kind of life is that?"

"Better than this." I looked at our dank surroundings pointedly. "Is this your grand hideout? Good job. Much better than obscurity."

"This is part of the plan." He stepped close and wrestled my phone out of my pocket. "Oh good. It's still on. Better plug it in though. Only seventeen percent. Wouldn't want it to die before they track us." He brought the phone to a tool bench on the far wall and plugged it in.

I realized with horror that he hadn't missed the cell phone. The guy was dumb, but I should have known he wasn't that dumb.

CHAPTER THIRTY

What the fuck are you doing?" I struggled against the duct tape, but there was a lot.

"I was going to run away to Mexico." He pointed at me. "Remember? I told you that was my plan. But then some dick arrested my pilot. So now I'm going to kill all those assholes. I might not make it to Mexico, but at least I'll be vindicated."

"'Kill all those assholes' isn't a plan, dickwad."

"Seems like an excellent plan to me." He opened a series of laptops on the workbench. They all showed video feed. It looked like we were at Grandma Brewer's place after all. We were just far from her house.

"You're using your grandmother's house for a bloody standoff?"

"Nana is still in county jail, thanks to you. And she will think this is a perfect use of her property." He went to the door to my right. It was a couple of feet behind me. Presumably, it was the door we'd entered through because I didn't see any others. "I'll be right back. Don't go anywhere, now." His laughter carried even after the door shut behind him.

I looked around the space. It wasn't particularly illuminating. The four laptops each showed four videos. I saw the front and back porches on one. They were paired with video from inside the house showing the front and back entrances. Another showed the entrance to the driveway. There was also a strip of road, presumably leading to the house. Two others showed sections of the fire road Laurel had parked on. I could see the front and back of the shed we were in. The wide-angle lens on the front showed the car we'd arrived in. Henry was pulling duffel bags of gear out of the trunk, which explained why he hadn't put me back there. The rest showed sections of forest.

The laptops were all plugged into a single power strip that was doing overtime. My phone was also plugged into it. So were the three shop lights overhead. And I couldn't see very well, but I was pretty sure there was another stun gun still plugged in. Henry was not paying attention to fire safety.

There was a hose spigot on the wall to my left. I knew it wouldn't help the burning in my eyes and nose, but I still wanted to dunk my head. I twisted to look behind me. It was all built-in shelving that looked like it had been there since Grandpa Brewer built the place. Old camping gear and yard equipment was shoved onto the shelves haphazardly. On my right was a rickety table. New camping gear was stacked underneath it. I saw a propane tank and a sleeping bag. Above the table was a narrow shelf with a tiny backpacking stove and a few cans of food. I wondered how many nights Henry had spent out here reveling in his self-righteous importance, surrounded by an unforgiving forest. I hoped it had been fucking cold.

He came back in and stacked the duffels on a table. Then he went back out and brought in more bags of equipment. I watched and looked for a way out, but there wasn't much for me to work with. I twisted my wrists, but there was still no hope of tearing the duct tape.

Henry started unpacking his bags. He started with the wearable stuff. A tactical belt with a thigh holster. A Kevlar vest. A helmet with webbing. He attached night vision goggles to the helmet. Then he started putting on his gear. He was methodical. After every piece, he checked the cameras for any sign of movement. He didn't know when they were going to come for me. I really didn't want him to be ready when they did.

"Hey, man, I see you're prepping for like a war or whatever, but I'm dying over here from the pepper spray." I knew damn well he had something to alleviate the pain. He was just waiting for a moment to be nice to me.

"Maybe you shouldn't have been such a dick when I was trying to get you in the car."

"Yeah, I've made some short-sighted decisions." Mostly just allowing him to be part of my life, but also getting pepper sprayed.

"I do have a bottle of baby soap." He shrugged. "That's what we used at the academy. I guess I could wash your eyes out."

"Please." I could play nice. Especially if it resulted in slowing his preparations. Getting the pepper spray out of my eyes was a bonus. A big bonus.

He pulled a sports water bottle from one of the bags on the ground. "This is a solution of water and mild soap." He held up the bottle. "I'm going to douse your eyes. Tilt your head back and to the side."

I did as he instructed and he gently held my eye open with his thumb. He squirted soapy water into the corner of my eye. I blinked and blinked, but the relief was almost immediate. He tilted my head the other direction and repeated the maneuver on my other eye. When he was done, he squirted the solution on my forehead, nose, cheeks, lips, ears. It ran and dripped down my face, but it was cool and soothing. He set the soap bottle down and pulled a couple of plastic water bottles out of the same bag. He cracked one open and poured the contents on my face. It gathered in my ears and hair. I shook my head. Water flew off me. I took a full, deep breath. It was exquisite. The collar and shoulders of my T-shirt were damp with a mixture of capsicum and soap and water. My skin itched, but it was an afterthought compared to the residual burning on my face.

"That feels a hell of a lot better. Thanks," I said.

"You're welcome."

"Any chance you've got drinking water?"

He huffed. "Yeah. Just a sec." He opened a second bottle and carefully poured some in my mouth. I drank greedily.

"More."

"If I give you more, you'll have to pee," he said.

"I already have to pee. I went out with a bunch of sorority girls tonight. They could drink most frat boys under the table."

"That sucks for you, man." He opened his own bottle and chugged the entire thing. "I got to stay hydrated. You know, so I can kill all your friends."

"Good luck with that." I'd never been so happy my default was sarcasm. I was sure he wanted to see fear and I really didn't want to indulge him. But also I was terrified. For me, for whomever was going to march into Henry's killing forest. I knew Michelson and Reyes wouldn't allow Laurel to join them, but I had little faith that they could actually stop her.

He went back to unloading equipment. He had a silly number of shotguns and an even sillier amount of bullets.

I saw movement on the fire road first. It was a dark SVU driving without headlights. Henry didn't see it right away. I wasn't going to tell him. They continued driving until they were out of the frame.

Henry put the neon handled Glock into his thigh holster. He put a few extra magazines in pouches on his belt. The rest of the magazines he laid out on the table. He clipped a knife sheath onto the belt. The unused stun gun got clipped next to that. He reached over the laptops to plug in the stun gun he'd used on me, which was when he missed the second dark SUV on the fire road. Pepper spray, which was officially the worse pain I'd ever experienced, went on the other side of his belt.

"So about that bathroom trip," I said.

"Piss yourself if you have to go that bad." He clipped another gun onto the belt. He was getting a little excessive with the guns.

"Come on, dude. It will take two minutes."

Two SUVs drove by the road camera. This time, Henry saw them. He whistled. "Showtime." He put on a Kevlar vest and adjusted the Velcro straps. The magazines he'd laid out got tucked into the pockets on the front of the vest. He grabbed one of the shotguns and slung it over his shoulder. The strap was loaded with additional shells. The two SUVs turned up the driveway. Henry put on the helmet and clipped the chin strap in place.

"Don't worry, man. I'll be back," he said.

"Asshole."

He yanked the extension cord for the shop lights. Everything went dark. My eyes adjusted to the dim light from the laptop videos. I saw a sliver of moonlight before the door closed and the lock clicked. On the surveillance video, I could see him running toward the house. He'd flipped down the night vision goggles. I took a small amount of comfort in the knowledge that he looked like an idiot. But then I heard the first shotgun blast. And another. And another. It kind of negated the comfort.

The video feed from the front porch showed two SUVs parked in the turnaround. Dudes dressed much like Henry were crouched behind open car doors. One body in tactical gear was already on the ground. I saw movement on one of the forest feeds, but it disappeared so quickly I wondered if I'd imagined it. Two shotgun blasts later, I saw it again. I didn't identify the slight shape as Laurel until she was outside the shed, trying to pick the lock. It took her thirty seconds. No time and an eternity. As soon as the door opened, an alarm went off. Henry looked up at the sound. He ran around the side of the house back toward the shed.

"Cash?" Laurel yelled over the alarm.

"Get out of here. He's coming back," I yelled.

She slid to her knees in front of me. "Are you okay?" She had a mini Maglite. She shined it on my face, then arms and legs. "Fuck." She pulled out a knife and moved behind me.

"Seriously. He's running back here right now. He'll be here in thirty seconds," I said.

"Let him. I'll shoot the motherfucker." She cut through the tape holding me to the chair and started sawing at the tape around my wrists.

"He's wearing Kevlar and he's armed to the teeth," I said.

"Shit."

"Put the knife in my hand and get out."

"Dammit, Cash." She pressed the knife hilt into my hand.

He appeared on the shed video. "It's too late. You have to hide," I said.

She stood and shone the light around the shed. "Where?"

"The duffel bags in the corner. Get behind them."

She dove and killed the light. The shed door opened.

"Hey, Cash, are you making friends?" Henry asked. He hit a fob and the alarm cut.

"Yeah, the sweetest little squirrel came in here." I angled the knife and was able to cut through another chunk of tape. "I named it Duke."

"That's strange. Because I don't think Duke the squirrel would set off my alarm." He moved around me, checking under shelves and in the darkened corners.

"Duke's a talented squirrel." I cut through the last of it. I leaned forward slightly to test and was able to move. Henry came around my left side, still studying the shelving built into the wall. "Oh look, there Duke goes, running out the door."

"Fucking cunt." He spun and dashed for the door. He left it open and I could see him studying the surrounding area.

I took the risk and leaned forward to cut my ankles free. The thick strip of tape stayed attached to my chest. The ends flapped comically as I sliced through the tape at my ankle. I got through one, but then he spun and stomped back to the shed.

"Where the fuck is she?" he shouted at me.

"Okay, I don't think I told you Duke's pronouns, but he actually uses he pronouns, not she."

He backhanded me again, then turned and resumed his search. He squatted and looked under the workbench. He was getting way too close to Laurel's arguably terrible hiding spot. I quietly leaned forward and cut the last piece of tape. Henry turned. I stood and launched myself at him. The chair was still partially attached to the tape on my leg. It went flying and slammed into the wall.

"How the fuck—" he started to say and then I jammed the knife up under his vest.

His gut was firm and soft. Warm blood dripped onto my hand. I gripped the knife hilt hard and twisted. Blood started to pour. I yanked the knife out, but after a couple of inches, my hand slipped and the blade stayed behind. I didn't realize Laurel had stood until she was behind me.

"You. You fucking bitch," Henry sputtered. He fell to his knees. He reached down. I thought he was trying to put pressure on the wound, but then I realized he was going for the Glock.

I grabbed Laurel and ran for the door. "Gun."

We barely cleared the doorway before it was splintered with bullets. Laurel yanked me behind Henry's car. We crouched, breathing hard, listening for a sign that he was following us.

"We can make it to those trees." Laurel pointed at a copse of small pines. They were across fifteen feet of bare ground. She started to stand.

I pulled her back. "Even if he's not following us, there are a fuckload of feds wandering around here, armed to the teeth, looking to shoot anyone running around."

"It's okay. I've got a plan."

"Last time you had a plan, you got shot."

"Technically, I got shot before the plan."

"Don't technically me."

"Do you trust me?"

I studied her face. The moonlight caught the edge of her hair, making it glow. She had half a grin like this was the most entertainment she'd had in a long time. I slid my hand behind her neck and kissed her. "Fuck yeah."

"Okay, stay in front of me." She shoved me to start running for the trees. I sprinted, her footfalls immediately behind me. I threw myself behind the first tree and she slammed into me. The tree wasn't much wider than we were. My back was to the tree. Thick scales of bark pressed against my shoulder blades. Laurel leaned against the length of me. She angled her head to watch the shed door. She had her gun out, but it was pointed at the ground.

"What now?" I asked.

"My phone is in my front pocket. Text Duarte. Tell him we're a quarter mile north of the house, coming in hot." She said it without a trace of irony and I found it stupid sexy.

I dug into her front pockets. She'd changed to dark thick pants. They were baggy—for her, at least—and felt like they could withstand battle. Did everyone except for me get the tactical outfit memo? I found her phone and unlocked it. I typed a message to Duarte.

This is Cash with L. 1/4 mile north of house. Coming in hott. I figured he would appreciate the extra "T" to really make the text come alive. I hit send as Laurel raised the gun and fired off two rounds.

"Time to move." She grabbed the shoulder of my T-shirt and hauled me with her to the next tree five feet away.

This tree was bigger. She knelt and studied the ground. She picked up a rock about the size of her fist. Then a second that was a little smaller.

"What are you doing?" I whispered.

She stood and grinned impishly. "Evening the playing field." She tossed one of the rocks six inches and caught it. "Head for that tree." She pointed to one about seven feet away. "I'll cover you."

I nodded. "Now?"

"Now."

I sprinted for the next cover. Henry fired off another shotgun round. Laurel fired back. I glanced back. He was moving slowly, but advancing steadily toward us. Laurel holstered her weapon. She took a breath and launched one of the rocks high and over his head. It arced and landed on the metal roof of the shed, then rolled and smacked the hood of Henry's car. He spun and fired into the side of the shed. She stepped out where she was fully exposed. He turned and she nailed him in the night vision goggles with the second rock. He roared and threw off his broken goggles. Laurel sprinted toward me.

"Come on." She grabbed my hand and yanked me after her. We wove through trees, leapt over dry underbrush, skirted brambles. We'd probably run a couple hundred yards when buckshot blew apart a young tree five feet to my left. "Fuck." She spun and dragged me behind another tree. She ducked and ran a few more feet. I followed suit.

"I'm going to get you, bitches. You may as well stop running," Henry yelled.

Laurel straightened with her back against a tree. "We're almost to the driveway. The guys won't enter the trees until we're out. You run through there." She pointed to our right. "After twenty feet, hang a sharp left. Don't stop until you're out of the trees."

"I think you mean out of the woods."

"Are you really doing this right now?"

I shrugged and grinned. "If we lose frivolity, the patriarchy wins."

"Run, Cash."

"Wait. Where are you going to go?"

"I'm going to run straight through here." She nodded perpendicular to where we were headed. Not toward the driveway of safety. "I'll see if I can tag him before I turn back to where the guys are."

"No."

"What?"

"We're not splitting up. We're in this together. You're not getting rid of me."

Another small tree splintered apart. He was getting closer and rapidly figuring out where we were.

"Come on, Cash. This is what I do."

"Too bad. I follow you. That's what I do."

She sighed. "Fine." She pointed a little to the left of where we were. "That's where we're going. I'm still going to try to hit him. When my magazine is spent, we run."

"Cool."

She dropped low and spun out from our cover. She methodically unloaded the remainder of her ammo in the direction we'd last seen him.

"Go." Laurel took off in the direction she'd told me. As we ran, she ejected her magazine and slammed another into her gun without looking. "Stay ahead of me."

It was difficult. She was a hell of a lot faster than I was. And I still couldn't breathe properly. We reached the driveway. The unobstructed moonlight was shockingly bright. Three guys in tactile gear sprinted out to cover us. One of them dropped to his knees in concert with a shotgun blast. Laurel tackled me and we landed behind one of the SUVs. We lay there breathing hard.

"Get up. Get up." Someone grabbed my bicep and hauled me to my feet. It was Malone. He shoved us around the corner of the vehicle. I was absolutely over people yanking me around. Except for Laurel. She could manhandle me all she wanted.

Michelson was on the far side of the SUV.

"You two okay?" he asked.

"Yeah," Laurel said. He looked at me and I nodded.

"How's Brewer?"

"He's got a knife in his gut and I think I winged his right arm. He's wearing a helmet and a Kevlar vest," she said.

Michelson nodded and relayed the information over his walkie. A shotgun round hit the other side of the SUV and shattered two windows. We all ducked instinctively. Michelson popped back up to look through a night scope.

"How is he still going?" Laurel asked. It didn't seem like she was directing it to anyone in particular, but the feds were a little busy.

"Pure white male rage, I think. Potent shit," I said.

Another round hit and we ducked again. Laurel looked at me incredulously. "Seriously. Even now?"

"If I see a misandrist opening, I've got to take it." I shrugged. "Plus, that dickwad pepper sprayed me. Twice. Have you ever been pepper sprayed?"

"Yes," Laurel said.

Michelson lowered his night vision goggles. "Yep. Hurts like hell."

"Why have you both been pepper sprayed?" I asked.

"Part of training for law enforcement. That way if it gets on you in the line of duty, then you will be better prepared." Laurel took my chin and tilted my face up to look at it in the moonlight. "But we wash it off five minutes later. You didn't."

"No, he was more focused on the kidnapping."

The gunfire ramped up and then a call went over the radio. "Got him. Suspect is down."

I started to stand, but Laurel pulled me back down. "Wait a second."

Michelson started talking into his radio. After a second, he tapped Laurel's shoulder. "Okay. We're clear."

Laurel led me away from the SUV surrounded by glass to the other SUV with only a little broken glass. She opened the back and directed me to sit. She dug through some of the gear until she found a first aid kit.

"There should be wipes in here that neutralize the pepper spray. Just give me a sec."

"It's okay. He washed my eyes and face with soap and water. It helped a lot."

"He did?"

"I saw you guys moving in so I bitched to distract him. He did it to shut me up."

"Nice." She grinned. "Are you hurt anywhere else?"

"Everywhere, I think. It all hurts."

"You're such a baby."

"I know." I stretched my hands. Henry's blood had dried. It looked black in the moonlight. "Can I wash my hands?"

"Probably not yet. You're evidence."

"Oh, good. I always wanted to be important. That sounds very important."

"You're important to me."

I pulled her close and kissed her. "Yeah, I noticed."

She smiled and kissed me again. "Okay, stay here. I'm going to get clearance for us to leave."

Chapter Thirty-one

When we walked in, the house was much louder than expected.

"No, you little shit. That's not cool," Lance shouted.

"Or is it?" Lane asked.

"No, Lane. It's very much not cool," Seth said.

Laurel looked at me. "So, you've still got *Mario Kart* hooked up?"

"You know it's the only game I own."

"But why would you only own one game?"

"It's the most perfect game. Why mess with perfection?"

"Right."

"Cash? Laurel? Is that you?" Lane called.

We rounded the corner as Lane vaulted off the couch. She stopped suddenly when she saw me. "What the fuck?"

"The blood isn't mine. Mostly." I put my hands up.

"What's wrong with your face?"

Lance and Seth came around the couch. "That's got to hurt, man," Lance said.

"She got pepper sprayed," Laurel told Lane.

"Are you okay?" Lane asked.

"Yeah, totally." I looked at Lance and Seth and tried to find a polite way to ask what they were doing in my house, but I came up empty. "Uh, what are you guys doing here?"

"Babysitting duty." Lance clapped his hand on Lane's shoulder.

"Big sis didn't think we should leave her alone with kidnappers running around," Seth said.

Lane rolled her eyes. "Which is silly."

"Really? How would you protect yourself if Henry had shown up?" Laurel asked.

Lane grinned at me. "Fluid mechanics."

"Okay, well I don't know anything about fluid mechanics, but I still don't think your scientific knowledge would help you fight off Henry," Laurel said.

"She's talking about the textbook she hit him with last time," I said.

"Oh."

"And obviously I can take care of myself. And Cash. Because I already did it once." Lane gave her siblings a withering stare.

"It doesn't matter. Brewer is in custody," Laurel said.

"My dude." Lance fist-bumped Laurel complete with an explosion noise. In moments like this, I was shocked that Lance was the tolerable brother. Somehow reminding myself Logan was worse didn't help.

"It's too early for you to be this much you," Laurel said.

Lance scoffed. "It's after eight. I'm just hitting my stride."

"Yeah, but we've been up all night."

The front door opened behind us and Andy strolled in with Nickels in her carrier. "Hey, Cash, next time you're in a safe house so you don't die, maybe don't escape and get kidnapped." She set Nickels on the floor and hugged me.

"You're so smart. Next time, I'll run my plans by you."

"Where's your mom?" Laurel asked.

Andy hugged Laurel. "I don't know. Still unloading the car, I guess."

"You little punk. Go back out and help her." I nodded at the door.

"We got it." Seth pulled Lance toward the door.

I sat on the floor and opened Nickels's carrier. "Hello, my darling. How was your vacation with Andy?"

Nickels walked out, headbutted me, sneezed, and ran down the hall.

"Wow. That reunion was the stuff fairy tales are made of," Laurel said.

"My life is basically a fairy tale, so yeah."

"Hey, Cash. Why are you covered in blood?" Andy poked at my crusty T-shirt.

"I stabbed Henry."

"Which fairy tale is that?" she asked.

The door opened again and Robin came in. She gasped. "Oh, honey."

"Not my blood," I said.

"She stabbed Henry," Andy said.

Robin gave me a cautious hug. It was like she didn't want to get blood on her or something. "That's very heroic of you."

"Hey, I shot him. I'm heroic too," Laurel said.

"Yes, honey, of course you are." Robin hugged her too.

"It was only in the arm. That barely counts." I pouted.

"This seems important and worth debating, but can we sit down with some coffee?" Robin asked.

Laurel groaned. "God, yes."

"I need a shower. You get coffee going," I said.

"Will do." Laurel kissed me. "Holler if you need us." She pushed me toward the bathroom.

Andy's eyes went wide at the kiss. She looked at Robin who shrugged. "Sorry, bud. I already knew."

I readied myself for a long conversation, but Andy just shrugged. Laurel went into the kitchen to start coffee. After I shut the bathroom door, I could hear Lance and Seth talking again. When I turned on the water, the voices dropped to a low din.

The shower was both pleasant and unpleasant. I felt clean and refreshed, but every time I turned, the water seemed to hit something that hurt. Cool water was excellent on my face, but every bruise and cut seemed to seize. Warm water made everything throb. I cut the water and slowly toweled off. The voices had disappeared. When I dried my back, the towel came away with blood. I tried to turn and see in the mirror. It looked like the taser prong had left a nice little hole in my shoulder. I opened the bathroom door.

"Laurel?" I called. Nothing. "Robin?"

"They're out back. What's up?" Nate called back.

I wrapped the towel around my waist and opened the door the rest of the way. "Come look at my shoulder. I'm probably dying."

"Bummer. I'll miss you." He came into the bathroom. "Ouch."

"I think it's from the taser prong."

"Yeah. That makes sense." He wiped away blood with a tissue. "I think it's fine. You probably don't need stitches or anything, but I can grab Robin if you want her to take a look at it."

"No. It's cool. Just slap a Band-Aid on it."

"Go sit on your bed. I'll be there in a sec." He opened the medicine cabinet and started pulling out supplies.

I ducked into my room and pulled on a pair of boxers. Nate followed me a second later. He cleaned my shoulder with peroxide and stuck a Band-Aid over the wound.

"Thanks, man."

"Sure. You bleeding anywhere else?"

"I don't think so."

"You've got an excellent shiner."

I pulled on a T-shirt. "I thought so, but there's a lot going on here." I waved my hand over my face.

"Yeah, that's a mess."

"But I'm still ruggedly handsome, right?"

Nate leaned against my dresser and crossed his arms. "So rugged. So handsome. I can hardly stand it."

"Hard same," Laurel said from the doorway. She'd changed out of her tactical gear. She was wearing chinos cuffed above her ankle and her feet were bare.

"That's good because I was lying," Nate said.

"It's cool. I already called dibs on her." Laurel smiled at me and I smiled back. "You two coming outside?"

"Yeah." Nate stood. "I got distracted from my coffee mission because Cash needed medical assistance."

"Everything okay?" Laurel asked.

"Taser barb thing. It wouldn't stop bleeding."

"Hot."

"I know."

"Come on. We're all out back." She held out her hand to me. I crossed the room to her. "You might want pants."

I looked down. She was right. No pants. "Pants are tools of the patriarchy."

"Actually, women wearing pants is a subversion of the patriarchy," Nate said.

"I don't like you," I said.

"Yes, you do." He punched my shoulder and left me to get dressed.

"You sure you're okay?" Laurel asked.

"Yeah. I'm fine." I grabbed a pair of cutoffs.

"Because I don't mind checking. I mean, if you want to take your shirt off, I support you." She was enviably stoic, but there was a whisper of a smile she couldn't drop.

"That's so kind."

"I know." She nodded very seriously.

I pulled her close and stopped just shy of kissing her. "Laurel?"

"Yes?" she asked. I held eye contact and waited until the hint of a smile fell from the corner of her mouth. "What is it?"

I took a deep breath. "I desperately need coffee."

She laughed. "You're an ass. You know that, right?"

I kissed her. "Also, I love you. And I trust that you love me. And I'm going to need you to stay for the next fifty years or so."

"I don't know. We might live longer than that."

"Fine. Accounting for modern medicine, I'm going to need you to stay for the next hundred years or so," I said.

"Yeah, fine."

"I'm going to have to be nice to your parents, aren't I?"

She shrugged. "Only as nice as I have to be to Clive."

"Deal."

"Come on." She took her hand. "The people we actually like are outside."

"Isn't your brother here?"

"Nope. He was giving me a headache. I told him to go away."

"This is why I'm into you."

We grabbed coffee and went out back. Andy was giving Nate a tour of the progress on Gracie-Ray. Lane was sitting on the stairs watching the tour.

Robin stood and wrapped me in a long hug. "I'm so glad you're okay."

"Same."

"Because you owe me a ton of ice cream."

I laughed. "I'll buy you so much ice cream."

The door we'd just closed opened. Kyra and Van came out. "No one answered so we let ourselves in," Kyra said.

"You'd think I would lock it after getting kidnapped," I said.

She laughed and hugged me. "Well, you're kind of dumb."

"She is, isn't she?" Laurel asked as she hugged Kyra.

"I think you're smart," Van said. "But I work with undergrads so my views might be skewed." He held up the white pastry box he was holding. "Sustenance."

Andy and Nate realized breakfast had arrived and made a beeline for the porch.

"Looks like donuts," Robin said.

"Donuts are sustenance."

"You brought donuts?" Lane turned from her perch on the stairs.

"Don't worry. I got you an apple fritter." Van grinned at her. "And there's chocolate milk in the fridge for you and Nate."

Nate took the stairs two at a time. "Excellent. Thanks, man." He disappeared into the house.

Van started distributing donuts on napkins. Andy retrieved her donut and took it back to sit on the bumper of Gracie-Ray. Laurel played it cool for all of two seconds before she went to join her. Andy jumped up and restarted the tour for Laurel.

"You sure you're good?" Kyra leaned against the railing next to me and bumped me with her shoulder.

"The bar is kind of low. I'm not being kidnapped or stalked so A plus, no notes, love it."

"You know what I mean."

I watched Andy shove half her donut in her mouth. Powdered sugar dusted her T-shirt as she climbed the sidestep to balance on the edge of the bed and the wheel well. She reached down to guide

Laurel up next to her. She bit through the donut and started gesturing with it in her hand. More powdered sugar dropped. Laurel grinned at something Andy said.

"I am. I'm so good," I said.

"You really are. I'm happy for you."

Andy and Laurel started laughing at something. They noticed us staring at them and it made them laugh harder. Andy started to lose her balance. She sat hard on the edge of the truck bed. Laurel joined her, still giggling.

Van and Robin were ensconced in Adirondacks on the other side of the porch. They were deep in conversation. The door behind me opened again. Nate came out with two cartons of chocolate milk. Lane reached for it, her hands grasping comically. She tried and failed to open the carton, then handed it back to Nate. He handed her the carton he'd just opened and took the one she'd mangled.

They were all messy idiots. But they were my messy idiots.

Coffee and donuts turned into beer and barbecue. I should have been tired, but I wasn't. Just content. Or I thought so until I dozed off in one of the Adirondacks in the afternoon. I woke up to Laurel shaking my shoulder. The sun was starting to drop. The sky was deep gold.

"Hey, let's get you to bed," she said.

"Yeah, okay."

She pulled me to my feet and led me inside. Robin and Andy called out good night as Laurel shut the door.

In my room, Laurel sat me on the bed. I immediately lay back. She unbuttoned my shorts and yanked them down. I started to make a joke about her wanting me, but I dozed off again.

"What are you grinning about?" she asked.

"You want me because shorts." It was not at all what I was trying to say. I laughed at myself.

"Sure." She laughed, but I was pretty sure she was laughing at me not with me.

"Get in bed with me." I scooted up so my head was on the pillow.

She kicked off her shoes and stripped off her pants. She climbed in bed still grinning. I rolled over and tried to kiss her. At the last moment she pulled away. "Okay, no. I can't do it."

"Do what?"

"Take you seriously."

"What? Why?"

"Andy and Nate drew a mustache on you."

"Assholes." I wiped my upper lip and my hand came away with a dark smudge. "You weren't going to tell me, were you?"

"Fuck no."

"Well, now you have to kiss me." I trapped her hands and kissed her. She tried to roll away, but she was laughing too hard. When I pulled back, her upper lip had a shadow. "There. Now we're even."

She flipped me and trapped my hands. "Not even close."

About the Author

Award-winning author Ashley Bartlett was born and raised in California. Her life consists of reading, writing, and editing. Most of the time Ashley engages in these pursuits while sitting in front of a coffee shop with her wife.

It's a glamorous life.

She is an obnoxious, sarcastic punk-ass, but her friends don't hold that against her. She lives in Sacramento, but you can find her at ashbartlett.com.

Blog: https://ashbartlett.wordpress.com/

Books Available from Bold Strokes Books

His Brother's Viscount by Stephanie Lake. Hector Somerville wants to rekindle his illicit love affair with Viscount Wentworth, but he must overcome one problem: Wentworth still loves Hector's brother. (978-1-63555-805-0)

Journey to Cash by Ashley Bartlett. Cash Braddock thought everything was great, but it looks like her history is about to become her right now. Which is a real bummer. (978-1-63555-464-9)

Liberty Bay by Karis Walsh. Wren Lindley's life is mired in tradition and untouched by trends until social media star Gina Strickland introduces an irresistible electricity into her off-the-grid world. (978-1-63555-816-6)

Scent by Kris Bryant. Nico Marshall has been burned by women in the past wanting her for her money. This time, she's determined to win Sophia Sweet over with her charm. (978-1-63555-780-0)

Shadows of Steel by Suzie Clarke. As their worlds collide and their choices come back to haunt them, Rachel and Claire must figure out how to stay together and most of all, stay alive. (978-1-63555-810-4)

The Clinch by Nicole Disney. Eden Bauer overcame a difficult past to become a world champion mixed martial artist, but now rising star and dreamy bad girl Brooklyn Shaw is a threat both to Eden's title and her heart. (978-1-63555-820-3)

The Last First Kiss by Julie Cannon. Kelly Newsome is so ready for a tropical island vacation, but she never expects to meet the woman who could give her her last first kiss. (978-1-63555-768-8)

The Mandolin Lunch by Missouri Vaun. Despite their immediate attraction, everything about Garet Allen says short-term, and Tess Hill refuses to consider anything less than forever. (978-1-63555-566-0)

Thor: Daughter of Asgard by Genevieve McCluer. When Hannah Olsen finds out she's the reincarnation of Thor, she's thrown into a world of magic and intrigue, unexpected attraction, and a mystery she's got to unravel. (978-1-63555-814-2)

Veterinary Technician by Nancy Wheelton. When a stable of horses is threatened Val and Ronnie must work together against the odds to save them, and maybe even themselves along the way. (978-1-63555-839-5)

16 Steps to Forever by Georgia Beers. Can Brooke Sullivan and Macy Carr find themselves by finding each other? (978-1-63555-762-6)

All I Want for Christmas by Georgia Beers, Maggie Cummings, Fiona Riley. The Christmas season sparks passion and love in these stories by award winning authors Georgia Beers, Maggie Cummings, and Fiona Riley. (978-1-63555-764-0)

From the Woods by Charlotte Greene. When Fiona goes backpacking in a protected wilderness, the last thing she expects is to be fighting for her life. (978-1-63555-793-0)

Heart of the Storm by Nicole Stiling. For Juliet Mitchell and Sienna Bennett a forbidden attraction definitely isn't worth upending the life they've worked so hard for. Is it? (978-1-63555-789-3)

If You Dare by Sandy Lowe. For Lauren West and Emma Prescott, following their passions is easy. Following their hearts, though? That's almost impossible. (978-1-63555-654-4)

Love Changes Everything by Jaime Maddox. For Samantha Brooks and Kirby Fielding, matter how careful their plans, love will change everything. (978-1-63555-835-7)

Not This Time by MA Binfield. Flung back into each other's lives, can former bandmates Sophia and Madison have a second chance at romance? (978-1-63555-798-5)

The Dubious Gift of Dragon Blood by J. Marshall Freeman. One day Crispin is a lonely high school student—the next he is fighting a war in a land ruled by dragons, his otherworldly boyfriend at his side. (978-1-63555-725-1)

The Found Jar by Jaycie Morrison. Fear keeps Emily Harris trapped in her emotionally vacant life; can she find the courage to let Beck Reynolds guide her toward love? (978-1-63555-825-8)

Aurora by Emma L McGeown. After a traumatic accident, Elena Ricci is stricken with amnesia leaving her with no recollection of the last eight years, including her wife and son. (978-1-63555-824-1)

Avenging Avery by Sheri Lewis Wohl. Revenge against a vengeful vampire unites Isa Meyer and Jeni Denton, but it's love that heals them. (978-1-63555-622-3)

Bulletproof by Maggie Cummings. For Dylan Prescott and Briana Logan, the complicated NYC criminal justice system doesn't leave room for love, but where the heart is concerned, no one is bulletproof. (978-1-63555-771-8)

Her Lady to Love by Jane Walsh. A shy wallflower joins forces with the most popular woman in Regency London on a quest to catch a husband, only to discover a wild passion for each other that far eclipses their interest for the Marriage Mart. (978-1-63555-809-8)

No Regrets by Joy Argento. For Jodi and Beth, the possibility of losing their future will force them to decide what is really important. (978-1-63555-751-0)

The Holiday Treatment by Elle Spencer. Who doesn't want a gay Christmas movie? Holly Hudson asks herself that question and discovers that happy endings aren't only for the movies. (978-1-63555-660-5)

Too Good to be True by Leigh Hays. Can the promise of love survive the realities of life for Madison and Jen, or is it too good to be true? (978-1-63555-715-2)

Treacherous Seas by Radclyffe. When the choice comes down to the lives of her officers against the promise she made to her wife, Reese Conlon puts everything she cares about on the line. (978-1-63555-778-7)

Two to Tangle by Melissa Brayden. Ryan Jacks has been a player all her life, but the new chef at Tangle Valley Vineyard changes everything. If only she wasn't off the menu. (978-1-63555-747-3)

When Sparks Fly by Annie McDonald. Will the devastating incident that first brought Dr. Daniella Waveny and hockey coach Luca McCaffrey together on frozen ice now force them apart, or will their secrets and fears thaw enough for them to create sparks? (978-1-63555-782-4)

Best Practice by Carsen Taite. When attorney Grace Maldonado agrees to mentor her best friend's little sister, she's prepared to confront Perry's rebellious nature, but she isn't prepared to fall in love. Legal Affairs: one law firm, three best friends, three chances to fall in love. (978-1-63555-361-1)

Home by Kris Bryant. Natalie and Sarah discover that anything is possible when love takes the long way home. (978-1-63555-853-1)

Keeper by Sydney Quinne. With a new charge under her reluctant wing—feisty, highly intelligent math wizard Isabelle Templeton—Keeper Andy Bouchard has to prevent a murder or die trying. (978-1-63555-852-4)

One More Chance by Ali Vali. Harry Basantes planned a future with Desi Thompson until the day Desi disappeared without a word, only to walk back into her life sixteen years later. (978-1-63555-536-3)

Renegade's War by Gun Brooke. Freedom fighter Aurelia DeCallum regrets saving the woman called Blue. She fears it will jeopardize her mission, and secretly, Blue might end up breaking Aurelia's heart. (978-1-63555-484-7)

The Other Women by Erin Zak. What happens in Vegas should stay in Vegas, but what do you do when the love you find in Vegas changes your life forever? (978-1-63555-741-1)

The Sea Within by Missouri Vaun. Time is running out for Dr. Elle Graham to convince Captain Jackson Drake that the only thing that can save future Earth resides in the past, and rescue her broken heart in the process. (978-1-63555-568-4)

To Sleep With Reindeer by Justine Saracen. In Norway under Nazi occupation, Maarit, an Indigenous woman; and Kirsten, a Norwegian resister, join forces to stop the development of an atomic weapon. (978-1-63555-735-0)

Twice Shy by Aurora Rey. Having an ex with benefits isn't all it's cracked up to be. Will Amanda Russo learn that lesson in time to take a chance on love with Quinn Sullivan? (978-1-63555-737-4)

Z-Town by Eden Darry. Forced to work together to stay alive, Meg and Lane must find the centuries-old treasure before the zombies find them first. (978-1-63555-743-5)

Bet Against Me by Fiona Riley. In the high stakes luxury real estate market, everything has a price, and as rival Realtors Trina Lee and Kendall Yates find out, that means their hearts and souls, too. (978-1-63555-729-9)

Broken Reign by Sam Ledel. Together on an epic journey in search of a mysterious cure, a princess and a village outcast must overcome life-threatening challenges and their own prejudice if they want to survive. (978-1-63555-739-8)

Just One Taste by CJ Birch. For Lauren, it only took one taste to start trusting in love again. (978-1-63555-772-5)

Lady of Stone by Barbara Ann Wright. Sparks fly as a magical emergency forces a noble embarrassed by her ability to submit to a low-born teacher who resents everything about her. (978-1-63555-607-0)

Last Resort by Angie Williams. Katie and Rhys are about to find out what happens when you meet the girl of your dreams but you aren't looking for a happily ever after. (978-1-63555-774-9)

Longing for You by Jenny Frame. When Debrek housekeeper Katie Brekman is attacked amid a burgeoning vampire-witch war, Alexis Villiers must go against everything her clan believes in to save her. (978-1-63555-658-2)

Money Creek by Anne Laughlin. Clare Lehane is a troubled lawyer from Chicago who tries to make her way in a rural town full of secrets and deceptions. (978-1-63555-795-4)

Passion's Sweet Surrender by Ronica Black. Cam and Blake are unable to deny their passion for each other, but surrendering to love is a whole different matter. (978-1-63555-703-9)

The Holiday Detour by Jane Kolven. It will take everything going wrong to make Dana and Charlie see how right they are for each other. (978-1-63555-720-6)

Too Hot to Ride by Andrews & Austin. World famous cutting horse champion and industry legend Jane Barrow is knockdown sexy in the way she moves, talks, and rides, and Rae Starr is determined not to get involved with this womanizing gambler. (978-1-63555-776-3)